CONTAMINATION

ALSO BY JAMIE THORNTON

Zombies Are Human Book One

CONTAMINATION

Jamie Thornton

IGNEOUS
BOOKS

IGNEOUS BOOKS
PO Box 159
Roseville, CA 95678

Copyright © 2015 by Jamie Thornton
Cover Art by Mayflower Studio
Copyedited by Melanie Lytle

ISBN-13: 9781091648920

TO ALL THE READERS WHO WON'T LET THE PAST DEFINE
THEM, EVEN DURING AN APOCALYPSE

CONTENTS

November

* * *

Which one should I talk about first, death or love? Or are they the same? I don't know how it was with anyone else. Dylan and I were holding hands on the sofa when those people came. I said to him I loved him. But I didn't know then how much. I had no idea how much—

CHAPTER 1

THERE WAS SOMETHING WRONG with the calendula flowers. The leaves had turned from celery green into a sickly yellow with spots.

This was a problem. I used the orange flowers to make a salve for Mr. Sidner's dogs because the pads of their feet often cracked during the winter. He'd tried everything: antiseptic spray, socks, allergy pills, the cone, and the only thing that worked was my lotion.

But the lotion wouldn't work without the calendula.

As I snipped off the offending parts, an astringent scent made my eyes water. The sticky oil transferred to my fingers. I hoped whatever sickness had befallen the calendula would disappear with my care.

I tossed those offending leaves in the trash as if I could throw away the past few days. My attempt made a pathetic pile in the garbage.

My eye caught on Dylan's waitering shirt casually thrown over the dining chair.

Did she know that shirt? Had they talked about me? Had she even known about me?

"Enough," I said to the cold air of the empty kitchen. I would make the calendula grow back. I would make Mr. Sidner's dogs their salve. Maybe coffee grounds would perk up the plant. Ms. Roche always liked to use that trick in the garden at work.

I pulled out the French press and ground some beans while staring out the window. Last night's chill had formed moisture droplets inside the single-pane glass. I rubbed my hands together for warmth—we'd stopped turning on the heat weeks ago in hopes of saving a little money.

The teapot overflowed with water and splashed onto my jeans. I dumped out the excess, set the pot to heat on the stove.

A shadow flitted across the side of the house next door.

I leaned over the sink for a better look.

The drops distorted the view of the strip of weeds that separated our duplex from the other houses. Was it some person scouting our neighborhood or just a loose dog? Some of the grass did seem to shift.

The hairs on the back of my neck prickled. I braced my wrists against the sink and leaned over. The wind, probably, but still—then I heard a sound, like someone singing. I shook my head, trying to determine the direction of the noise.

"Are you trying to climb into the sink?"

I jumped, banging my hip on the countertop rim. "Ow! You scared the hell out me."

Dylan had put on jeans and a long-sleeved shirt. I always liked how he would roll them to his elbows to wash our cooking pots by hand, sudsing his forearms and soaking the front of his shirt to a translucent white. He had a smile that disarmed many a salesperson, male or female, it didn't matter.

He smiled and raised an eyebrow at my wet jeans.

I rolled my eyes. "The teapot overflowed."

"It's a good look on you."

"Anyway," I said, forestalling any further jokes at my expense, but glad our first words to each other hadn't been about last night. "Do you hear the singing?"

He opened the fridge and pulled out the orange juice. I stared at his back, his brown hair, his neck still damp from the shower. I didn't think I wanted too much for us: a big, sunny yard, a garden to grow food, two children, three dogs, and someone who loved me like my father had loved my mother before they'd both died. But sometimes I felt sick at night with how far away we were from it.

If Dylan and I could just speed through this hard stuff, maybe things could be better on the other side.

The singing grew louder and—familiar.

He still didn't answer. He had that half-smile on his face— that joking smile he got when not answering me was part of his secret master plan for something. He walked out of the kitchen.

I followed him and then stared at the speakers like they were living things.

"I was going through some boxes last week and came across the CD. I thought about throwing it away." He faced the wall, as if embarrassed. "And I couldn't do it. I played it, not...expecting it to affect me, and then," he shrugged, turned to me and produced a lopsided grin, "couldn't get you off my mind after that."

"Haha," I said and couldn't help but smile back. Dylan had

gifted that CD to me after we'd started dating. All twenty-three variations of *Corrina, Corrina*. "I'm glad you found it."

We sat on the sofa and listened to Bob Dylan's version, his favorite, and then Taj Mahal's version, my favorite.

I wrapped my hand in his, let the music soak into me, and refused to think about how all the people I loved most in the world eventually found a way to abandon me.

"Look," he said. "I need to tell you—"

"Please, Dylan. We made a deal." He always did this. He couldn't let things go.

I focused on the greenery framing our patio door. It formed the illusion of lush, vibrant growth. A bright red pot for the rosemary, a paisley-printed blue pot for the thyme, plants in several stands, a strawberry hanger waiting for spring.

"Corrina."

I tore my gaze away from the patio garden and looked into his blue eyes. They showed kindness, anxiousness, guilt.

"I've missed you," I said.

He flinched. "This is important. I can't just keep this from you." He ran a hand through his hair.

The song ended. I steeled myself for whatever Dylan thought he needed to say next.

And yes, I knew how ridiculous all this would sound to most people. Jane had lectured me many times. Yes, I knew I was eighteen and he was twenty. Yes, I knew there were other fish in the sea and all that crap.

None of that mattered to me.

But if I knew everything, if I could imagine every touch and kiss and smell, how could I ever forgive him? If he knew the same about what I'd done—if our mistakes took the form of real people, how could either of us banish them into the past?

"If we're going to make this work," Dylan said, "if we're going to be real with each other and stop hiding what we're afraid of—"

"I'm afraid I'm not good enough." I hated how weak this made me, admitting it out loud, but it wasn't news to either of us. I could fight with the best of them. I could stand up for what I thought was right and other people be damned. But when it came to someone I loved, all that self-confidence evaporated.

A knocking sound started. Thinking he must be tapping his foot against the coffee table, I looked down, but his legs were still.

We both looked to the glass patio door at the same moment.

The dirt-caked face of a middle-aged man pressed up against the glass. Mud-covered hands flanked either side of his face, and he was tapping his fingertips in unison with the next song.

"What the hell?" Dylan said.

The strangled ring of the doorbell cut through the house. Someone pounded on the front door.

"Call 911," Dylan said. He stood up and turned off the CD, but the man continued tapping as if he hadn't seen Dylan move.

I grabbed my cell phone and dialed.

"Door's locked," Dylan said from behind me. "It's okay, I remember locking it."

Nothing but a strange tone. I tried again.

Fear squeezed my stomach. I forced myself to stop compulsively dialing. "My phone must be broken." I tried to remember when we had last paid the bill. "Or maybe they shut off service."

"Dammit," Dylan said. Tension strained the veins along his neck.

"Look at him," I whispered. "He's crazy, he's gotta be on

drugs, right?"

"Come here, Blitz," Dylan said.

But Blitz was dead. That knowledge dawned across Dylan's face for the hundredth time.

It was an automatic thing for both of us. We had adopted him not knowing he already had cancer. He would have thrown his 100 pounds of mutt at this guy and used his deepest, fiercest growl. Neighbor kids knew better than to jump over our fence for a lost ball. They rang the doorbell. Salesman never pushed their way through our front door during their pitch. They took three steps back down the walkway.

But four weeks ago Blitz's pain had become too great.

The pounding on the front door started again. A piercing "Dylan?" A pause, and then, "Corrina?"

"Jane?" I stood up from the sofa.

"Are you crazy?" Dylan said. "Don't answer the door, Corrina. You don't know it's her."

"It's Jane. That was her voice." She lived on the same block as us. It had been her parents who had rented me a room so I could prove to the courts I deserved to leave the group home. I would know the voice of my best friend anywhere.

"Stay here," Dylan said. "None of this feels okay."

"Too bad we couldn't have said that to each other a month ago." I regretted the words as soon as they were out of my mouth.

He moved toward the front door but I was already at the linoleum entryway. My shoes squeaked on the plastic. I wanted to throw open the door, but Dylan might be right. I peered through the eye hole.

Jane was alone on the porch.

Dylan pressed his hand against the door to keep it closed.

"Let it go," I said. "She's out there."

"I don't care who's out there. You're not opening the door."

"We can't ignore her!"

He sighed. "Step aside."

My blood was pounding in my ears and I wanted to keep fighting with him. It felt easier than trying to talk things out and admit what horrible people we'd been to each other.

I forced myself to step back.

"I don't think this is a good idea." He unlocked the door and Jane burst through. Behind her, a layer of fog partially obscured the street. Shadows, or maybe a trick of the light. A chill swept across my skin as she rushed inside. I slammed the door behind her.

"They got into my house," Jane said, breathless. "They came in through the back and I ran out front, but there are more on the street—"

"More what?" I said.

Dylan's arm wrapped around my waist. I froze, caught between wanting to lean into him and wanting to throw off his arm.

Jane seemed to stare at Dylan's arm. "—at least a dozen more."

"I'm getting the gun," he said and let go. I felt the loss of his body heat like a flu ache.

We owned one gun, a cheap handgun that always jammed. His father had given it to him. Dylan had described once watching his father pry out a twisted bullet—digging in with his fingers and a letter opener. That was when they had still been talking.

And now that gun was all we had.

"And my knife," I said, remembering the big chef's knife in

the kitchen.

Dylan left to gather our meager arsenal.

"We'll be okay," I said, reaching out to hug Jane. "We just have to watch out for each other."

She brushed me off. "You didn't see them."

Dylan returned, handed me the knife, gave Jane a baseball bat we kept in the closet, and held the handgun nervously at his side.

"Are you seriously going to shoot someone?" I asked. "He doesn't look like he has any weapons."

"Even if he doesn't, someone else might," he said.

"This is not Krista all over again."

"Don't bring her up right now." The look on his face told me he'd already been thinking about his sister.

"It's going to be okay," I said.

"I don't think so," Jane said.

"Stop it, both of you," I said.

"We should see if the front is clear and leave. Try someone else's phone," Dylan said. "Jane, did you call the cops?"

"I tried, but my cell phone's dead."

"Battery dead?" He asked, "or—"

"No, the phone works," she said. "I keep getting a beeping signal. I think the network's down."

I shook my head. I headed back to the living room.

Dylan grabbed my arm. "What are you doing?"

"I want to see if the guy is still there. Why didn't he break the glass? Why didn't he yell anything at us?"

"How am I supposed to know?" Dylan said. "Plenty of people do crazy things all the time!"

"Seriously, why don't you two just get it over with and break up?" Jane said.

"Because I still love her," Dylan said without missing a beat.

They looked at each other like my foster parents had when they'd been talking about me behind my back.

"Then can we save the arguing and making up until later?" Jane said. "There are slightly more important, sort-of-serious, things to deal with at this moment."

Jane and I had grown distant over these last few months, but I didn't understand how she could say such cruel things. I thought about how this morning was supposed to be a new beginning for Dylan and me. "I'll be careful," I said in a softer voice.

"You shouldn't—"

"She's not going to listen," Jane said. "You know how she gets."

Dylan gave Jane a weird look. "I'll go first." He held the gun in front of him and crept into the short hallway, peered around the wall toward the patio door, stilled.

I became impatient and pressed in next to him.

My breath caught in my throat. The intruder had smeared yellowish saliva across the glass.

I didn't stop moving until I was within a couple feet of the glass. I told myself not to show fear. If people see fear they take advantage of it.

"You get away!" I waved my knife. "I'll cut you up. I'll do it. Get out of my backyard!"

Dylan came up next to me.

The intruder began banging his head against the glass. The dull thud shook the entire door.

"You hear us?" Dylan said. "I have a gun!"

No change.

The knife began to feel slippery in my hands. "Institution?"

I whispered. There was one a few blocks away.

"Maybe," Dylan said.

"We can't hurt him if he's sick."

"Why not?" Jane responded from behind me.

In spite of the panic of the moment, maybe because of it, I saw this scene as if from a movie, as if I was watching from outside myself. Jane carried the baseball bat like an Amazonian warrior, her blonde hair framed around her hazel eyes, her tall body ready to throw its weight into a swing. Wild fear flushed her cheeks and brightened her eyes. I hated her for a second. "He's sick," I said. "He probably doesn't know what he's doing."

"They came into my house. A whole gang of them tried to put their dirty hands on me," Jane said, raising her chin. "They deserve whatever they get."

"I don't think he knows what he's doing," Dylan said, "but he's still dangerous. If he tries anything…" He raised the gun and pointed it at the man's chest. "I will shoot you." Then he glanced at me before refocusing on the intruder. "But I agree. He's obviously sick."

"Oh, this is stupid," Jane said. "He's crazy. He'll kill us all and, what? We let him because he sick?"

"We'll do whatever we need to protect ourselves. But if we can help him, we should," Dylan said.

"And what about the others outside?" Jane demanded.

"We're not outside." I examined the man's street clothes. A rip or two in his jeans, but that could have been how he bought them. Dirt covered his hands and wrists, but otherwise he wore a clean collared shirt. His face was flushed and slick with sweat, his hair thin and receding. He kept his eyes closed. His forehead formed a pink circle where he kept hitting it. Suddenly a little blood streaked across the glass.

"Stop that," I yelled. It reminded me too much of watching a girl cut herself. She'd scraped scissors against her thigh until it bled. That's what this guy looked like he was doing—hurting himself physically so he could stop hurting emotionally, even if just for a few moments.

He kept up the banging, further opening the gash on his forehead.

"Hey!" I tapped the flat side of my knife against the glass.

He stopped. Opened his eyes.

"Oh, crap," Jane said.

His eyes stunned me. They were completely bloodshot, unseeing, as if he were sleeping with his eyes open.

"Wow," Dylan said.

The front door rattled against its hinges. I flinched. All three of us turned as if following some dance cue.

"Not more," Jane cried, bat raised for a swing that would knock me in the head if she didn't step away first.

An eerie quiet settled over the house. I looked back. The intruder was gone. Left behind were trails of black potting soil, smears of yellow saliva and red blood on the glass, a tipped-over rosemary plant, a shattered pot of lavender, my boneset ripped to shreds. My beautiful, pitiful mess of a garden, destroyed.

CHAPTER 2

"CORRINA!" A MUFFLED SHOUT made it through the door.

"Stan," Dylan said, disdain in his voice.

Stan was our neighbor two houses down. He liked to over fertilize his lawn, creating pesticide puddles that had made Blitz sick once. I'd said something to Stan about it, but I guess in such a nice, subtle way, he had acted as if I had made up the excuse just to talk to him.

Dylan had not been so subtle.

"We have to let him in," I said.

"The hell we do," Dylan said.

"Dylan."

"I'll look," Jane said, walking back to the front door.

Dylan and I hovered behind her as she peered through the eye hole.

"Corrina! You in there?" Stan yelled.

Jane turned around. "He's alone."

Dylan raised the gun.

"Open it up then," I said.

Jane shifted the bat to her right hand and opened the door.

Stan looked at the three of us, his face flushed. I almost laughed at how piggish the red made his cheeks look. Stan was very fit for a man in his late forties. He liked to talk about how often he worked out and how many miles he'd run over the weekend. His cologne always gave away his presence.

It swamped me now—that newly revamped, Old Spice musk. The front pocket of his shirt was torn and a smudge of dirt marred his khaki pants, but his oiled brown shoes still looked untouched. He could probably have any woman his age. He preferred to chase women twenty years younger than him instead.

"You coming in or not?"Dylan said.

"Dylan," I said again, but he ignored me.

Stan's regained control. "I've come to save you. The whole block is overrun so I've decided to save the lot of you—whether you deserve it or not."

Stan glanced at Dylan while he said this last bit, then looked at the gun still pointed at his chest. "You don't want my help, that's fine. But you should know, there are no police in sight and they killed Mrs. Crozier on her front porch. They're—"

He shook his head.

"—You don't need to know what they did. But here's what you do need to know: I'm getting out of here. Corrina, you were always the nicest to me in the neighborhood, and that might not mean much to some people, but it matters to me. So, I came to see if you needed help, but we have to leave right now."

He pivoted without waiting for an answer and hurried back to Luna—his luxury RV. He'd parked it halfway up our lawn.

He liked to tell us how Luna cost more than the median American home and how he planned to sell his house and go RVing around the country, maybe even dip into Central America, meet lots of women on the road, throw off all responsibilities.

Dylan called it Stan's mid-life crisis on wheels. I called it a rich man's pedophile van. Jane had laughed and said rich was right—she'd peeked in the window and seen granite flooring and white leather bench seats.

I figured the story about Mrs. Crozier being dead couldn't be true. No way that cranky old widow opened the door to some strange men, not when she kept the chain on even when Dylan and I visited.

Breaking glass sounded from across the street, from Mr. Sidner's place. He lived alone with his two golden retrievers with the sore paws.

A woman standing on his porch had smashed her hands through his front window.

"Hey!" I shouted, moving out the door and across the lawn. Fog swirled dense in the sky and in all directions, creating a sort of bubble. There was Luna, the brilliant green of the grass, the open street, Mr. Sidner's porch.

"You get away!"

Didn't matter if the woman was crazy or sick. Mr. Sidner should be left alone with his two dogs and the memory of his dead wife.

The front door opened and Mr. Sidner appeared, trying to reason with the woman. She removed her bleeding hands from the broken window, let out a scream, grabbed Mr. Sidner by the shoulders and tossed him down the steps onto his lawn.

I sprinted across the street, made it to the other side, and tripped on a cracked piece of pavement. I went down hard on one knee but bounced back up. I crossed the last few feet at a galloping limp and prayed I hadn't fractured anything.

Mr. Sidner grappled with a woman who looked to be in her twenties. He was beneath her and both pairs of feet pointed at me so that I could make out plenty of strange details. She was supposed to be another escaped hospital patient, or maybe a homeless woman, or a drug addict. But she wore a pastel blue pencil skirt, torn pantyhose, black, low-heeled pumps. A piece of pink gum was stuck to the bottom of her right shoe.

Mr. Sidner screamed.

I dropped the knife and barreled into the woman's backside, sending both of us flying.

The fog-soaked grass wet my clothes and chilled my bones. The pain in my knee flared up and I stared at the white blankness of sky and waited for the dizziness to pass.

The woman's face was less than a foot away from mine. She must have been unconscious, her eyes were closed and she didn't move except for what looked like some sort of involuntary twitching. Blood covered her exposed skin—I feared I'd done that, face-planted her into a rock or something. Her breath stank of rotting food. Her hair was a ratty brown, her white-ruffled shirt had torn, exposing a matching blue bra, and there were bite marks up one arm and purplish bruising around her neck, as if someone had choked her.

"Corrina?" Dylan's voice.

"I'm okay," I said shakily.

"You shouldn't have done that," Dylan said.

I ignored what was usually an opening line to one of our arguments and tried to still the dizziness in my head. "Is Mr.

Sidner okay?"

Silence.

"He's dead. It looks like she...broke his neck."

I closed my eyes and forced myself not to throw up. When I opened them, the young woman twitched again. "I don't know what I did to her. I only pushed her—"

She opened her eyes. Bloodshot eyes. Blown pupils.

Dylan lifted me up and dragged me backward across the lawn.

"What's going on?" Stan bellowed from across the street. A car alarm started blaring. A low boom echoed down the block, setting off more alarms.

Dylan stumbled on the same piece of sidewalk as me and unbalanced us both. I dropped to my hurt knee. The woman teetered to a standing position on her black pumps and then fixated on me.

"Uh," I said, and then air rushed past me. Stan ran toward the woman, Jane's bat in hand, and slugged her on the side of the head. She toppled over Mr. Sidner's body.

I placed both palms flat on the grass and puked my heart out. It wasn't much since we'd never gotten around to breakfast. Next to my pitiful pile of vomit, I saw my knife. I picked it up. This was supposed to be a street of people who held petty grievances against each other about tree pruning, lawn watering and dog walking.

"That's right," Stan screamed at the woman's unconscious form. He waved the bat around.

Dylan helped me up. Stan tucked the bat under his arm and supported my other side.

"Let's get you inside Luna," Stan said.

"It's just a bruise. I can walk. Give me fifteen minutes for the sting to wear off and I'll be able to run," I said.

"We don't have fifteen minutes," Dylan said quietly. "The fog is making it difficult to see, but I'm pretty sure there are more."

Shadows continued to move in the fog, just far enough to stay indistinct, to maybe believe it was my imagination. Two, three, a dozen, there was no way to know.

Jane waited inside Luna and secured the door after we entered. She tilted her head to the window. "Stan was right. They took out Mrs. Crozier too."

I didn't want to look. My eyes skipped to the sycamore trees lining the street. They were taller than most of the houses with roots strong enough to have cracked almost every section of sidewalk, except for the mulberry tree that Stan nubbed into a garish skeleton every year because he thought the leaves were too much trouble.

If you stood in the middle of Grove Street on a sunny day the trees combined overhead into a beautiful canopy, with trunks you couldn't fully reach around, with limbs grown into a complex system of crooked mazes, with leafy crowns that didn't quite meet each other across the road.

This neighborhood was supposed to make things right again.

"Corrina," Dylan gently shook my shoulder. "Don't ever do that again. What were you thinking?"

"Stop it, Dylan," I said, knowing I was taking out my sadness on him, but not being able to stop myself. "Don't treat me like I can't take care of myself. I did just fine before you came along."

He looked away from me.

The bench rocked under me as Stan took off down the street. The rumble of the road and the engine soothed me, but did nothing to release the tension in Dylan's face.

I sighed. "You take risks, too. Mr. Sidner needed our help." My stomach roiled as if thinking about cramping again. "But we didn't help him."

Luna made a wide turn. My stomach flipped and the dizziness came back. I focused on a potted cactus sitting on the back of the opposite bench. Stan turned again and the cactus moved an inch. I grabbed for the pot before it fell.

"How's your knee?" Dylan asked quietly.

I thought about his question for a long second and then my mind tripped away into a different thought. "Sidner's dogs! Wait, Stan, we have to go back for them!"

I rushed to the driver's seat, but my shoes slipped on the granite floor and I went down hard on my tailbone and jammed my knife wrist on the side of a cabinet. The pain seared away the rest of my dizziness.

"No way!" Stan whirled the steering wheel counterclockwise, forcing my forehead into the bench siding. "Those dogs are dead, dead, dead. What do you think made me bring out Luna?"

Dylan helped me onto the bench. "Just sit here for a minute, Corrina. Please." He stood behind Stan and grabbed the back of the chair. His other hand held the gun like it was part of his body now. "Take us back out by your house. That's the quickest way out of the neighborhood."

"I know it. You think I don't know that?" Stan gunned the engine. "I came to save you when I could have just left. You don't need to tell me."

People ran around—none of them our neighbors. They crossed in front of us and then disappeared in bushes or behind trees or jumped fences, or vanished into the fog. Dozens of shapes in motion. And another dozen shapes, people-size, lay still in front yards, across porch steps, along the sidewalk. Our neighborhood looked ransacked, pillaged, looted, and now the survivors were abandoning it, letting the weeds grow unchecked, leaving the doors left ajar, the lights on, the alarms ringing.

A thick column of smoke rose a block away, transforming the fog into a poisonous brown. No police or firefighters were in sight. Would the entire neighborhood burn? I almost said we needed to go back for the *Corrina* CD, for the computer hard drive with all our files, for the picture of my parents, for Blitz's collar.

Stan turned Luna onto the outlet street. I remained silent. I would not be that person—the one who puts those she loves in danger because of things that don't matter. I had Dylan and Jane with me. No thing could be more important than them.

Jane moved to the passenger seat and placed the blood-stained bat across her lap. Luna's windows were meant to showcase beautiful mountain vistas and long stretches of prairie hills, but now they gave a panoramic view of the destruction. Even inside Luna with all the windows closed, everything sounded wrong. Sirens, alarms, rumblings, and booms like the last time a transformer had exploded on our street, sounds like gunfire, and the screech and crash of cars colliding.

And yet it was otherworldly too, sounds that drifted in through the fog, detached from sight, like an old radio drama. No picture, only sound and imagination, which felt somehow worse.

Dylan turned to me, his face whitewashed and sallow, the stubble standing out. "There's a girl," he said. He nodded through the window. "That girl who moved in with her uncle last week, same age as Krista."

Krista, his dead sister. It's part of what had connected us at first, being in the club with other people who'd lost loved ones.

"Let's go get her," I said without a second thought.

"We don't even know her." Stan whipped his head around, then turned back to the windshield. "She's some Pakistani or something, just moved in. Don't think she even speaks English. Besides, Luna doesn't like backing up or making u-turns. Better just to keep moving."

"Just stop then," Dylan said.

"She could be like them," Jane said. "She could be crazy like the others."

I refrained from shouting at Jane to shut up. Didn't she know how deep a trigger Krista was for Dylan? Instead, I focused on what might convince Stan to stop. "I thought you came to save us," I said, knowing it was a lame attempt as soon as the words came out.

"Yeah, you…" He glanced back at Dylan. "All of you. Because you're my neighbors and all, and you treated me right."

"Stop, Stan." Dylan's voice was pitched low.

My panic increased, something that should have been impossible with the day's trauma. But Dylan never used that tone of voice, not unless he was thinking about the drunk driver who had murdered Krista while Dylan had been driving, about the helplessness he felt being unable to save her, about how if he had just been a few seconds slower or faster that everything would have turned out different.

Dylan raised the gun. A silent scream mounted in my brain. Dylan wouldn't do anything that crazy. Except, I wasn't totally sure.

I grabbed my knife off the floor, pushed Dylan aside and pressed the blade into Stan's throat. The adrenaline made me lose all feeling in my hand so that I wasn't sure how hard I was pressing. "Stop, Stan."

Stan's eyes bulged, but he kept driving. "Come on, Corrina. Don't play stupid now. Me and Luna will take care of you."

"Stan," I said.

"I know you don't have it in you," Stan said.

"You don't know me," I said, letting my fear of Dylan's gun dig the blade in a little deeper. Not enough to break skin, but enough for him to notice. "You don't know the trouble I got into when I was in school. You don't know how well I know how to use this knife. You don't know how much it pisses me off to hear you want to leave that girl behind because she's Pakistani. I'm Egyptian, Stan. What do you think about me?"

"You're not Egyptian. Where's your accent? Sure, you tan real nice, but you didn't come from any foreign country."

"The girl could be like them," Jane said.

I stared at Jane and the coldness that had entered her hazel eyes. "The only way to know," I said, driving ice into every word, "is if we stop and find out. Otherwise, we're leaving a defenseless little girl to die."

Stan kept driving.

If I didn't follow through now it would be as if we crowned him king of the RV. And then there was what Dylan would do.

Stan was calling my bluff, and I knew, just as surely as I'd known in school before a fight—it was always better to take the first punch. Most people saw it as an act of courage. I knew it for what it was—an act of desperation. Can't take the beating, too afraid to turn the other cheek, so you hide behind violence and act like you asked for it.

"Stan." I held my breath and nicked his neck with my knife.

Stan slapped a hand to the bleeding scratch. His eyes rolled into the back of his head and he slammed on the brakes. I tumbled forward. The steering wheel punched me in the chest.

"Back up, people!" He licked his lips. "I saved you all, didn't I? I'm all about saving people." His knuckles turned white on the steering wheel.

I coughed. Blood dripped down Stan's neck and disappeared into his shirt collar.

I had done that.

I had never done that before.

"I just want to be careful about it," Stan said. "What if it's Ebola or rabies or something? You don't want to catch it. You want the girl so bad? All right. I'll turn at this roundabout." Luna teetered a bit as he sped around the circle. "But we've got to get out of here."

"We will," Dylan said. "After we get her on board." His voice sounded strained, but I dared to look at him now. He pointed the gun at the floor.

"It's not Ebola," I said. "That makes people sick. Not violent."

Stan shook his head. "Doesn't matter what it is. It's here and that means we shouldn't be."

The girl, wearing a pink hoodie and jeans, stood in the middle of the street a few yards away, the fog closing in behind her like a curtain. She must have run after us.

Her eyes were big and round, examining our faces through the windshield. "Are you normal?" She yelled, the windshield glass muffling her voice.

My breath quickened as I wondered what she meant. She pulled the sleeves of her hoodie down to cover her hands as if she were cold. She looked to be only thirteen years old. Skinny and short and trying not to show her fear by standing as tall as possible in front of a giant RV with the sounds of the whole world falling apart surrounding her.

I stood by the side door and opened it to a clear street, except for three figures mostly obscured by the fog further down the block.

Dylan pushed open a side window and waved at the girl. "We're your neighbors on Grove Street. Get in here."

She appeared, small and scared, like a rabbit. She dashed through the door, skidded on the granite floor, and fell onto the dining bench with a big, gulping breath.

Dylan closed the window. "Get going, Stan. There are three coming our way."

"So how come she's okay and not those three?" Jane demanded. "Or are we letting those three in too?"

"Look at them and look at her," I said. "Can't you just tell?"

They were close enough to make out details in the fog now. A brown-haired woman, dressed as if she had just gone to the mall. She wore cowboy boots and I watched as one of them caught on the asphalt and forced her to her knees. The two men seemed to be together. Like coworkers just getting off from a construction work site. All three had blank gazes when they opened their eyes, and all three cradled or cocked their heads as if enduring a great deal of pain.

One of the men frothed saliva at the mouth. The woman's muscles spasmed, interfering with her ability to walk in a straight line. They seemed drawn to Luna's engine noise, or our voices, or I don't know. Something about them looked so, disturbed, so angry. And they were making their way down the street fast, faster than I would have thought possible with their loping, crippled gaits.

"Shut the door, Corrina," Dylan said.

"There's got to be something we can do to help them. Something…"

Dylan wrapped his hand over mine and pulled the door closed. Stan went through the roundabout again and we rumbled down the street.

The shapes disappeared into the whiteness like vanishing ghosts.

"Maybe once we can figure out what's going on," Dylan said, "but we can't risk—"

"I know," I said, remembering Mr. Sidner. Were they part of some sick gang? They couldn't all be from the mental health institution, especially since these three looked as if they had just walked off their jobs.

The girl hunched over the bench,. Her sweatshirt failed to hide her trembling.

"I'm Corrina," I said. "This is Dylan, Stan, and Jane," I pointed to each person in turn. "You're safe here."

"I'm Maibe." She pushed back her hood. "My name is Egyptian for grave because my mother died giving birth to me and my father sent me away to my uncle," she said. "We just moved here, but the zombies killed him and now I'm alone."

All of us stared.

"Oh wow, this is just great," Jane said.

Maibe rolled up the sleeves of her pink hoodie, and her arms were skinny things. Two gold-colored bangles clinked together on her left wrist. Her hoodie revealed dark, thick hair pulled back into a ponytail with a matching pink band.

"Maibe," I said. "These people are sick with something. Something mental, or on drugs, or…" I looked to Dylan for help.

He sat across from her and carefully folded his hands onto the tabletop. He stared at Maibe for a second and then looked away. He always handled kids like this. He was careful not to make them anxious by invading their space. "Maibe," he said quietly. "Sometime people are capable of horrible, monstrous things—"

"No. That's not what's happening," she said.

I opened my mouth to contradict her. Dylan gave me a warning look.

"Maibe," Dylan said. "Did you see what happened to your uncle?"

She nodded. "He went outside to scare off the zombies, but they killed him in our backyard." She stared at the table and fiddled with her bracelets. She rubbed hard at her eyes. "I was scared. I didn't think I would be. It's not like that in the movies. I wasn't ready, so I ran and hid behind that big flower bush in the front yard, that's when I saw you all drive by."

"It's okay, you're safe here," Dylan said.

I could tell Maibe didn't buy into his comfort. I didn't. We were a long way from safe, but if we could escape the neighborhood, find a fire station, call the police, maybe we could get some answers at least. "Does anyone have a working phone?" I asked.

"No good," Stan yelled. "I tried a dozen times."

"We just need to try again," Dylan said.

"Phones are gone," Maibe said. "My uncle and I have been

watching…We just didn't think it would spread so fast. We were planning to leave tomorrow. Thought we had plenty of time. The zombies only now got to us, but they took over most of downtown last night."

"If you don't shut up with that crazy talk, I'll throw you back out with the crazies," Stan said. He didn't bother turning around, but Jane did and the look on her face said she agreed with Stan.

I didn't understand how she could be so callous. "Jane."

She shook her head and turned away.

"How do you know all this?" Dylan said.

"My uncle listens…listened to the police scanners. It was bad all night."

"What was bad?" Dylan asked.

"Fires and murders and stuff."

"Why are you calling them zombies?" He asked like he was talking to a butterfly.

She shrugged and looked at Dylan with her huge brown eyes. Serious, in control of herself again. "What else would you call them?"

"Sick," I said.

"It doesn't matter," Jane said. "They're trying to kill us. That's what matters."

I tugged on Dylan's arm. "Stay here," I said to Maibe. I pulled Dylan into Stan's little bedroom of love. That was the only way to describe the red satin sheets, incense holder, and the huge mirror hung on one wall. This room made my skin crawl, which was a pretty amazing accomplishment considering all that had happened.

"This is nuts," Dylan said.

I could see our profiles in the mirror. Both of us looked paler than usual, though Dylan looked downright ghostly next to me. He always turned pale and red when he got scared, while I turned pale and yellow. I was shorter than Dylan and Jane, not short, just shorter. The top of my head hit the bottom of Dylan's chin. I began tucking in my flyaway hairs as if the act might magically make everything normal again.

Dylan laid his hand on my arm to make me stop.

I sighed. "What should we do?"

"Obviously the girl is in shock. We just have to be careful with her."

"She's a kid who watched her uncle murdered. Why are Stan and Jane being so harsh?"

"I don't know." He turned the knob to go back out, then drew me close to his chest so that I could feel the warmth of his body and the beat of his heart. "We need to get hold of the authorities and figure out what's going on."

"There's so many of them," I said.

"I know. Look, before we go back I want to tell you—"

"I love you too—"

"—You've got to be more careful."

Embarrassment flushed my cheeks and a spark of anger lit inside my chest.

"Considering whether to help the intruder at our patio door, and then running after Mr. Sidner, and then thinking, for even a second, about helping those other three? You're risking yourself for strangers trying to kill us."

"And what about Maibe?" I tried not to raise my voice.

"I know, I know." He brushed a strand of hair off my forehead. I imagined slapping his hand away.

"I'm not saying we shouldn't help people, but I watched you tackle that woman, and I saw what she had done to Mr. Sidner, and all I could think was that I was about to watch you die, and how…God, I'm not good at this."

The part of me that didn't want to slap him wanted to kiss him and forget what was happening for a moment.

But I let that moment pass too.

He pulled me into him and wrapped his arms around me.

"All right," I said, my words muffled in his shirt. The smells of cotton and his skin enveloped me, comforted me. "I will." But even as I said the words I remembered too many people who had stood on the sidelines of my life, unwilling to help when I needed it. I would not turn into one of those people.

I felt the door open behind me, startling me with its whoosh of air. Dylan didn't let go.

Silence. Darkness. The smell of his shirt, the warm dampness of my breath.

"We're coming up on the fire station." Jane's voice.

Dylan let go and I followed him back into the main part of the RV. The bay windows provided a stunning view. Thinning fog, moving shadows, smoke trails, broken glass.

"Why are there no cars on the roads?" I said. But no one answered my question, if they even heard it. I thought I knew the answer anyway. This early in the morning on a foggy Saturday—the streets were usually empty. But surely others had tried to escape?

Jane climbed back into the passenger seat. Dylan and Maibe crowded the driver's seat. Stan turned the corner. I leaned with Luna's sway and let out a moan.

"I told you," Maibe said.

Stan rolled his window down and craned his head out for a better look. The air suddenly filled with the smell of burning plastics. A stench that made my eyes water and blurred my vision. The alarms grew louder, overlapping, grating on me. Booms sounded at random, some far away, some close by.

I stepped forward, the floor slick underneath my shoes. The windshield was grimy and moisture gathered on it. I bent over to peer through. Someone had broken all the windows in the brick station. A person in firefighting gear hung out of a bottom level window, his suit halfway off and his head and torso...bloody. A red fire truck sat part of the way out of the garage, all tires flat. The fog amplified the low roar of Luna's engine. The fire station alarm came through as a low buzzing underneath the shriek of the car alarms. Something like a shotgun fired. More shots.

"How far away are those?" Jane asked.

"Hard to say with the fog," Dylan said.

"Turn the radio on," I said. "Try the radio. Stan, get us out of here. Please close the windows again."

"But where do we go?" Maibe said. "There won't be any place safe."

Jane fiddled with the tuner buttons.

Stan labored to reverse Luna down the street. "There's a police station about a mile from here," Stan said.

"This neighborhood is already gone," Dylan said. "Whatever's happening is a lot bigger than a gang of sickos taking over a neighborhood."

"Maybe it is zombies," Jane said.

Smoke rose from a house down the street, its column of yellow infecting the fog around it. Ours was the only vehicle running, though from the several crashed cars we'd passed, we weren't the only ones who had tried to leave by vehicle.

A large RV, with purple swirls, revving its engine. We were a target for whatever had been let loose here.

"Why hasn't the National Guard been called in?" Dylan asked. "Where are all the first responders?" He stared out a side window looking like he was memorizing every house, every street, every broken window, trying to x-ray vision what waited. "And where are the ones who did this? Where did they go?"

Maibe turned and looked at me, wide-eyed. "Do you believe me yet?"

My shoulders trembled. My knee ached from my falls. I felt about ready to yell at Maibe myself, and then the tuner picked up a signal.

CHAPTER 3

"...ARE REQUESTED TO VOLUNTARILY EVACUATE DUE TO MUL-
TIPLE CIVIL EMERGENCY INCIDENTS. EVACUATION CENTER
HAS BEEN SET UP ON CAL EXPO FAIRGROUNDS. RESIDENTS
SHOULD TAKE PRECAUTIONS AGAINST LOOTERS. RESIDENTS OF
SURROUNDING AREAS ARE REQUESTED TO REMAIN INDOORS.
PREVENT OUTDOOR ACCESS TO YOUR RESIDENCE AND COVER ALL
WINDOWS. BULLETIN - EAS ACTIVATION REQUESTED. CIVIL EMER-
GENCY MESSAGE. THE FOLLOWING MESSAGE IS TRANSMITTED AT
THE REQUEST OF THE CALIFORNIA EMERGENCY MANAGEMENT
AGENCY. RESIDENTS OF SACRAMENTO CITY..."

Before my gardening job I'd been a seasonal employee for
the fairgrounds. They often assigned me to events near the
horse track. I had sneaked onto the river bike trail that ran
along it many a time while on a smoke break with coworkers
when that had still seemed cool. The fairgrounds were a place
for entertainment, for overpriced food, for horseracing, but I

realized its concrete acres and tall, chain-link fencing could easily be put to other uses.

"Try another station," Dylan said.

Jane obliged. The next station sent out the same Emergency Alert message.

"That can't be all of it?" I asked.

"The government is probably doing this on purpose," Maibe said. "They don't want any stations to get on the air and say what's really going on. That always happens in the zombie movies."

"Girl," Stan said, this odd twist to his voice, like the word came from the back of his throat at the last second instead of a different, harsher word.

"Maybe she's right," Jane said.

"Stop it, Jane," I said.

"Do you have a better idea?" Jane turned an accusing stare at me. "They're monsters, or they might as well be, so you tell me, Corrina—what's going on here?"

"It's not zombies," I said. "I would buy some sort of sickness, a version of rabies or maybe a poison." I refused to flinch under her stare. If that's where it needed to go, I could give it as good as she could dish it.

A banging on the back froze Jane's features into panic mode. Maibe yelped. A cold determination swept through me. My life had been filled with people banging on doors, ushering themselves in, invited or not. I had learned I could deal with whatever waited on the other side, though, admittedly, this situation was a little different than what I'd experienced in the past.

"Luna is only parked," Stan said.

"Help us." A muffled male voice.

"Go. Just go," Jane whispered. She placed the bat across her lap and squeezed it until her knuckles turned as white as her face.

Stan's hand hovered over the shifter and I wondered if we were really going to repeat this whole scene again. "We have to at least see if…" If what? If they slobbered? If they walked like cripples? If they wanted to kill us? Did I really want to open that door and check?

But then the squeal of the door sounded anyways. I whirled around. Maibe.

Faces peered into the crack of light.

"Wait." I raised my hand in a stopping motion, forgetting it held the knife. The blade clattered onto the floor.

"It's a family," Maibe said. She threw the door wide. "Come on. Get inside." She waved her hands as if to make them hurry.

I retrieved the knife. Three adults and two children pushed into the space.

"You're the one who's talking about zombies," I said to Maibe, "and you let these people in like it's no big deal?"

"I…" Maibe looked away. "The bad ones can't talk. That's how you know the difference. They can't say words anymore, just noises."

"Thank you," the older man said. He looked to be in his early fifties. His hair was longer than I'd usually seen people in their fifties wear it. More an unkempt style that fell just past the top of his ears, like a hipster. His pants were torn at the knee and streaked with dirt. His hazel eyes examined each of us in turn. His dark eyebrows accentuated his stare. There was something odd about his skin, a weird webbing of lines and an ashy cast to his color.

"I'm Christopher." He waved toward the two women. "This

is Gracelyn and Mai. The kids are Samara and Joseph. We're not family, but we are all neighbors. Sort of. I was visiting my sister when they came through our houses this morning. We've been hiding until we saw you drive by the first time. When you came back around, we took our chance."

Dylan motioned for everyone to sit down. Gracelyn tucked Joseph, who looked to be about five, into her lap. Samara was maybe eight years old and pressed herself into Mai. "How did you know we wouldn't be like...whoever's done this?" Dylan asked.

"They're like animals," Christopher said. His eyes lost their focus, as if he were reliving a terrible moment. "They aren't capable of doing something like driving an RV." Christopher tilted his head. "How'd you know we would be all right?"

"We didn't," Dylan said, "but Maibe here didn't give us much of a choice."

"All right...listen up," Stan yelled across the RV. "This is my place." He swiveled his chair around. "Everybody better watch where he or she sits. I want Luna kept as clean as when you all walked in. You better watch those kids, too. You'll have to pay for anything that gets broken."

I felt a small hand reach for mine. I looked down as Maibe's pink arm intertwined itself with mine. "I'm sorry. I promise they're not zombies," she said. "I've watched all the movies. I know the signs. They're still okay."

This kid was alone when she had watched her uncle brutally murdered. I pulled her close for a moment and caught Dylan's eye.

"Everything okay?" He asked.

"No," I said, smiling through the tears welling up in my eyes.

"Okay. Now that everyone knows Luna's rules, we have a problem. Luna's been in storage. We need gas if we're going to make it to Cal Expo," Stan said.

"May we use the bathroom?" Mai asked, Samara still pressed into her side.

"Absolutely not," Stan said. "I haven't had the septic tank checked in awhile. You can wait to go once we stop for gas."

I was about to protest, but when Mai returned her focus to the top of Samara's head without argument, I let the matter drop for the moment.

The group looked cold, exhausted, shell-shocked. I'm sure we didn't look much differently to them. No one else bothered to speak up, except for Joseph who complained about his hiccups. His cheeks were streaked with dirt and his eyes watered. Gracelyn held him in her lap and crooned into his hair.

"Do you have any water?" Christopher asked. Even though it was cold inside the RV, sweat beaded on his forehead.

I went into the bathroom, poured a cup of water and handed it over.

Christopher took a sip and then passed the rest to Joseph. He cleared his throat. "I know a gas station where we could see anyone coming at us for miles. Along the railroad tracks from here."

We all waited to see what Stan would do.

"Give me directions," Stan said.

We drove out of the neighborhood and followed the railroad tracks away from downtown.

Everything had become eerily still, as if the city had gone comatose after a violent seizure. The different alarms filled the air, making it impossible to hear anything else except for the person right next to you. There was plenty of broken glass, car accidents, blood, a bicycle twisted into the front end of a truck, a spilled bag of groceries, milk dribbling into the gutter, streaks of blood showing where something was dragged away. Odd-shaped lumps lay unmoving in doorways, bullet casings lay in a small pile next to a car with its windshield busted, but there were very few bodies out in the open and no one moving around.

I hoped that meant the worst was over, but I feared it was just a lull.

On the other side of the railroad tracks from the gas station were open fields full of starthistle, foxtails, goathead—weeds for as far as the eye could see. Flat, open fields on one side, and except for a few buildings and the station's convenience store, flat, cracked pavement on the other.

Luna sputtered to a halt as Stan downshifted, and I searched for anything that moved outside. It looked quiet, abandoned, safe, for the moment.

We decided that Jane, Stan, and I would get the gas. Dylan would go with the gun, Mai, Gracelyn, and the kids to find a bathroom. Christopher would stay and guard Luna.

"Maybe we shouldn't split up," I said to Dylan, even though I was the one who had argued the gun should go with the bathroomers.

Dylan raised an eyebrow. "Do you trust Stan not to do something stupid?"

Everything in me wanted to keep together in a large group, as if we were in elementary school playing bunch-ball soccer. Luna was the soccer ball and we should all be hovering around her, not leaving her sight. "Jane could go alone and help him." But I knew that wasn't fair to her. "Never mind," I said. "Just be quick and be safe."

He kissed me, a deep, sorry-I-gotta-go-but-I'll-make-up-for-it-later kiss. And I wished for time later to make up for this rushed kiss, and for the last few months.

Dylan opened Luna's back door. "All right, come on out." He motioned with his free hand for everyone to step onto the pavement.

My knee still ached, but Christopher had checked it, saying he was a paramedic. He concluded it was only badly bruised.

I held the kitchen knife more like a security blanket than a real weapon, and yet I felt stronger for holding it and for being given a reason to not look at the pathetic group of people exiting Luna as if she were some spaceship landing on a harsh alien planet.

Maibe came out last, her pink hood up and her hands drawn into her sleeves. Christopher poked his head out of the door and gave an all-clear thumbs up before closing it.

Stan closed Luna's door with a soft click. We tried the hose. The pump was shut off.

We would need to go inside the store and see about switching it on before heading back to safety. That's how I thought of Luna now, as safe. As if we were playing baseball and as long as we made it back to base before the other team tagged us, we were safe. I didn't know who this other team was yet, but I forced those questions away for when there was more time to think.

Dylan and his ragtag group walked alongside the railroad tracks, around the back of the store to look for an unlocked bathroom or the privacy of a wall.

They went out of sight and suddenly I couldn't breathe for fear I would never see Dylan again.

I forced myself to follow Stan and Jane instead of running after Dylan. The store was pretty much gutted inside except for what one man might need to operate the pumps. A countertop, a cash register, and somewhere, a pump switch. On racks by the register hung a few trinkets and what looked like empty Slim Jim's wrappers. The place was little more than a shack to protect the owner from the weather. Stan pulled open the doors without any problems.

Something grabbed my hand. I yelled and jerked away.

Maibe.

The bat in Jane's hand shook from the vibrations of her body. Stan had his flare gun pointed at Maibe, and then grimaced and lowered it. I tried to calm the trembling of my own body. Her surprise entrance had made blood rush to my ears, which blocked out sound and balance. Not a good reaction. I shook my head and took a deep breath. "Come on," I kept hold of Maibe's hand.

"I'm sorry," she said. "I didn't mean to surprise you."

"What were you thinking?" Jane yelled. "Running around by yourself? Are you stupid?"

"Let's just get this done," I said.

Stan pointed the flare gun into the store like he actually knew how to use the thing. He led the way. It would be easy to follow him, the oldest adult, and pretend that had any meaning.

Yes, there were people in the world capable of doing horrible acts, but just because they all seemed loose in our area didn't mean that someone wouldn't get things under control. The police, or the National Guard, or whoever. All we had to do was not die before that happened.

I laughed quietly to myself. Easy. Just don't die, Corrina,

then everything will be fine.

"Found it." Stan bent behind the cash register counter. Something clicked and then there was a whirring sound, like liquid running through a pipe. Stan stood up and brushed dust off his hands.

Jane stood by a door at the back of the store. "I think this is a food closet."

"This whole thing is a closet," I said.

"The owner had to have a little sink area or something," she said. "A microwave, a little pantry."

In spite of everything that had happened, or maybe because of it, my stomach rumbled. I wondered if we'd find enough food for everyone and how we would go about splitting it if there wasn't.

"Don't open that door," Maibe said with all the conviction a thirteen year old could muster.

"Shut up, kid," Stan said.

Maibe looked first at Jane and then back to me. "This is exactly like in the movies. You don't go opening closed doors, ever. That's one of the first things you learn after a zombie apocalypse. There's always something bad hiding behind a closed door. All the movies are like that. You just know the movie plans to kill someone as soon as you see them thinking about opening a closed door. That's how it—"

"I told you to shut your mouth," Stan said.

"Calm down, Stan," I said. "She's been through a lot. We all have."

Jane remained silent, as if she were also considering what may or may not be waiting on the other side.

The door was a flimsy-looking metal sheet. Shoe marks

covered the bottom half as if someone routinely kicked it closed. The place smelled like grease, sweat, dust. If there was any food it wasn't out here with us.

"Look," I said. "It wouldn't hurt to be cautious, but what if there's food? We wouldn't have to stop again." A part of me knew that if I gave into Maibe's superstition I'd never want to open another door for as long as I lived, because wasn't she right? Hadn't all the doors today brought nothing but one horrible thing after another?

"Just open the goddamn door," Stan said. "There's nothing there, alive anyways. Otherwise we would have heard something."

"I don't want to. You do it," Jane said.

Stan stomped over to her. He leaned his head close to the door. "I don't hear anything," Stan said. "There's nothing there." Yet he still didn't pull it open.

"Knock or something," I said. I immediately felt embarrassed. I waited for Stan to shoot me a withering look, but he seemed thoughtful instead.

Jane shifted from foot to foot.

"Yeah, okay," Stan said.

Maibe moved away from the rest of us. Closer to outside.

Stan took a small step back, kept the flare gun in his right hand and raised his left. He froze for a moment, and then knocked softly. He stopped, and then knocked harder.

Silence filled the room. The four of us strained to hear something, anything, coming from behind the door. There was noise, but it came from outside, muffled by the closed gas station door—the low whine of alarms, the screech of far-off car brakes, the low rumblings of who knew what. The booms had started up again too, sounding like gunshots, but there was no way to know for sure. I did catch a glimpse of Joseph and Samara straggling back to Luna. They must have finished, and here we were, standing stupid, not yet done with our one task, risking all our lives by not getting the gas and then getting the hell out of there.

"There's nothing," I said. "Open it and let's get back to Luna."

"Stupid kid," Stan muttered before jerking the door open.

Maibe squeaked and pulled on my arm hard enough to tweak it.

"Nothing," Stan said as he walked into the room with Jane on his heels.

"Maibe, ease up," I said.

Jane poked her head out of the door. "The lights aren't working, but there is some food. Crackers and some water bottles."

Maibe buried her head into her hands. "I'm sorry," she said. "I thought for sure—that's always how it works. People never get away this easy."

"It's okay." I tried to take a step, but my knee buckled. I swore and touched the tender spot under my jeans. Not a good time for injuries, even if it was just a bruise with some swelling.

Jane and Stan came back out with a few boxes and a depressingly small stack of water bottles in their arms.

Maibe drew up her hood and pulled the strings tight so that the pink cloth hugged her face, like in one of those photo shoots where they dressed babies in enormous flower costumes. I decided not to mention this to her. I'd yet to meet a teenager who would feel thrilled with knowing they reminded someone of a baby.

"It's okay, Maibe," I said. "Remember this is real life, not the movies."

"You didn't see them up close like I did. You didn't see what they did to my uncle."

I decided not to tell her about Mr. Sidner. Better to just try and forget about it. I would want to do a lot of forgetting once this was all over. But I had gotten pretty good at that skill while living in the group home with other fosters out for blood at any accidental insult.

"They always demand payment." Maibe bowed her head, and then raised it again as if inspiration had just struck. "Oh. Why didn't I think...you can't ever get away with something like this, getting food or gas or something, without a cost, but maybe it's not supposed to come from us."

She stared at me as if waiting for a response to her brilliance.

I closed my eyes. "Are we done here?"

"This is all there was," Jane said.

"It's enough," I said. I pushed open the door to the outside.

That's when we heard the shouting. The gunfire. The roar of an engine.

"Luna!" Stan yelled. "They're trying to leave without us." He dropped the boxes and sprinted.

Luna remained exactly where we'd left her. Everything looked okay from our side of things, but it did not sound okay.

"If it's not us who has to make payment," Maibe said from behind me. "It's the people who went to the bathroom."

I ran across the parking lot in spite of the jelly my legs seemed to be turning into. I ran, but it felt so slow, it felt so late.

Stan reached Luna and shook the driver's side door, scream-ing for someone to let him in.

I rounded Luna's back side and saw the doors to a box van

that hadn't been there before. They closed shut on a glimpse of Dylan's jacket. Before I could raise a shout, it sped off in a whine of engine noise.

If Dylan stood beside me, then whatever happened next, it would be manageable, it would not be the end because we would get through it together. Wasn't that what this morning had proved, that we would get through whatever life threw at us—together?

I ran after Dylan as if my life depended on it. I ran like I used to run for my father when Bettina's gang of girlfriends chased after me in elementary school.

The van turned a corner and then another corner. I gasped for breath and wished for longer, faster legs, the same wish I'd had when I was nine. My nightmare come to life—home base just out of reach and I ran and I ran and I ran, and home base moved further away.

My knee flared and I lost my balance. Asphalt grated my cheek, made my face burn, matched with the pain flaring in my knee, but it could not match the pain inside. It could not stop the despair welling up in me like a black hole, its gravity sucking me down and about to break me apart. I screamed.

A WILD THOUGHT jolted me back—maybe Dylan had let one of the others borrow his jacket. Maybe he was safe. Maybe he was hiding somewhere, and I would find him in the weeds by the railroad tracks.

I forced myself to rise from the pavement and return to the gas station at a fast limp. I walked past the first dead body, that little hiccuping boy, Joseph. As soon as I realized he was too small to be Dylan I did not look closer.

Joseph's body was the only one on the pavement, so I moved to the field. My mind was fuzzed out, as if nothing existed beyond waiting for Dylan to sit up from the middle of a bunch of starthistle and say, "I'm okay."

I do not know what Jane and Maibe and Stan were doing while I conducted my search. I did catch the shadow of a figure out of the corner of my eye. I think it was Maibe and I think she may have said something like, "They might come back," but I can't be sure and besides, I hadn't found Dylan and I knew he was waiting for me.

The world would not be so cruel as to have allowed us to see we were still worth saving, and then not allow us to save ourselves. A voice whispered in my head that, yes, the world was definitely cruel enough to do that. It had taken both my parents from me and dumped me in a group home, hadn't it? I kept searching anyways.

I found five bodies of people who looked sick like the man at our patio door, now dead from what must have been bullet wounds. I did not find Dylan, and suddenly I was glad, because no one I had found was still alive.

Jane's voice cut through my search. "Look at this." She held up something small. Dylan's gun.

"There's blood on it," she said.

That's when I grew calm. I walked to Jane as if I were passing through a swarm of paper wasps. Let them get a good look at me. They could recognize faces. They knew whether you belonged in their section of garden or not. I took stately, relaxed steps across the field, over another body. I examined Jane's hands as if I could tell whether it were Dylan's blood. On the ground was a flattened goathead plant and boot prints. Not Dylan's shoes. He'd worn sneakers like me.

There was blood. Little enough that I could breathe again.

The barrel of Dylan's gun looked twisted in on itself, as if hit by something small with great force. It must have been shot out of his hand.

Jane let the broken gun drop into the weeds.

"They took him then," I said, hope rising in me. "He's still alive."

He was alive, but for how long? As if this thought woke me up, I noticed Stan sobbing. He had dropped to his knees next to the wreck that used to be Luna. Her tires were flat, blood streaked the purple swirls on the side. Bullets had punched holes in the front hood, making something inside smoke.

"Luna! My God, what have they done to you?" Stan looked around at us and then pointed at Maibe. "I saw them. Those criminals who shot up Luna. All dark-eyed foreigners."

I lost all my calm.

I walked over to Stan and punched him.

He babied his jaw in his hands. He narrowed his eyes so that his cheeks seemed to swallow his face.

I turned and began to limp away.

"You can't leave. You need me."

CHAPTER 4

STAN CURSED at me and shouted stuff about being a true American. It took another block before his voice disappeared among the alarms. It was a third block before I was sure that Jane had decided to follow Maibe and me.

By the fourth block, I knew it had been wrong to leave Stan. It left a sick feeling in my stomach, running away like I'd done. His face, the way it had hardened against me—I'd caused that, and then I had run. He was still my neighbor. He had tried to help. I would go back and apologize and beg him to come with us.

Footsteps crunched behind me. I whirled with my knife raised, hoping it was Stan, afraid it wasn't. Jane raised her bat. Maibe dropped the water bottles and a box of crackers. She landed on her knees and scooped some puny rocks into her hands. All three of us brandished our weapons as if we actually meant to use them. I held back a hysterical laugh that bubbled in my throat. We were children brandishing toys.

"Who's there?" Maibe shouted.

I looked at her like she was crazy.

"Whoever it is knows we're here," Maibe said. "If it's a real person, they'll say something. If it's zombies, they'll just groan—so we'll have our answer."

I held back the desire to yell at her. There was no way to know if we'd been seen, but they'd definitely heard us.

"Stan," I said. "It's all right. Come on out. Just promise you'll stop being a jerk, then you can stay with us, okay?"

"Come out if you're real," Maibe said.

A cat screeched over the droning alarms and dashed across the street in front of us. Something else made a scratching sound, and then scuffling, and then a low moan.

"Is that our answer?" Jane asked, raising an eyebrow.

"I think so," Maibe said.

A figure separated itself from the wall of a building about fifty yards away. "Isn't that Christopher?" I said.

"I know where they've taken him," Christopher called out.

I froze. "What are you talking about?"

"I don't want to…to be a bother," he huffed out, and then almost fell over. "Could I…can you help me?" And then he collapsed like a deflating balloon.

I dropped my knife and ran over. Blood soaked the front of his shirt. Three bite marks on his arm wept more blood. His forehead was slick with sweat, his face flushed with fever.

His eyes still seemed normal. Not like the others. Not yet at least.

I was careful not to touch the open wounds. I didn't believe in zombies or Stan's Ebola theory or Jane's invasion remark. Rabies, maybe, but that took weeks to incubate.

I tried to sit him up. We splayed his legs while he took deep gulping breaths. His eyes were still closed, but he mumbled under his breath, as if dreaming.

"I don't see anything worse than the bites. Jane, help me with him."

She pulled her sleeve over her hand and covered her mouth. "I don't think so."

I had time to wonder if the only reason we'd stayed friends was because we'd always said we would, before we'd known what that really meant. Then I wondered what she and Dylan had been saying behind my back.

Christopher groaned and shifted. Jane jumped away.

"Wake up, Christopher," I said, shaking him because I couldn't shake Jane. "Where did they take Dylan? What do you know?"

His eyes fluttered open, focused on me. "Cheyanne?" He waved a hand in front of his face. "No, you're not Cheyanne."

"Who is she?" I asked.

"My wife…She was killed."

"I'm sorry."

"Please don't leave me behind. My heart isn't very good." He took in another galloping breath. "And the fever is getting stronger. I don't have much time before I'm going to go unconscious for a little while."

"What are you talking about?" Jane asked. "What's wrong with you? Is it the same as the rest of them?"

"No…it's different."

"But where were you?" I asked. "We searched the field—"

"What happened?" Jane asked.

"You said you know where Dylan is? Where is he?" Just saying his name out loud fluttered the panic inside of me. What had been my last words to him? Why had we argued that morning? Why hadn't I tried harder?

"I was in the RV when the infected came."

"The guys in the van?" I asked.

"No, like in our neighborhoods. Those kinds of people. Five of them came in, like they were running from something—usually they run after something. They…they…everyone started fighting. I ran out to help. I pulled out a," he swallowed and laughed, "frying pan from one of the cabinets. I went to help, but it was as if one of them knew I was inside. He was waiting for me when I opened the door and he pushed me back in…I killed him. And I tried to go back out, but then the van arrived. These were military-like people, and they had guns and shot everyone else. I stayed inside the RV. And then something happened with my heart. I don't know. I passed out and I woke up to Stan shaking me and telling me to get out. To get gone with you three. And then he took off."

"With Luna?" Jane asked.

"No. He couldn't get her to start. He took off on foot," Christopher said.

That sick feeling returned to my stomach. Now I could never take back what I had done. I shouldn't have run away, no matter what he had said.

"They took him," Christopher said, his voice hoarse. "Dylan was alive. Holding his right arm, I think. But he was definitely alive. I'm sure they took him to Cal Expo."

"Maibe," I said. "Bring some water over here."

"But why? We were headed there anyway. That's where the radio said to go. Why did they shoot everyone? It doesn't make any sense!" Jane said, her voice rising after each word until she was practically screaming.

He broke into a heavy cough.

"Maibe," I said. "Where's the—" Maibe hadn't moved from her position a dozen yards away. "What are doing?"

"He's been infected," Maibe said. "He's going to turn. That's how it always happens. He'll get sicker and sicker and then die and then come back to life and kill us all! He's already sick!"

Jane took several steps back from Christopher.

"Maibe," I said. "He's probably had a heart attack. That's why he's sick."

"It's not quite a heart attack," Christopher whispered. "I was born with a heart defect." His eyes fluttered closed and then opened again. He saw me but somehow I knew this time he wasn't really seeing me. He began mumbling under his breath.

"We need the water," I said, "to clear out his wounds, or he will get sick from infection and it will be your fault."

Maibe almost wailed. "Don't you see? He's a nice old man now, but when he turns on us, it won't be him, it will be some monster and then we'll all become zombies. We can't let him near us. We just can't!" Maibe held the water fiercely to her chest.

My hands went numb with the thought that she might be right. But I couldn't let him die from coughing either. "If this was your uncle, if Christopher was your uncle, you mean you wouldn't give him water just to ease his pain? Even though he hasn't 'turned' yet? Even though he's still a 'real' person? You mean you would withhold something that could help him?"

Maibe began to cry but didn't move. I hated myself a little bit then. "You would withhold water from this good man, from this man who was trying to help us? Then you're already one of them. You've already turned, and I don't want to be anywhere near you."

I turned an accusing look onto Jane. She knew I meant the words for her too. I didn't need to say them out loud. She flinched but held my gaze.

Christopher's head rolled to the side. I propped him up as best I could and worked on unsticking his shirt from his skin. A water bottle was thrust into my hand.

Maibe said a quiet, "I'm sorry."

I twisted off the cap, gave him a careful sip, then began ripping apart the sleeve of his shirt to get a better look at the bites.

"We need to get inside somewhere," Jane said. "This is too exposed."

I looked over our four-person group. Three women and an old, injured man on the asphalt of a long abandoned part of town full of weeds, trash, and car alarms. At least each store on this block was an island onto itself, surrounded by mostly empty lots except for the spurge, burdock, and yarrow growing up through the cracks and along the edge.

How quickly could I go after Dylan? How much would Christopher slow me down now?

Alone, with an injured man, a freaked-out girl, and a friend I wasn't sure I could count on.

I shook my head as if to banish the thought. I could count on Jane. When it mattered, I could count on her.

Jane positioned her hands to brace Christopher to a standing position. "We need to get him inside somewhere."

"Then go find us a place," I said, frustration leaking into my words. "I have to stay with him."

She headed over to the first building, tried its doors. Locked.

She went on to the next one.

I motioned Maibe over. "Follow her," I said quietly. I didn't want to say it was because I feared Jane would ditch us, but for all of Maibe's crazy zombie talk, she was a smart girl. She knew.

I dragged Christopher over to prop him against a brick wall. His shirt stunk of sweat, fear, and blood. I'm sure I smelled the same. The sun should have been somewhere in the middle of the sky by now, but the fog and smoke obscured it. A brownish yellow glow tainted everything.

How far away was Dylan now?

I'd clean Christopher's wounds and I'd find a way to talk Jane into staying with him while I went after Dylan. The faster Christopher got fixed up, the faster I could leave.

Maibe waved at me outside the door of an Army surplus store then ran back to help get Christopher inside. She used her sleeves to cover her hands when she touched him, but then again, so did I.

Just because I wasn't going to abandon him didn't mean I had to be stupid about it.

The door was made out of sturdy tempered glass. It had a hefty handle and slightly bent hinges that made the door stick as I forced it open. It was only slightly warmer inside than outside. I tried the lights, but nothing came on. Just as well. Lights might give us away to anyone watching.

What windows existed were small, cloudy, and above eye level. Empty store shelves ran along both walls. Though the cash register no longer existed, its presence had left a square mark on the wood countertop. The rest of the counter was rough, pock-marked oak.

I settled Christopher and checked the shelves. Empty. But

there was a box of musty blankets, another filled with plastic holsters, a third that had the look of a clearance bin dumping ground, and a half-full box of dusty MREs. My stomach growled at the sight and I almost hugged the box in relief. There would be food at least.

On either end of the back wall were doors. The left one opened to a one-stall bathroom that had seen better days. I did not try the light switch. The sunlight was enough to reveal the cracked porcelain, peeling paint, and exposed plumbing.

The important thing was the toilet still flushed and the faucet ran water. I wouldn't normally trust it to be drinkable, but this wasn't a normal kind of day.

The other door led to a small, lockable storeroom. I twisted the deadbolt and opened it, no knocking this time. The shelves were bare. I returned to the main part of the store and listened to the swop-swop sound my shoes made on the cement flooring. The sound slapped back from the walls, accentuating the hollowness of the place. Hollow was good, hollow meant there wasn't anywhere for things to hide.

I went behind the counter and rifled through one final box. Inside were a half dozen rusting machetes still inside army-green cloth covers. I set the machetes on the countertop and pulled one out of its sleeve. I tested the weight and length of it with a few swings through the air, and then looked at Maibe. No way her small body could carry one of these.

I handed her my kitchen knife. "This is yours now." I stuck one of the machetes in the back waist of my jeans.

Maibe examined her knife and then looked sideways at the machete in my hand. "These are some sorry kind of weapons," Maibe said.

I laughed. "This is some sorry kind of zombie movie we're starring in."

She laughed and then stopped and stared at me for a second.

"Joke," I said.

"Oh. I thought maybe you were starting to believe me."

I shook my head. "Nope." I smiled again to tell her I meant no offense. Just because people were sick didn't make it okay to treat them like monsters. Even if that made me a fool.

I brought one of the blankets over to Christopher. Sweat slicked his forehead but the cement floor was ice cold. I found some gloves and cleaned the wounds on his arms with more of the water, but it wasn't a very good job. Not with the angry red they were already looking. Then I remembered the yarrow outside.

People mostly grew it for its yellow flowers or because bees liked it. But it could also be used as an antiseptic.

I went outside into the chilly air. Goosebumps rose on my skin and I shivered. I wrapped my arms around myself. A person-shaped figure flitted between two buildings then vanished. Either there were people around after all, or I was imagining things.

I didn't want to wait to find out. I ran over and grabbed up the yarrow. It's roots flung dirt and moisture around. Its leaves were fuzzy, its flowers soft. There might just be enough to make a poultice. I went for a second plant.

"Corrina! Behind you!" Maibe yelled.

A man was sprinting toward me, his hands raised like a claw machine in an arcade game, ready to grab a stuffed animal.

I ran for the surplus store, my bruised knee slowing me down. I focused on Maibe's wide eyes, the way her hands jiggled the door as if it would make me go faster, the way my breath caught in my chest and my blood pounded in my ears. A sort of growl sounded behind me.

I jumped over the curb and tumbled into the store. Maibe slammed the door shut behind me. The guy slammed hard into the tempered glass a second later, smearing its film with yellow streaks of saliva.

"What was that?" Jane said, hair disheveled, hands frozen mid-air while eating an MRE.

I bent over, breathing hard, feeling dizzy from the adrenaline rush, feeling like a scared animal that had reached its burrow barely in time.

The guy banged against the door again and it shifted an inch from its frame, knocking dust into the air. This was not the polite knocking of the patio door man.

I noticed the checkout counter—a boxy rectangle of metal, glass and plywood—wasn't attached to the floor. "Help me drag this."

We dragged the counter against the door. The pounding continued, but the door seemed more solid now and the counter blocked most of him from sight. I rechecked the rest of the store. It was empty, and the windows were too small and high for anyone to break through.

But as I peered through the filmy glass, more people appeared in the street.

The pounding stopped, but the other shadows didn't leave. They seemed to be milling about, or if they left the area, more came soon after. They hovered like flies over something that died. Or was about to die. It was as if everyone was waking up at once.

A sick feeling entered my stomach. There was no way I could go after Dylan in the middle of all this, not unless I had a death wish.

I returned to Christopher and made the yarrow poultice as best I could. There wasn't much. I'd lost most of it while running.

Jane didn't speak a word to me as I worked. She sat herself on a table, huddled in a blanket, and stared out a grimy window, watching the shadows pass by. Maibe curled on another blanket on the ground, asleep.

I felt that exhaustion pulling at my muscles and eyelids. The faint light outside disappeared altogether. Christopher settled into a hallucinatory sleep and I tried to do the same. I lay there, awake and obsessing. Rabies could make animals violent. People were animals. But how did so many people get sick so fast?

In the early dawn light, I saw that Christopher no longer slept. He looked wrecked, old, but aware of himself again. I wondered how angry-red his wounds were now. If he didn't get some antibiotics in him soon, well, I wasn't any sort of doctor, but I knew it would be bad news if the red lines reached his heart.

He saw me staring and tried to paste a smile onto his face but broke into a cough instead.

"It seems like you know a lot for being someone who was just visiting his sister," I said.

"Not sure where it started." He wiped his hand across his mouth. "They didn't think I needed to know that kind of thing."

"What are you talking about?"

He coughed again, then paused as if considering what to say. "People are catching a type of rabies virus. One that our normal vaccine can't prevent, and one where the incubation period is more like thirty minutes instead of three weeks."

"Why should I believe you?" But even as I said it, I knew deep down it had to be true. It was the only thing that made sense to me.

"I'm an EMT," he said. "I'm also one of the first people who managed to get the new vaccine, if you can call it that. We've been dealing with this for months already."

"I thought you said there was no vaccine."

"I said the old one didn't work."

A dark object flew through the air and dropped into my lap, startling me. It was square and leather and still warm from Christopher's body heat.

"Take a look through my wallet. You'll see."

"It's dark." Another object fell into my lap. I picked it up.

"Use my lighter to see it."

"How do you know where to throw?" I said.

"You're talking, aren't you? I can tell where you are by the noise you're making." Irritation pricked his voice.

I flipped on the lighter and fumbled open the wallet. The sudden warmth stung my chin.

Jane and Maibe were huddled forms on the ground, still sleeping. Christopher sat up on his blanket. Shadows danced across the walls and his face. He looked old but talked like someone younger.

"How old are you?"

"Thirty-one."

The flame from his lighter must have shown the surprised look on my face.

"The vaccine makes the body age quickly," he explained. "My

insides are fine, for now. Heart issues run in my family. It's the epidermis that's affected. And the nervous system."

I had no idea what to make of his statement so I turned to the wallet instead. I held the lighter up to the plastic covering his ID. I saw his EMT license but nothing to indicate he was otherwise special. There was a picture of a young woman holding a little boy and girl against her. She sat on the grass while they stood on either side of her. They were dressed in summer clothes and smiling. I returned the picture.

"Do you believe me now?"

"It's definitely an EMT license, but I don't know what that's supposed to prove except that you're an EMT."

Christopher sighed. "Look in the billfold."

I re-opened the wallet. The billfold contained a couple of twenties and a folded piece of paper. It looked like some sort of report. The title read: "Test results for patient: Gurnman, Christopher." There were a bunch of numbers and labels. Cholesterol, blood pressure, triglycerides.

"Near the bottom," he said.

I scanned down the page. A line read: "*Lyssavirus iratus*: positive. *Borrelia alucinari*: positive," and then a handwritten note: "Congratulations, we'll retest to confirm."

CHAPTER 5

"I'LL TELL YOU what I know, but I don't know much."

I woke up Jane and Maibe. Christopher re-explained what they'd missed. The dawn light became bright enough they could read the folded paper without help from his lighter.

"You need to have both infections to survive with any sort of sanity. The bacterial infection fights off the rabies virus inside the body," he said. " But it's not really a cure. I'm infected with both now."

"They infected you with a bacteria? On purpose?" I said, incredulous.

He shook his head. "Not just any bacteria. It's a form of Lyme disease."

"This is crazy," I said. "Who would do that?"

"They said it was the only bacteria they found that stood a chance of fighting off the rabies. I doubt they chose Lyme on purpose."

"But what about the rabies? Who made that?" Jane asked.

"I don't know. Maybe it was just nature, or a bioweapon, or an accident. If they knew, they never told me."

His eyes began to take on a certain glaze I recognized. "Your bites reinfected you with a dose of the rabies virus," I said, not really asking a question.

He nodded. "They call it the Lyssa virus. The bacterial infection fights it off, but there are side effects."

"So your bites," Jane said. "They're from people who caught the Lyssa virus but not the other one."

"I told you!" Maibe said.

"No, it's not like that...I have both," Christopher said. "That's what I'm trying to tell you. I'm infected with both," he lowered his voice even though there was no one else in the room, "so I'm protected."

"Or sick twice over."

"Both are probably true," he said.

"If everything you've said is actually true," I said, "then why didn't you explain all this earlier? Why did you wait until now to tell us?"

"If I only had the mutated rabies virus, you'd all be dead by now and I wouldn't be able to put two words together."

"But only if you're actually protected, and only if it's supposed to work as fast as you say," I said.

"And only if these new bites don't do anything," Jane added quietly.

Christopher covered one of the festering bites on his left arm with his hand. "That's why I'm telling you now. I don't know what's going to happen. I mean, I think I'll be all right if I don't end up dying from a regular old infection, but I...When I went through this the first time, when they injected me with both at once, they said I fell into a sort of coma. The bacteria attacks the virus but can't destroy it, not completely. It does something to the body's skin and brain...I don't know which one causes it, but something still happens to the mind. To your memories. It's like you relive them. They become tied up in the present."

"You've already fallen into a coma," I said and explained about the mumblings from earlier.

"It's probably going to happen again," he said. "At least until my body gets back to some sort of equilibrium." He wiped a hand across his forehead. It was cold in the room but he had broken out in a sweat. "A lot of this is me just guessing. By the time I was inoculated, things were happening pretty fast. I woke up and everyone was gone. I needed to find my wife, my kids. They had been staying with my sister."

"And then?" Jane asked.

Christopher didn't answer for a long time.

"They all had the Lyssa virus," I said.

He shook his head. "I tried to help them..." He buried his head in his hands. One of his makeshift bandages slipped and revealed the angry bites on his arm.

He looked old enough to be my grandfather. Could he really be thirty-one? Had I gotten any of his blood on me?

"Once you kill them," Maibe said, "do they—the people who only catch the Lyssa virus—do they come back?"

"Dead is dead," he said.

Maibe looked about to challenge him but I interrupted with another question. "What happens if you only get the bacterial infection?"

He looked at me, surprised. "I don't know. I've never thought about it."

"You should leave," Jane said. "You're going to make us sick. You might have already done it."

The glaze over his eyes deepened. "You'd be feeling it by now if I had," he said.

I inventoried my body for signs of sickness. I felt sore, bruised, exhausted, hungry, but not sick like the flu, if that's what it was supposed to feel like.

"Please. I'll do whatever you want to prove that I'm not going to hurt you. I don't have anyone left." A drop of sweat trailed down the side of his ashy cheek.

"We should get the hell away from him," Jane said.

I secretly agreed with her and I hated that I did. I wanted to find Dylan. I didn't want to get sick.

"We can't leave him," I said.

Maibe whimpered.

Jane turned her head away.

"We'll lock him in the storeroom and wait it out," I said.

"As long as you promise you won't leave," he said. "Promise me."

"We won't leave," I said, "until we know what's going to happen to you."

Christopher managed a comical wave before we closed the door on him.

CHAPTER 6

WE ATE A MEAGER LUNCH that finished off the crackers—Maibe and I. Jane hadn't spoken to me in hours.

I handed Maibe the packaging so she could lick out the crumbs, and then set aside a bottle of water for Christopher. If we stayed inside the store for another day, we'd need to resort to the bathroom sink water.

Loud, clattering noises erupted what seemed like right outside.

"What's going on out there," Christopher shouted through his door.

I checked the front entrance to make sure it was still locked and barricaded, then returned to where Maibe stood on a countertop looking outside. I scrambled up next to her and we pressed our heads together. I smelled the stink of our combined sweat and fear from the last twenty-four hours. I ran a couple of fingers through my hair, felt oily build-up, and pushed all of it back behind my ears. The window was grimy and hard to see through. I pulled up my sleeve and wiped it across the glass.

People trickled down the street, sometimes alone, sometimes in groups. Sometimes aimless, sometimes running with an unknown purpose. I couldn't tell whether they were all sick, or if some of them were normal like us.

I jumped down and began pacing the room. Back and forth across the cold floor. The air in here was stale, dry, cold. Dust kept tickling my throat, making me want to cough. Every time I decided to risk going outside, find a car, drive like a mad woman to Cal Expo, some new sound obliterated my courage.

I tripped over the water bottle and forced myself to stop pacing. I picked up the bottle and went to Christopher's door.

"What are you doing," Jane said as my hand touched the deadbolt. She sat cross-legged on the counter next to a window.

"We forgot to give him water," I said.

"And?"

"And I'm going to give him some."

She pulled her hair back into a ponytail, smoothing it down with her hands. "Don't open the door. Are you crazy?"

I didn't remove my hand and instead observed the texture of the door's surface like it might be life or death. We needed to have it out, whatever 'it' was. Still, I wasn't looking forward to it.

"I don't think giving a sick man some water counts as crazy," I said finally.

"And why do you," Jane raised her voice, "get to decide?"

I pressed my back against the door for support. Maibe ducked her head into her blanket.

"I don't 'get' to decide anything, Jane. But keeping water from him is cruel."

"Don't start with that high-and-mighty 'it's the right thing to do' crap. I've known you too long for that. Please, you've been pulling that line since middle school."

I squeezed the water bottle, making the plastic crinkle. "What's your problem?"

She raised her left hand and began ticking off fingers with her right. "You ran after Mr. Sidner like nothing else mattered, putting me, Dylan, and Stan in danger—"

"I didn't—"

"You took in this girl and those others, like psycho-Christopher over there," she ticked off another finger, "without even asking if that was okay with Stan and me."

"I did ask. We discussed it."

"No, you didn't, Corrina. Sure, you pretended to discuss it, but you'd already decided to take them on, and it didn't matter who disagreed with you."

I shook my head in frustration. I didn't remember any of it going that way. Did it happen like that? Maibe had opened the door to the others, but had I already decided to let them in? "No. You're remembering it wrong. We wanted to check them out first, and then decide."

"Whatever," Jane said.

"Why are you assuming the worst in people? I am not out to get you."

"If the shoe fits," she said. She ticked off another finger. "There's still this last year of all the crap you like to throw at the people you're supposed to care about."

"And what about this last year?" I demanded.

"The way you've been so self-absorbed. When was the last time you asked, and actually cared, about what was going on in my life, my job? I'm the head ophthalmologist now at the office. Have been for a while—"

"How long have you been itching to have this conversation with me?"

"That's not the point," she ticked off another finger. "The point is you couldn't be bothered to notice. This last year has been all about your drama, all about grinding Dylan down for losing his job. I've watched the two of you for years. He already feels so much responsibility for you, and you take advantage of it. You play the needy-guilty-orphan card—"

"What did you say?" My fists were in the air before realizing it. She knew me and what saying that would do to me. "Congratulations on the job promotion. Sorry I wasn't paying attention because I was too busy keeping us from getting evicted. But in case you haven't noticed, the world is kind of ending right now. Is this really the time to have all this out?"

"Yeah, Corrina. It's not news you think you're better than me."

Some sort of infuriating half-growl, half-protest sound left my throat. I wanted to slap the sarcasm out of her. I hated that she sat there cool and collected, as if she'd mapped out this conversation a dozen times already and felt bored needing to repeat it for me. "Is that all of it? Are you done? Feel better yet?"

She paused, took in a long breath, as if debating whether to speak her next words. I wondered what cruelty she would dish out now. Maybe bring up some old high school wound, skewer me with a childish insult, pretend she never cared.

"It was me. It was me with Dylan. I was there when you weren't and he was going to leave you." She stood up, wrapped the blanket around herself and went to stand by the barricaded front door.

Maibe stared at me with huge drowning eyes. No wait, I was the one drowning. The rushing sound of water filled my ears, my brain, my shaking body.

"What?" I whispered. I rolled my eyes to the ceiling and examined its patchwork of cobwebs. "Is that why you ran to our house? Because it was…to him?" But then what was I to do with the last day, the forgiveness, the intimacy, the promises to make things better? My mistake had been with a coworker, but his—my best friend?

"He didn't leave," I said, struggling to hear myself over the ocean waves filling my ears. "How long, how did you…What did you…?" I'd once punched a girl in the eardrum for calling me a filthy name and my hand had made a satisfying swop noise and I wanted to hear that noise again.

"We were friends for a long time," she said while staring through the little bit of door not covered by the barricade. "But things change." She turned from the door and tightened the blanket around her shoulders. "The only thing that matters right now is figuring out how to get to Cal Expo, to Dylan, and—"

I didn't stop until I was inside the bathroom and had slammed the door shut behind me. Either I got her out of my sight or I really would hurt her.

The bathroom fell into almost complete darkness with the door closed. I slid along one of the walls until I sat on the tile floor. I took long, slow, deep breaths. The air stank of mold. The tile chilled my hands and quickly seeped through my jeans. I would not give her the pleasure of hearing me cry.

I punched the tile wall. A sharp pain shot up my arm and into my shoulder. The feeling of wetness spread across my knuckles. I cradled my hand in my lap and focused on that pain instead of all the other kinds of pain I could feel. I had been stupid, pathetic. Dylan had made me a fool and I had believed him, and none of it had been true, and Jane had come out with it like it was nothing.

There was a knock on the door and I gasped out the breath I had been holding. The handle shifted. I shot to my feet and scrambled backwards until my tailbone cracked against the porcelain sink.

"Corrina?" Maibe's tentative voice.

I relaxed my grip on the porcelain. "I'm here." I didn't mean to, but it came out as a growl. I sighed. Maibe didn't deserve my anger. "I'm here, Maibe."

"I'm sorry about Dylan," Maibe said. "And your friend. You don't deserve that."

I let out one sob at her kind words and then I gulped down more air and choked on it, coughed, and turned to the sink for water, quality be damned. The coldness of the liquid hit my lips and I splashed some on my face, shocking myself into the here and now.

There were worse things happening out in the world than this commonplace betrayal I faced.

"Corrina, will you come out?"

"I just need some time."

"I know, it's just…It's a little less scary with you out here."

I gripped both sides of the sink and let my head hang over it. I didn't know if Maibe knew how much her words helped me in that moment. I had no idea if she was mature enough at twelve to understand that she had just given me something to keep me from wallowing in my misery. She probably was. I couldn't stay in the bathroom any longer, not if Maibe was brave enough to ask me for help.

"Thank you, Maibe." I kept my voice soft and low. "I'm sorry I stayed in here as long as I did."

I walked out of the bathroom, stiffening my back in anticipation of facing Jane again. She'd curled up in a nest of army blankets in the far corner, already asleep, or pretending. This was so stupid. This was so high school drama. The world was ending and she had gone for the cheap shot. I couldn't let myself think about her or Dylan right then, all of it mixed up now. All of it treacherous and ready to suck me into an abyss.

The air in the main room seemed fresh by comparison to the moldy air I'd just been breathing. Maibe grabbed the hand I had used to punch the wall. I winced but did not pull away. I deserved that pain for abandoning her to Jane, for being a fool, for believing things could have gotten better so easily.

By how chilly the air felt already, I knew it was going to be a cold night. I only wore a few layers, and Maibe only had her sweatshirt. She guided me to a pile of blankets and I helped her set up layers of bedding. She crept into the makeshift bed and I tucked several layers of blankets around her before wrapping myself in several more blankets and curling up next to her for warmth.

I tried to fall asleep. Failed. Tried not to feel bad for myself. Failed at that too. I spent the hours examining the last few months like a forensic anthropologist. There must have been clues and signs, and of course I found them, obsessing about it now, reading into every word and look and doubt and intuition. And she had been my friend and he had been my boyfriend and my stomach flipped and I went into dry heaves.

I crawled out of the blankets, the cold floor painful against my hands. The blankets tangled and then slid away. I needed water.

Water.

Christopher.

I'd meant to give him water. I was determined to make up for forgetting. For letting Jane get the best of me. I crawled in the shadows, careful not to make noise. Everything was silent except for the almost hypnotic rhythm of their breathing. I swore I could almost see the frost of their breaths in the moonlit darkness. Two humps of gray, fuzzy blankets and two puffs of white mist. I could almost forget about the madness outside.

The MREs were set next to several bottles of water. It took almost a full minute to open the MRE silently with my numbed hands. The MRE tasted like paper on my tongue and sucked up what little moisture had been left. I swigged the water and swallowed, then waited a moment to see if it would all stay down.

It seemed okay, so I grabbed an unopened water, another MRE, and went to Christopher's door. Before thinking about it too hard, I undid the locks, and forced the door open in one go. It made a horrible squeak and I froze, but the rhythm of breaths continued and I entered Christopher's cage. A dim shadow seemed stuffed in the corner. It began to stir, but before it could rise up, throw off the blanket and overtake me—which in the dark on this night after everything, I suddenly had a great fear of exactly that happening—I set the MRE and water on the floor and retreated to the main room. Adrenaline pulsed through me as I raced to redo the locks as best I could in the dark, unsure if I got it right, but not believing it really mattered.

I headed back for my blankets when Jane's voice cut through the cold. "You shouldn't have done that."

I paused, thought about ignoring her, then said, "No, Jane, YOU shouldn't have done that."

She did not respond and I went back to my blankets satisfied in a small way that I had kept my self-control and maybe showed a shred of self-respect.

This time, while sleep did not come quickly, it did drift in eventually. I dreamed Dylan was sick and injured and abandoned on some dirty asphalt street, calling out my name. All my limbs felt heavy, immobile. Something, someone was calling me. Dylan, I thought. He's dying and calling out for me and I tried to force my limbs back to life, but felt resistance.

I awoke and expected to feel sharp stings as blood returned to my limbs. Instead, I felt rope around my wrists. My eyes flew open to darkness. I tried to move my legs and felt the ties around my ankles as well.

"Jane—"

"Shh." Fingers pressed against my lips.

Every muscle in my body contracted and pulled against the ropes. I opened my lips again, ready to shout for help but the fingers pressed harder, mashing my lips onto my teeth. My mouth tasted the finger. Salty and rough. My eyes focused enough to see an outline. The bulk of someone hovered over me. The person leaned close and I smelled rotted food and something akin to a school locker room. Suddenly, cold water washed over my hand.

"Cheyanne, you're sick," Christopher said. "It's for your own good. Please don't fight me. It's your only chance. Cheyanne, you have to trust me."

Pain sliced through my hand. I cried out.

He sniffed at my ear and nuzzled the space between my neck

and shoulder with his nose. I tried to separate that part of me from him. He was touching some other person's neck. He was not touching me, he was not touching me.

"This will protect you."

Something warm pressed against the pain.

I heard sniffling. "Maibe?"

"He bit me," Maibe said. I strained to see where she lay but only made out a dark lump against a darker wall.

The meaning of his actions sunk in. He was mixing our blood, infecting us with whatever he had. With a mutated form of rabies and some awful bacteria. I struggled to take my hand away but he only pressed his palm more firmly against mine. I watched a light flare. His lighter. It revealed Christopher—the lines on his face, the flush in his cheeks, the glaze on his eyes. I saw the rope around my wrists was shoelace pulled from my own sneakers.

"Jane?" No answer. "Jane?"

A headache pounded in my temples. My limbs were dead weights and my chest hurt.

Christopher scratched his eyes with the hand not infusing blood into mine.

I tried to think, could I break through the shoelace?

"There." Christopher removed his hand from mine. "I'm sorry, Cheyanne—"

"That's not my name!"

His eyes cleared and he seemed to see me. "What's happened?" He looked down at my palm, the knife, the blood. "Oh God, I'm sorry. I'm so sorry. I had a memory-rush. It happens..." His eyes lost focus again. "I love you, baby. You'll be safe now. I promise. You and the kids."

"You're a bastard," I said.

Maibe moaned. "I'm so hot. I don't feel good."

"It's probably going to be painful. It was for me. But don't tell the kids." He stood up and sorted through our meager pile of supplies. He returned with a bottle of water and supported my head. I was thirsty, but my throat felt swollen and my tongue thick. I sealed my lips and turned my face away from the water.

"It causes hydrophobia at first, but you've got to drink something, while you still can. Come on, baby." He forced my lips open with the bottle and tipped a small sip of water into my mouth. I almost spit it back in his face, but thirst overruled me. He laid my head down and stood back. The relief at his distance was immediate. I was still tied up, bleeding, infected, but at least he wasn't touching me.

Waves of heat rolled across my body, I broke into a sweat, I swore my hand wasn't clotting and I was going to bleed out on the floor. The muscles in my shoulder and around my knee spasmed. My eyes felt so heavy.

I fell into the memory-rush and the fevers, and everything disappeared.

December

***

—until the knocking started. That sick man came and pressed his dirt-smudged faces against our glass patio door. Doesn't matter what everyone else believes. They're not zombies. Zombie is just a made-up word to scare people into horrible—I can't talk about all that yet.

Please.

I need more time.

Dylan and I wanted to start over. We were putting ourselves back together when everything else fell apart. Like Humpty Dumpty, except that with the two of us, I just knew the broken pieces could be glued back together and made stronger and more beautiful because of it. The glue lines would create a mosaic. A fingerprint of our love; unique to the two of us. It would never look perfect or new or unused, but what's the point of having something if you don't use it, enjoy it, break it in like a new pair of shoes? Our love was like an old t-shirt, the more beloved the more we used it. Our love was like an iron filing ready to fly through the air and latch onto its magnet. Our love was like the olive oil vessels filled to overflowing, spilling over the ceramic and into the dirt and becoming a part of the earth, and making feet dirty as people walked through the oil slick puddles and took our love out to the rest of the world...

...did a van come for you too? I will try to make you understand how it was. How it is now. Don't you see that you all are like me and Dylan?

CHAPTER 7

FATHER ALWAYS WAITED in the front yard for me to come home from the fifth grade, the grade I remember the most for all the wrong reasons. He usually kept his hands behind him, holding back some kind of present—almost always an orange, his favorite afternoon snack. The unspoken rules of our game: first my father would ask, "How was school?" and then I shared a good story before winning whatever he hid.

One day I didn't want to play. I didn't want to talk about fighting the girl who'd called me 'foreigner' and said she wished my mother died from her cancer. I brushed off his question and headed for our front door, books heavy in my arms.

"What happened?" He'd asked.

I'd stopped and stared at the grass and then shook my head, my braid whipping across my back. I yearned for a hug, but fifth grade was the year I decided to stop acting like a baby.

I felt a tug on my braid. "Here."

I turned and saw my father offering me one of his hands. "Make a wish," he said, and held out a wishflower even though I hadn't followed any of our rules.

I imagined how my breath might release the feather-like pods to gallop into the air and travel a chaotic path away. But I felt too old to fall for these tricks anymore. I forced the spines of my textbooks to dig bruises into my arms. "This is stupid."

"Okay. Try this." He brought out his other hand.

Air caught in my throat. He held the largest bouquet of wish-flowers I'd ever seen, inches from my face. Dozens of globes hung together by the barest of connections and blotted out the rest of the world. Each stalk contained potential, hundreds of seeds ready to tornado into the sky and then blanket the yard, maybe land on Mrs. Harrit's grass and anger her when they sprouted in a week.

I took a deep breath.

Before I exhaled, my father used all his strength to blow.

A rushing wall of pods plunged into the air around me. Feathery tails twirled across my cheeks, eyebrows, into my open mouth. I smelled the oranges my father loved.

He blew again, hard enough to snuff out fifty birthday candles, his cheeks puffed into a pair of red balloons and I couldn't prevent my smile or the giggle that materialized deep in my throat, because yes, he'd gotten me, was getting me, and, oh, what a good trick!

I dropped my books and searched the grass. Broken stalks poked from the yard like bent drinking straws. I laughed while brushing seeds out of my mouth. "Did you pick them all?"

He waved his hands at the pods still floating in the air. "Just about."

The seeds settled into a white carpet on the grass and did not pay attention to property lines. I couldn't wait for the look of horror on Mrs. Harrit's face once hundreds of wishflowers grew up in her perfect lawn. Then I saw it—a scraggly stalk with half the seeds already blown off the flower head, hiding in the crack where the house met grass—it was enough. "Mrs. Harrit is going to be mad," I said.

He looked toward Mrs. Harrit's front door. "Promise you won't tell on me?"

"Okay." I picked the flower and hid it behind my back. "But only if you get my books."

"Done."

I crept closer and readied my attack stance. I blew at the wishflower as he turned, but he blew at the same time. The seeds twirled as if caught in a hurricane, some going this way, some going that way.

My father laughed. I giggled as a couple of seeds caught in his eyebrows and disappeared into his gray-streaked hair.

"I think your father wins this round."

We froze at the sound of my mother's voice. It came out of nowhere, reminding me we were still three, though no one knew how much longer that might last.

She leaned against the door post. I noticed she wore sweats, not a bathrobe. One of her good days.

"You both look like you're wearing very silly white hats," she said.

I ran fingers through my hair, pulled out a handful of white tufts and stuffed the seeds into my pockets for my collection.

My father stepped onto the porch and kissed my mother's cheek. "Did I tell you how," he said, turning back to where I stood in the grass, "when we first moved here, your mother returned to her old neighborhood to pick some wishflowers? She couldn't find a single one growing on the whole block here. To your mother, this was a travesty." He lowered his voice and glanced toward Mrs. Harrit's house. "So your mother walked the neighborhood, under the cover of night, and blew an entire flower's head of seeds into each front yard, for five houses down, in both directions and both sides of the street."

"But I didn't plant anything!" My mother laughed. "I was like a strong breeze, nothing more."

"I don't think the neighbors would agree." He winked at me.

She replied, "Well, too bad."

RAIN BEAT AGAINST the roof of the store, startling my memory-rush—there was nothing else to call it except what Christopher had named it. Memories that wisped in and then away like weed-flowers turned into wishes.

"Yes, momma. I know you love me." My throat spasmed and I wished for her to get better. I thought maybe if I made the wish over and over again, one wish for every wishflower pod that my father and I had ever blown at each other, that it would come true.

I woke enough to remember my mother had died six weeks after that day. All my wishing for nothing. It couldn't stop my father from dying of pneumonia and grief two months after I turned thirteen. I went through several foster homes. I ended up at a group home that asked me to find a new place to live after I'd gotten into a bad fight at school. I moved in with Jane's parents. Got a job at the garden. Met Dylan.

Dylan.

The infection grew, swirling together old and older memories. I came out enough to drink a little water, and then I sweat it out, and then I fell back into it, but not before seeing Maibe lying next to me, and then the fever of memories settled on my brain like a humid blanket.

I lived my father dying. I lived my high school fights. I lived endless pasta dinners and tuna sandwiches, the calls to Jane that held me together, the classes and papers and bills. There was nothing particularly poignant about grief and poverty and loneliness. I'd folded those memories into a black hole of time, but they came back.

My father had died, but he'd done so slowly and his will asked he be cremated and shipped back to his family in the old country. There was no proper funeral for him, just an ache and emptiness. I lived much of my memory-rush time with him, and felt some gratitude to the virus for this.

I wondered if all of the memory-rushes would be so kind, and then I understood how people might get so lost in the fevers they never came back out.

HOURS OR DAYS OR WEEKS LATER, there was no way to know, the gnawing pain in my stomach cleared my head. Like the knife-edge feeling after a migraine has left. This sense of openness, yet fear, because the migraine might be waiting around the corner.

I lay flat on the floor. I tested my muscles. I stretched and felt the tingle of increased blood flow. The shoelaces no longer bound my limbs. I sat up and looked around.

"Jane?" No answer. I raised my voice. "Jane? Maibe?"

"Here," Maibe said.

I saw a lump. Both of us had retreated to corners of the room, as if we'd turned into wild animals licking our wounds in privacy.

"Do you hurt still?" I thought about trying to stand, and tested putting weight on my feet. They held up okay.

"I guess. I feel kind of empty," Maibe said.

I tried not to think about what might or might not be going on inside my body. My spine creaked as I forced myself to stand. My muscles felt weak, my bones fragile. I tried to take a step. "What the hell?"

"What's wrong?" Maibe said.

I couldn't tell her how everything was wrong. But it was, everything felt wrong. My skin felt tight, my joints ached, my entire body felt as if it was pulling my toes and my head into my middle. I tried to straighten my hunched back, pain seared up my spine.

"Corrina?"

"I'm okay," I gasped. My body felt old and rickety. I feared taking a step. I feared I wouldn't be able to take a step.

Pain lanced through my feet. I shifted my weight without moving an inch. Once I felt steady, I took another tentative step. More aches, but not as intense. I hoped the grinding feeling would disappear altogether once I moved around enough. I hoped all of it was caused by bad circulation and not something else.

"Maibe," I said. "I want you to go very slowly. We've been sick and are both very weak. Be careful, but I want you to try standing up now and describe for me how you feel."

I heard the scrape and shuffle of her shoes and then a small cry of pain.

"Maibe?"

"I'm okay," she said in a small voice.

I stumbled over to her in the semi-darkness, pushing away the stinging in my joints, ignoring the way my body seemed incapable of standing straight. When I reached her corner she stumbled. I tried to catch her.

Both of us went down. My elbow hit the cement, shooting pain up my arm. Maibe sprawled across my stomach. I laid my head back on the ground and stared up at the ceiling. What was wrong with us?

"I'm scared," Maibe said.

I shivered and wrapped my arms across my chest. "Me too."

Maibe snuggled into the hollow of my armpit. I moved to embrace her and we lay still, together on that cold cement floor. I felt the warmth of her small body against my arm. The weight of her constricted my lungs, but I didn't say anything. I just held her tighter and tried to find some comfort. Tried to tell myself to be happy that our hearts were still beating.

"DID IT MEAN ANYTHING?"

Dylan paused for just a little too long. "No."

"No? Then why did that take so long to say?"

"Why was it so easy for you to tell me?"

I didn't know what to fire back with. I didn't know how things had gotten so bad so fast. His knuckles turned white on the back of the chair. I feared he would break it and there wasn't any money left to buy another, but I didn't dare say something and have him accuse me of nagging him.

After a long moment of looking at each other, tears pooled in my eyes and in the space of that pause, next to my anger, I felt what really lay underneath.

Loneliness.

I missed him. I missed him and I didn't want any of this to end, but I didn't know how to stop it either.

"Corrina."

I held up my hand to give me time to fight the lump that had closed up my throat. "Just...let me cook the dinner. Just leave it for now. Please."

He stood there as if about to argue with me and I steeled myself for the next round and told myself I would not cry in front him.

I waited for it, whatever was too much for him to keep in, whatever was going to hurt really bad and crush this moment of truce, this possible new beginning, and then the moment passed.

His dark eyebrows softened and a different light came into his eyes and it was his move and he kissed me. It was long and deep and tentative, like he feared guttering a candle. His five o'clock shadow scratched my cheek. He smelled like the almond-scented soap we both used. We made love as an offering to each other and we made love to banish the lingering ghosts. We made love as if we feared it wouldn't be enough.

CHAPTER 8

I PUSHED MYSELF UP from the concrete and crawled to the door. There was a stillness to the air I didn't understand.

I checked to make sure the door was locked. It was, but from the outside, as if someone had left and barricaded it behind them to keep us from leaving.

My tongue felt thick with dust, like I'd been dreaming with my mouth open. The air was chilly and stale, yet humid from our sweat. Maibe shivered on the floor, moaning, tossing around. In the haze of gray cloudiness in my brain I went over and shifted the blanket to cover her.

I tried not to think about how much time I'd lost, how I was going to find Dylan. Thinking about him sent a new hurt through me.

I steadied my hand against the door.

Where was Christopher? Where was Jane?

Before I could search for them, I lost myself again.

THE PATHFINDER STARTED with only a slight cough and rumble.
I tied my hair into a ponytail and rolled down the window since
I couldn't afford the gas to run the air conditioner, even if it had
worked. The radio spouted a song from the 50s and I cranked
up the volume to compete with the rushing air.

I'd upped my time at the community garden to three days
a week. The garden had helped put my life back together. I
loved working in the dirt, planning out a new section of plants,
discussing which species to cultivate next.

I made good time to Ms. Roche's little blue cottage. She'd
painted her stone porch a bright yellow the neighbors hated. I
loved her courage.

"Hello, dear," Ms. Roche said as she opened her front door.
She wore a large dream-catcher pendant with plastic, pink beads
that clinked together in the canyon between her breasts. "Come
around back and let's quickly get the starters in your car. Did
Leiko tell you the water's been off on my block for two days?"

"I thought it was only for overnight?"

"Yes, well," she hummed a couple of notes to herself and
then looked sideways at me once we stepped into her backyard. "There was a water problem in Golden Estates and they
dropped everything to go deal with that. And so here we are."
She fluttered her hands at the sky.

We loved to gossip about Golden Estates, but Leiko was
waiting for the starters. "So what's the deal?" I saw about a
dozen starts of wilted kale, wilted lettuce, and a single pathetic
blueberry plant covered in yellow leaves.

"I haven't watered in two days. I managed to put by enough
for me to drink, but that's it." She laughed. "I'm staying back
all these feet so you can't smell me."

I smiled and said, "Ms. Roche, you always smell like a butterfly and you know it."

She giggled and then fingered the blueberry, sending a leaf twirling to the ground. "The blueberry is bad off. Most should bounce back once you get them to the garden. Not sure the blueberry's going to make it, but, well…" She shrugged her shoulders.

I rummaged in my purse. I shook an almost empty bottle over the blueberry plant to release the last few drops. The heat seemed to laugh at my misting attempt.

"Let's get 'em in my car." We loaded up the plants and a wheelbarrow, and I waved as I drove off with my precious cargo.

The community garden was two miles away, but the first half-mile crawled, and then brought me to a standstill. Lights flashed far in the distance. I turned left onto an empty side street—the alternate route would triple the distance, but who knew how long the accident might hold things up. I sent out a hopeful thought that no one was seriously injured.

I turned the radio up and hummed along. Several miles later, I stopped at a light to turn left. I tapped my fingers on the steering wheel and glanced back at the plants. This intersection always took forever. Whenever I stopped I swore the car's temperature increased by ten degrees.

My detour had taken me past city limits and into a section of vacant lots turning back into country. Two out of the four corners were cracked cement and starthistle. The other two corners were graveled dirt.

Plenty of cars broke the speed limit racing through the intersection. Lunch hour. A bicyclist in bright blue clothes and matching helmet crossed before the light turned. "He's got the right idea," I said to the plants. Soon it would be too hot to bike, but he seemed better off than me right now.

The light changed and I pressed the gas. My car rumbled to life, and then coughed, and then died. I sent out a frantic wish for enough momentum to reach the curb, but my car halted in what seemed like the exact middle of the intersection. I tried to restart. Nothing. The car didn't whimper, but I did.

The light changed, cars inched past, and then picked up speed. A black BMW made a lane change that almost forced a red truck into my front fender.

I opened the driver's side door and tried to ignore the irritation rolling toward me like heat waves. I took a deep breath, held the air in my lungs, and pushed the car with all my strength.

The car moved like a ton of rock. It didn't budge.

I tried again, moved the car an inch, but then the grade of the street moved it back two inches. Sweat streaked down my face, arms, inside my clothes. I wiped my hands on my jeans and repositioned. "C'mon. You can do this."

I lunged into the push. I grunted. The car moved an inch and then another inch and then a few more. I was doing it! I was also headed into oncoming traffic, but I dared not lose momentum by trying to steer.

"Grab the wheel!"

I startled and lost my grip, but the car continued moving without my touch. The blue bicyclist was pushing at the back of my car. His bike lay in the street behind us.

"Just get in and steer it," the biker shouted. "Make sure this coffin doesn't jump the curb!"

I hopped into the driver's seat, steered, and the car rolled onto the shoulder. I hit the brake, regretful that I was ending all that had gone into moving this stupid hunk of metal.

"Thank you so much," I said, jumping out of the car, ready to heap him with compliments. "It just stopped—"

"Hold up," he said. "Let me get my bike."

He jogged back to the intersection, ignored the lights, the Don't Walk sign, and stopped traffic like he had a god-given right to it. He reached his bike. I heard him swear. He gave the finger to a honking car, and came back through the intersection. The bicycle's wheel wobbled like badly tossed pizza dough. "Goddamn," he said every few seconds and kicked out once at the passenger side door of a car that refused to let him pass. The car paused, and I thought I might witness some sort of road rage incident, but the biker's fury must have given the driver second thoughts. The car sped off.

When he reached the shoulder, he flipped the bike onto the seat and handlebars, and began fiddling with the wheel.

I didn't know anything about bikes, except that a wobbly wheel wasn't good.

"They tacoed the damn thing," he said without looking up. "I just retuned the spokes. What a mess."

"Umm," I cleared my throat. "Thank you for helping me, and I'm sorry about your bike. I—maybe I could help buy you a new one, as a thank you?" I could probably scrounge together fifty dollars. Maybe pay my rent a little late, forgo the seed donation money this month.

He kept his head bent over the wheel. "The hub has lost some teeth. The wheels alone cost me $350 to build and the hub is ruined, that's another hundred bucks."

My head began to swim. "I…"

He looked up. Dark eyebrows and a shaving shadow framed

sunburned skin and piercing blue eyes. "Not your fault," he said.

"But…"

He returned his gaze to the wheel hub and then back to me. I drowned in multiple waves of embarrassment.

"You didn't happen to notice the license plate of the car that did this?" He asked.

"I…" God, why couldn't I finish a sentence or even put two words together? Maybe it was situational stress, the adrenaline lessening, the embarrassment rising again, the monumental mechanic's bill waiting for me in the near future.

"Never mind," he said.

"I'll help out," I said. "I have maybe fifty bucks at home. I could at least help you get a new hubber thing."

He laughed. His facial features relaxed. "Hub," he said. "Wheel hub. And really, it's not your fault. I should have left it on the corner sidewalk, not in the intersection, but you looked so alone out there with all those cars honking at you." He shook his head and spun his back wheel, but the wobble caught on the frame and stopped the movement halfway through a rotation.

I remembered the plants. "Oh!" I said and ran to open the back of the Pathfinder. The plants looked much worse. The blueberry had all but given up. "Do you have any water?" I removed the wheelbarrow and pulled over the plant containers for closer inspection.

"Uh, yeah." He handed me the sports bottle from his bike.

I unscrewed the cap and portioned water out for the blueberry. I drained half the bottle and then finished it off on four other starts. The rest were goners. "I was on my way to the community garden on 7th street and…" I trailed off as I saw the look on his face.

He stared at his empty water bottle. "Did you know," he said in a strangled voice, "that there isn't any potable water around here for at least another two miles?"

I dropped the offending bottle to my side. "I didn't know that."

"Did you know today's going to break a hundred degrees?"

I laughed, the sound choking a bit in my throat. "I did know that."

After a long pause, he said, "It must be important to get these plants back to the garden alive."

"Oh, it is," I said, and then rushed into a long explanation of each plant's history, genetic value, the mission of the garden, the blueberry's varietal uniqueness.

He laughed and held up a hand for me to stop. "Save your energy," he said. "I believe you."

"I'm sorry," I said, breathless at the warmth of his laugh. I wiped the sweat from my forehead.

"You've got some dirt." He moved closer and brushed his hand along my face. He pushed back a strand of my hair. Our eyes caught and held.

He stepped back. "Sorry."

"No," I said. "That was...I should be saying sorry." I brushed my face again with my hand and froze. "I totally didn't mean to do that." I could have slapped myself. I turned my back to him, took the edge of my shirt, and furiously cleaned my face with it. When I turned back, he had set the wheelbarrow upright on the street and was filling it with the plants.

"Since the plants can't stay here, but the car looks like it won't be going anywhere for awhile, I'll walk the wheelbarrow if you walk my bike. There's a bus stop about a mile away. No water, but the driver on this route should be cool about the wheelbarrow and he'll get us to water."

"I don't know how to thank you," I said. "Nobody stopped to help but you. And now your bike is ruined because of me."

"True," he said seriously. "All true." And then he smiled. "The bus will let us off in front of a grocery store. Treat me to a bottle of ice cold water…and a date."

"I…yes, yeah. Okay." I unsuccessfully hid a smile. "I'd love to."

He handed his bike over, and then closed the back of the Pathfinder. I didn't bother locking the piece of junk. It'd make things easier if someone stole it.

The wheel made it difficult to steer the bike, but I was determined to get the hang of it. Soon the shoulder gave way to hard-packed dirt wide enough for us to walk side by side.

"I'm Corrina," I said.

"Dylan," he said. He hummed a song melody, and then sang the words.

"Yeah, my dad was a Bob Dylan fan." I searched for something else to say. "I'm glad I met you."

He shook his head.

"What?" I asked.

"Do you mean that, considering the circumstances?"

A little put off, I lost control of the bike and the front tire bumped into the side of the wheelbarrow. I steadied it and said, "Obviously I didn't want my car to die like that, and using your water for the plants was—"

He busted up laughing.

After a moment I joined in. "Thanks," I said between breaths. "I really appreciate a person who can laugh at me when I'm in trouble."

"With you. Technically, you're laughing, so I'm laughing, with you, at all your troubles." He pointed to one of the plants. "So what kind of blueberry is this one again?"

"Well." I touched the bare skin of his arm, feeling warmth, sweat, electricity. I pushed his arm so that his pointing finger moved a foot to the right. "First, this one's the blueberry."

I BABBLED and I woke to my own noises. Christopher pressed against me, and I rushed back into a coma full of memories. I was next to my dying mother's bedside. I was tied up in the army surplus store. I was listening to Maibe sob in the darkness. I was sitting next to Dylan. He was telling me how much he loved all my ideas: how beautiful I could make drying on a clothesline sound, how romantically I described a weed garden in every front yard, how inspiring I was when I talked about people trading in their gym memberships for bicycle-powered washing machines. But he knew me well enough to understand it was partly about fear, about not relying on others because maybe they couldn't be relied on. People always died, people always left.

Suddenly I was drinking water from a cup. I woke enough to eat the MRE that Christopher pressed into my hand. My body felt weak from sickness and dehydration. I realized he'd tied me up again.

"Sometimes the memory-rush is too strong," he said. "It can make you do things. Hurt people. You were walking around. This is safer."

"Where's Jane. What did you do to her?"

"She's gone."

CHAPTER 9

"DID YOU KILL HER?" I couldn't generate much emotion at the thought. Not that I didn't care.

Even with what she and Dylan had done, she didn't deserve to die. But my head ached and my limbs were dead weights and my chest hurt and the memories had wrung out my emotions. I didn't have the energy to care about much of anything.

"She left, Corrina. And I didn't do anything to her. She got out of the ropes before I could infect her. The memory-rush… She made it through the barricade and was out the door. That was over two weeks ago…I think."

It was too much information to digest at once. Two weeks? Jane gone? Was he even telling the truth? "She wouldn't have abandoned us without trying to help," I said with conviction. Jane was many things, but she had never been a coward.

"That's what happened."

"You've done something to her." I strained against the bonds and pushed myself up a few inches to look at her sleeping place, but it was empty. The floor was bare of any blankets, bare of anything that gave the impression Jane had slept there. "And there's no way it's been two weeks. You are a liar."

"I think it's been about two weeks," Christopher said. "It could be longer. It...it's hard to keep track." He began talking about his wife, his kids, his job. He smelled my hair. He went to Maibe. She tossed about on the cement floor, but she did not open her eyes. He lifted her shirt. His hands hovered over her chest. Her nipples were two red dots on a flat surface.

"Get away from her!" My tongue felt thick in my mouth.

He sprang away from Maibe and he looked at me and he brushed imaginary cobwebs from his eyes. "I'm sorry. I...I... My child was sick and I had to rub menthol."

"Cover her up," I said, and I fought the constriction of my throat. We lay helpless, locked in by ropes, bound up by sickness, possessed by a man gone crazy.

He pulled Maibe's shirt down, scuttled across the room, and pressed against the wall. "I'm sorry." He did look sorry. He looked horrified. He rocked on his heels and stared unseeing into the air.

I WOKE UP and found him next to me. He cradled me, and disgust shuddered through me, but I did not pull away. I pressed my body against his, and I encouraged him to stay by me. He stayed by me, and he did not go near Maibe, and I wished for the fever, but this time it did not come.

Christopher only slept pressed against me, and I spent those next few hours thinking about how far away Dylan was, how if he hadn't stopped to help push my car out of the way we never would have met. How I might never reach him, and if I did, it might not matter anymore.

Christopher woke and loosened the bonds enough to allow me to stretch. He loosened Maibe's rope as well. He went into the back room, mumbling about foraging supplies.

I searched Maibe for injury—her bedraggled hair and smudged hoodie, her cross-legged position on the cement. There was nothing.

Relieved, my attention turned to the cold, how it seeped into my legs, deep into my bones.

"He's turning us," Maibe said. "We're becoming zombies."

I didn't respond because I didn't know what to say. He had made us sick with something deadly, something that had torn apart the whole city and taken Dylan away. Maibe's explanation made as much sense as Christopher's. And it didn't matter what the truth was, it mattered that it was here and it had infected Christopher, and now—but I forced my thoughts away from this. My wounded hand throbbed and I pretended Christopher had only wounded me. A flesh wound, nothing deeper, nothing more profound. Please.

The fever rose up in me again—a slight tick in my calf muscle, a sluggishness in my blood, a thickness in my throat and brain, a sense of floating through multiple dimensions.

An image of Dylan from when we first met appeared next to Maibe's right shoulder. He wore the biking shorts and held the blue helmet the way he had just before the car had crushed his bicycle. He flickered and disappeared, and then my mother hobbled to the bathroom door in the robe she never took off during those last weeks. I closed my eyes, but her image remained. I opened them and she disappeared to be replaced with Jane, high school Jane.

I heard a whimper and did not know whether it came from me or Maibe. With painful effort, I ignored the illusions for the moment and focused on Maibe's flushed cheeks. The fever was ready to rage up in us again. I wondered how bad the memory-rush would get this time around, how long it would last, how much time we would lose.

"I was sleeping on a piece of glass," Maibe said. "I'm trying to cut through the rope, but I'm so weak, and then I go to sleep."

She turned her wrist to show me her progress. She had such a long way to go. If the fever hit her like it hit me, her muscles were weak and hard to control.

Christopher came back carrying another water bottle and some rags. "Just a few more days, and then it will get easier to manage," he said.

Maibe turned her wrist away and closed her hand around the glass.

"Christopher," I croaked, trying to focus his attention on me. He came quickly to my side. His breath still smelled of sour, rotting food and I wondered if that was part of the infection, and whether it would become a part of me as well, and whether I would ever leave that smell behind.

"It's okay, it's okay. Shh." He brushed the hair off my forehead and allowed his fingertips to touch my collarbone. He looked at me with a mixture of love and lust and madness.

I was determined to keep his focus on me instead of Maibe. "Hold me? I can feel the fever rising and I'm scared."

He paused, squeezed the water bottles, and then set them down. "Of course."

"Maibe," I said. The fever rushed up and fuzzed over my eyes. Christopher lay down beside me. He curled his arm around my waist. "Close your eyes and go to sleep." I could not see well enough to tell whether she listened. I tensed my stomach muscles to keep them from flinching at his touch. "Stay with me, Christopher."

"I will."

"Promise," I said. "I saved your life, remember? Promise me— don't leave me for a single moment."

"I promise."

The fever took me. This time I welcomed it, jumped inside of it, asked it to keep me under a spell long enough to not remember a single moment of what came next.

THE OLD VICTORIAN house was well taken care of. The porch was painted a cheery white, the grass and landscaping were a happy balance of care and growth. It was the sort of house I took pleasure in walking by. The sort of house that looked humble, settled into itself, inviting.

Where the house met the sidewalk there was a straggling line of weeds. Coarse grasses and some sort of delicate purple weed-flower poked through the cracks in the sidewalk, over- looked, for now. They caught my eye, like they always do. Living organisms that don't belong in the spaces they inhabit. Living organisms that hang on to their chosen ground with a tenacity that few other plants could match.

In spite of Dylan's earlier warnings, I thought surely we would find enough common ground with a home as lovely as theirs. If they saw beauty and enjoyment in morning glory vines, a miniature weeping willow tree, chamomile bushes and a patch of wildflowers, then Dylan's parents would be welcoming. They would.

"You okay?" Dylan squeezed my hand.

"What? Oh. Just worried, I guess." We locked our bikes to a street sign pole. I used my free hand to straighten the summer dress I'd bought specifically for this brunch. A cute yellow paisley pattern that showed off my legs.

Since that first meeting, Dylan had coaxed me into bike riding with him to our various coffee, dinner and hang-out dates. He had a car hidden away somewhere, a green Saturn, he said, but I'd yet to see it. I appreciated having a reason to dust off my beach cruiser. Dylan had tuned it up for me. His insistence and care as he worked on it touched me more than if he had brought me flowers or jewelry.

Dylan tugged my arm to his chest. "You'll be fine. It's my family I'm worried about."

"Did you grow up your whole life in this house?"

"Pretty much," he said. He pointed to the weeping willow tree. "That used to be as tall as me when I was five." He pointed to the porch. "I cracked my chin on those steps several times while playing army soldiers with the neighbors." He held open the fence gate that enclosed the front yard. "But this fence is newer because I backed into the old one the first day I drove by myself."

"No," I said, laughing. "And did that begin your aversion to cars?"

"Ha, no. I don't have an aversion to cars, I just like bikes better. Cars are good for some things, but bikes are good for most things. Why would I pay for a gym membership, and then pay for a car to drive me there, when I can just ride my bike and—"

"All right, all right." I lifted my hands in mock surrender.

"Right, you've heard this a few times by now. Sorry."

"No, it's fine." I kissed him and felt the stubble on his face against the softness of my lips. The feeling was now pleasantly familiar. He dropped his hand to cup my butt through the thin cotton of the dress. We had first slept together a week ago and all of it was still so new and wonderful. I loved the smell of him and I breathed just a bit faster at the heat of his hand through my dress. I smiled against his lips.

He stepped back reluctantly, allowing a soft breeze between us. He cradled my face with his hands, kissed my forehead, and then kissed the space between my neck and shoulder, sending a shiver down my spine.

"My place tonight?" He asked. "I even cleaned."

"Yes," I said, and left it at that. If I said more my voice might crack. Instead I refocused on the evening's agenda. Meet Dylan's parents. Get them to like me.

"Ready?"

I nodded.

We walked to the front door and he rang the doorbell.

I had expected one of Dylan's parents. Instead a young man who looked a lot like Dylan opened the door.

"Good to see you, bro," Dylan said.

"You too, big brother." The brother turned his gaze upon me. He had Dylan's hair color and build, but a longer hair cut and a paler shade of blue eyes. "This Corrina?"

"Yep," Dylan said. "Corrina, this is my brother, Denny."

"Our parents liked names that started with the letter D for boys," Denny said, "and K for girls."

K as in Krista. His sister who'd died.

Denny smiled and held out his hand and I shook it. "What-ever you do, don't bring up how pretty the front fence is, it'll get both Dylan and my parents going."

Dylan laughed.

"Oh, I see my warning has come a bit too late." He ushered us both into the house. "Mom and Dad are barbecuing in the backyard." He pointed to a landscape painting of some hills at dusk. "That's Mom's favorite painting so make sure you com-pliment it. Dad loves to fish and some of his catch is on the barbecue tonight, so make sure you mention how good it is. Bathroom is down the hall, did you need it?"

"Yeah, might as well," I said. Now that we were officially inside Dylan's house and seconds away from meeting his parents I wanted to give myself a once-over. I walked to the hall bathroom and was about to close the door when I heard Denny's voice.

"Nice catch, bro. But did you warn Mom and Dad ahead of time?"

"I told them I wanted them to meet my new girlfriend."

"Did you tell them about her?"

"Not really, that's what tonight is for."

"Did you tell her about them?"

"She's already nervous enough. It'll be fine."

Denny snorted. My hand slipped off the doorknob and made a squeak, but they didn't notice.

"Dad's already in the booze. Mom's all set to launch into Darren stories. Well, she's been going all week. His anniversary is next week."

Dylan sighed. "I know it."

"All right, bro, maybe you know best, but I wouldn't bring my girl in here without warning her, especially when she looks

Middle Eastern. She is, right?"

"Yeah. Egyptian, if that makes a difference."

"It won't."

"It will. I'll make it matter."

"You serious about her?"

"No question, man. I'm serious."

A pause in their conversation made me realize I was holding my breath. I continued to hold it, afraid letting it out would give myself away.

"I'll do my best to play interference."

"Thanks, bro. I appreciate that."

"How'd you end up with someone so hot?"

Dylan laughed. "Man, my blue Marin."

"Your bike? What the hell? No way you're cruising along on that baby and she, what? Can't help but fall in love with your manly calves?"

"Not quite like that. I had to retire the Marin…" Their voices drifted away from me. I guessed they must have moved to the back of the house.

I locked the bathroom door, sat on the closed toilet seat, and wiped the sweat from my palms onto my dress. After a long minute, I gathered my courage, ran the faucet, and sprinkled some water on my neck to cool down. When I opened the bathroom door Dylan was leaning against the hallway wall. "Ready?"

"I guess," I said.

"Before we go out there, I need to tell you something. I'm sorry I didn't warn you sooner. Denny kind of pointed out I was being an ass by keeping this from you, but I didn't want you to worry or think it mattered or—"

"Just tell me, please."

"Alright, I had an older brother, Darren. He was killed in the war. And my dad, well, he's not okay with it, and sometimes that comes out when he drinks. And my mom isn't okay with it in a different way. They hold it against, well, they believe all of the Middle East is the enemy now. It's been a lot for us. First Krista and then Darren…and if you want to back out, I'll figure out something to say to them."

"I'm sorry about your brother. I wish you had told me before, but no, I won't back out. Not unless you think I should."

"No, I want you to meet them. They're good people, just, well…you know how bad things can get after somebody dies."

"I'll be fine. I'm sure your parents will be fine. But I kind of want to get this over with. Unless there's another secret you should tell me?"

Dylan half-smiled. "Just that, according to Denny, I can be a real ass sometimes."

"You know, I really like Denny." I linked arms with him. He laughed and we went outside. Just before they saw us, he grabbed my hand and kissed it. "It'll be fine."

But it hadn't been fine. The awful awkwardness, the painful silences, the not-so-silent comments that Dylan's father made as he finished off one six-pack and started another. Denny tried to help play interference. I tried to help with serving the food, cleaning up, making conversation about my job, asking about their lives, complimenting the house. Dylan tried to be a bridge, talking about the things we must have had in common.

Denny took the leftovers into the house and I cleaned up our plates. Dylan jumped in and asked about the last fishing trip, and then I complimented him on the fish and Dylan's dad asked, "Are you Muslim?" I said I wasn't. My father had been an

Egyptian scientist and culturally Muslim, but I didn't remember anything of that since I'd been born in the United States, and by then my parents had declared themselves secularists.

"So you're telling me my son is dating a Muslim and an atheist?"

"Dad, you should stop talking now," Dylan said.

"You're the one who brought her over." He drained a can and popped open the next one. "Like you aren't purposefully shitting on your brother's grave or his childhood home or the—"

"Stop it," Dylan's mother said. "Stop this right now. Corrina can't help who she is."

I felt a glimmer of hope at her defense.

"But we can't help what happened either, or how we feel about it. Dylan, you know this isn't going to work. You must know."

I waited for Dylan to defend us. I feared he wouldn't. My very existence was causing people deep pain. Even if I didn't deserve it, I couldn't blame his parents. I didn't want to start things out that way—as enemies fighting over Dylan.

Dylan held my shoulders and leaned me against his chest. "I think we should leave," Dylan whispered in my ear. "It's not you that's the problem. It's not."

"All right," I said. "It was nice to meet both of you, but I think it would be best if I leave now."

"Thank you, dear," his mom said. "I believe that would be best."

"We'll talk about this more tomorrow, Mom. Once Dad is a little more sober." There was a hint of disgust in Dylan's voice, and I thought it wasn't right for him to talk to his parents like that. They were grieving. However wrong that made them react to me, they did it because of grief.

"You're leaving, too?"

"I love her, Mom. I love her, and if she goes, then I'm going."

"But Dylan, how can you—"

"Come on." He tugged me back into the house and closed the back door on his mother's words.

It was the first time either one of us had used the word love. I felt overwhelmingly sad about it.

Denny stood at the kitchen island. He motioned to three shot glasses and a bottle of whiskey. "I know, I know, Dad isn't a shining example of alcohol's miracle-like benefits, but I do believe you two need a shot before getting the hell out of Dodge."

Before I thought about it too hard I swallowed mine. A couple of tears slipped down my cheek. I wiped them away, furious with myself.

"I'm sorry, Corrina," Dylan said. "I shouldn't have brought you."

His statement felt like a punch in the gut, like I wasn't worthy of his family after all. Like maybe even after the declaration of love, he was having second thoughts about me being worth the trouble.

"You're an ass, bro," Denny said.

I didn't know why I couldn't speak for myself just then, but I couldn't, and I was grateful to Denny for doing it for me.

Dylan crushed me into his embrace. "I love you."

I feared he would come to regret it, but I cared too much to stay silent. "I love you too."

"We're leaving," Dylan said over the top of my head.

I kept my head buried in his shirt and took comfort in his clean soap smell. We'd figure this out. We'd find a way to work it out with his parents. To make it right.

"Yeah, cool," Denny said.

I turned at the kitchen entrance and waved. "I'm glad we met," I said. "Come over for dinner soon."

Denny smiled and nodded. "Absolutely."

"And thank you," I said and turned away. I don't know why but I looked back one more time. Denny faced the back window and the smile had disappeared from his face. He looked like he was preparing for battle. He grabbed the whiskey and drank directly from the bottle, wiped his mouth, then went back outside.

Dylan latched the front gate behind us and unlocked our bikes from the pole. "You up for a longer ride? I need to burn some of that off," he said cocking his thumb back to his parents' house. "I don't think I can sit still or be pleasant until I've worked them out of my system."

"Yeah, let's do it," I said. I pedaled after Dylan until all I could think about was the burn in my legs. When Dylan brought us around to his place we fell on each other without a word, but with a ferociousness that both scared and thrilled me.

I WOKE TO DEEP COLD, the kind that sinks into the bones, that makes you forget what heat ever felt like. I wondered if this virus had taken Dylan's parents and his brother, if they were still normal, or if they were like me, except their memory-rush would include all the ways I had injured their family.

I woke up as if hit by a wave of cold water. Someone had pushed my jeans down to my ankles and my shirt up to my neck. My dingy, sweat-caked sports bra was skewed, mashing my breasts. Christopher loomed into view. He rested a hand against my bare stomach. I jerked against the ropes before I told myself to hold still. Hold still. Hold still.

"I love you, Cheyanne," Christopher said.

Dylan's image rose like a ghost before my opened eyes. His face superimposed over Christopher's. A part of me shriveled up. There was a chastising look on Dylan's face and his voice echoed inside my head. "You're not stronger, so be smarter." I couldn't remember when or why he'd said that, but I remembered the voice and the worry inside of it and an idea bloomed.

"Can you untie me? I would like to touch you." I held my breath. Could you hear during a memory-rush?

He ran his hands up and down my body. He touched me gently, as if I was his wife and he loved me and wanted to show me kindness and passion.

I withdrew myself. I turned my head away and stared at the shoelace around my right wrist. I stared at the threads and the dirt and thought about whether it was a half-inch or one-quarter inch across. The threads swam out of focus. I brought them back into focus, and then forced them back out of focus.

Air rushed across my ear. There was a loud thump, like a stick hitting a couch cushion. Christopher's hands stopped. His weight fell onto me.

I screamed and fought with his weight. Hands were at my wrist, and I struggled harder to prevent Christopher from pinning me down.

"Let me untie them." Maibe's voice.

Christopher's shirt collar shifted and stuffed into my mouth so that I could only groan and hold still to show her I had heard.

"Okay," she said as the bonds fell away.

I pushed Christopher off and pulled my clothes back together.

Maibe held Jane's bat in her hands. She gripped the bat so hard the blood drained from her fingers, turning them white. The bat had a smudge of blood on it.

"Thank you," I said. "If you think you can put the bat down, I could use some help moving him."

We pushed Christopher back into his old prison. This time we did what Jane had argued for. We laid him out spread-eagled on the cement floor, ran the rope through some pipes and back to him, and we made sure he couldn't bring together either his hands or feet. Then I closed the door, but it wouldn't lock because he had pried off the lock during his first escape. For all I knew it had been my fault for not locking the door correctly.

We both took turns using the toilet. I wondered how long we'd been out. Hours? Days? The water in the bathroom had stopped running.

I forced myself to sip from one of the last remaining bottles. Maibe did the same. Ghosts and voices and emotions appeared. My muscles shivered with fatigue. I checked the box of MREs before my legs collapsed. One bar left. How many had we started with? How many had Jane taken and Christopher eaten?

"What are we going to do?" Maibe asked.

"I have a friend in New York," I said, making a joke.

Maibe twisted her mouth and looked at me sideways.

I laughed. "Too far? Yeah, just a little."

I didn't say what I was really thinking—that part of me wanted to go to Cal Expo to find Dylan, and part of me never wanted to see him again.

CHAPTER 10

MAIBE WAS STILL very much a thirteen-year-old girl, but spider-web wrinkles covered her skin now, and her face and mouth showed even deeper lines, like someone four times her age.

I could feel some of it—the dry, papery texture of my face, the way my bones creaked at the joints. I pinched my skin and let it go. It stayed up and took an eternity to melt back into place.

My brain felt like someone had taken a wire brush and bleach and scoured the inside of my skull, erasing all the boundaries. My thoughts felt sharp and purposeful, and also crowded.

I saw Maibe, knew where I was and what we were doing, but I also looked at her and saw myself at twelve with that same hair and those same dark eyes, and remembered how it had been at the mall with Jane.

"I can't stop thinking about things that have already happened," I said.

"Me too," she said. "Will it stop?"

"I don't know." I pulled her into a hug. Touching her pink cotton hoodie, feeling her heartbeat against me, helped steady my thoughts. This is now. This is real.

Whatever we were sick with, we needed to get help from real doctors with real medicine, real knowledge, not from a person who was already living on the wrong side of crazy.

Christopher might be telling the truth as he knew it, I believed that, but it might not be the whole truth. Maybe there was a way to undo the sickness etched into my skin and flaring in my brain. Cal Expo was where the doctors must be. It was where the radio said to go, it was where, if Christopher could be believed, they took Dylan.

In spite of everything I knew, or maybe because of it, I needed to know he was still alive, I needed to face him again, I needed to hear the truth from him.

IT WAS TIME for us to leave, but Christopher was still tied up and I didn't know what to do.

"We should leave him," Maibe said.

"I know," I said.

"He infected us. He was hurting you, he was—"

"I know," I said.

There was a long pause where Maibe just stared at me.

"You're not going to leave him," she said finally.

I shook my head. "I can't," I whispered.

"He's going to follow us."

I knew she was right, but I didn't know what choice I had. He had done a horrible, unspeakable thing to us. And yet, and yet. He had lost his wife, his children. He had gone more than a little crazy.

I could not bear to think of him suffering and dying of thirst. So I untied him.

He sat up, rubbing his wrists and ankles where the ropes had been.

Maibe held the bat, knees bent, arms cocked. She must have played baseball before. It looked as if she knew what she was doing.

"It wasn't me. It was me, it was, but I was living in the memories and I didn't see you. I saw my sick child and my wife and—"

"That doesn't make it okay," Maibe said.

"It doesn't," he said.

"We don't want you following us," I said. "You can't think we could let you. You infected us, you—"

"I promise you will thank me for that," he said.

I raised my hand in a fist. He flinched.

"Don't EVER think you did right by us. You didn't ask. You didn't explain. You just decided you knew what was best for us like we weren't even real people." I lowered my arm. "Don't follow."

We left the army surplus store, Maibe and I.

Christopher stayed behind. He pretended to listen to us, but I knew Maibe was right. He would follow. But we would deal with it when we had to.

I took my first step outside, listening, watching. The sky was clear and soon we would gain some warmth from the sun, though not much. My heartbeat flooded my ears and filled the silence. It was as if all the world had gone to sleep. No white noise of cars. No blinking street lights. No car alarms. I searched every shadow and corner and window for movement.

There was nothing.

But even still, the stench gave it away. The decay of something gone rotten.

A flash of something. Blonde hair. Someone stood up from behind a car.

"Jane," I said.

"Where," Maibe said.

I pointed. My arm wavered, my fingers trembled. There was an odd outline to her shape. A waviness that made my eyes swim.

She was supposed to be gone. She was supposed to have abandoned us to our fate.

Maibe clutched my hand. "I don't see her. I don't see anyone."

I willed her shape to either solidify or disappear. I wasn't quite sure what I wanted more.

She didn't move. She didn't disappear either.

Maibe tugged on my hand. "'Let's go."

We left Jane—we left it behind and it stayed behind. When she was out of sight, I remembered to breathe again and then I thought I might dry heave.

I ordered her shape to go stand against the wall of my mind. I tried to make myself believe it had to obey. I held my breath as the memory did back off, slowly, making me fear it would not quiet down like the others, but finally, it faded into the background, and Maibe pulled me to the tracks, and they looked so much like the tracks where Dylan was taken, where Luna had stood mute and Stan had stood yelling. That memory was running from the walls of the room to the very center, ready to slam dunk itself across my vision.

"I don't know if I can do this."

"Squeeze my hand," Maibe said. "It helps keep it away."

I did, and I felt her return squeeze, and then felt the prick of her nails as they dug into the back of my hand, and it was that pain which drove the memory back against the wall.

I looked at Maibe.

"Sorry," she said.

Four drops of blood welled up from the crescents her fingernails had made. I shook my head. "Don't be. I was about to lose it."

Maibe closed her eyes. "I think this is going to be hard."

A laugh erupted from me.

Maibe's eyes flew open.

"Going to be hard?" I said.

Maibe hid her face in her hands and stifled a giggle.

Okay. I rested a hand on her shoulder. "Time to go."

We walked alongside the railroad tracks in a type of ditch. The tracks took us away from houses filled with who knew what. The tracks felt safe. Relatively speaking.

Talking, we realized soon, helped keep the memories in check, so we dared it, even though silence would have been safer.

The tracks passed by a café that Dylan and I used to go to for breakfast. The shape of the building and the topmost windows, they triggered ghost-memories—that's what I decided to name them—something different than the fevers.

The memory-rush took over completely, but the ghost-memories superimposed themselves onto the present, making it feel like I was watching a 3-D movie without the special glasses.

I saw Dylan and me joking over pancakes and orange juice and how the morning light filtered through the windows and voices bounced off the walls. And I saw too how it looked now, all burned out with a body lying on the sidewalk in front of the entrance.

At the café was when we noticed that Christopher had caught up to us. A scratching footstep had given him away. Maibe said she caught a glimpse of him.

Of course, we couldn't be sure, not with the ghost-memories. But then I caught another glimpse of him a few seconds later. He had dashed around the corner of a building when I bent to retie my shoelaces.

We decided it was unlikely we would have the same ghost-memories.

We hoped we were right about that.

We decided to take a break against an old sentinel oak across the tracks from the café. I pressed my fingers into the rough bark and felt the air sing in my lungs. Stopping for just these few seconds brought the memories clamoring back.

"I could walk forever," Maibe said.

I dug my fingers deeper into the bark to keep myself anchored in the present. "Let's keep walking then," I said with desperation.

I couldn't think much beyond sending those memories back to the wall to shut up. What hurt the most were the good memories with Dylan. I couldn't utter a breath without those memories crowding in and making me regret everything I had done to sabotage us.

Maibe grabbed my hand and we scrambled back up the gravel together. We stepped onto the middle of the tracks. It felt as if we were traveling a horizontal ladder above the city.

"Do you see that?" Maibe pointed to smoke curling into the sky from one of the downtown skyscrapers.

A smaller building off in one of the neighborhoods also sent up a curl. "There's another one," I said. I did a slow circle and saw multiple smoke trails.

Three weeks later and there were still fires burning. It must have been bad while we were in the fevers.

"Did you see that?" Maibe said. She pointed into the neighborhood next to the café.

"I don't see anything."

"There's something. I don't know," she said.

"We should keep going," I said, not sure what would be worse, if something really was out there, or if she had just seen a ghost-memory.

I turned in a full circle again, got halfway around. Froze.

Christopher had stopped trying to hide. I didn't know how long it had taken him, or what had changed, but he was out in the open now. On the tracks. A few hundred yards behind us.

Running.

A dark figure flashed in the corner of my eye and disappeared around a building.

"There." Maibe said. "Christopher?"

"He's behind us." I readied myself to run.

The dark figure, small, moved again, this time into the middle of a shadowed street.

The object moved again, this time out of the shadow, revealing four legs and a proud head and tall shepherd ears that swiveled at us, then to the side, then behind, all without the dog moving its gaze an inch.

"Whoa," I said, not realizing I had been holding my breath. I followed after the dog and allowed memories of Blitz to crowd in: how safe I felt burying my fingers into his fur, how he greeted me with a dozen circlings every time I returned from work, how he liked to lick the shower water off of my legs.

Like a whip he flipped around and let out a low, deep, throaty growl at something that had come up behind him—a larger shape, clearly human, the shape that Maibe must have seen.

A second person loped into view, followed by a third and then a fourth. The dog crept backwards even as it growled and bared its teeth. Anyone sane would have stopped in their tracks at such a sight, but these people kept going until they cornered the dog against a wall. The dog's tail tucked between its legs and its butt pressed against the wall.

One of them reached out a hand. The dog snapped at it, but caught only air.

Christopher came running up, gasping for air, yelling. "There's more!"

Four heads turned and the faint light hit one face just right to see the sickness in him.

The dog dashed through their legs. A woman tumbled onto her side. The dog galloped across the open space straight for us, tail between its legs, hair still raised on the nape of its neck.

Maibe gasped.

The dog shot up the incline to where we stood stupefied, yelped as it passed alongside us, raced down the other side and then disappeared into the fields.

"Hey," I said, "here boy, come back." But it did not turn.

Maibe tugged on my arm. "There's no dog! Snap out of it! We gotta go. We gotta go now!"

The dog hadn't been real? But I was so sure.

Before I could stop it, I saw the bloody mess on our neighbor's front yard, the sickening crunch of bone as I bowled into that woman, the slap as Stan took a bat to her. No, no, no. This was not the time, but my brain wouldn't stop and I fell to my knees, the wooden tracks digging splinters into my palms, the strings of puke glistening in the light. I tried to force myself back up.

Come on, come on.

The crunch of gravel told me I hadn't moved fast enough.

My stomach heaved one more time. The memory cleared.

Maibe was up ahead a few dozen yards. I willed her to keep running, but she stopped and turned and waited and flapped her arms as if it might speed me along.

I yelled at myself to get up, get up, get up.

"Run!" Christopher said and flung himself in their way.

I set my sights on Maibe's sweatshirt and ran like an old woman.

Christopher screamed and then his scream cut off.

Something snarled behind me. I risked a glance over my shoulder—but that was a mistake.

I fell, scraping my hands and knees. One of them bared his teeth as he reached out his hands. I got back to my feet and sprinted after Maibe, realizing too late that I was leading the gang right to her.

Maibe ran to a building that backed up to the tracks, it's clay-colored paint peeling and familiar. The café. She struggled with the back door and then got it free, slamming it open against the wall, the sound ricocheting through the air.

I veered off the tracks. For a split second, I thought about passing her by, leading them away, but then something moved in the shadows behind Maibe, inside the building, and I found speed I didn't think I had.

She wasn't looking behind her. There was something behind her and she couldn't see it.

My feet crossed the threshold of the door, slapping against tile. My body bowled into something big and solid, cushioning what otherwise would have been a bad fall. My cheek felt the hot breath of something alive, its hands wrapping around my chest, squeezing, squeezing, squeezing.

I fought back, but the arms pinned me in place.

Searing pain in my shoulder. No, this was wrong, no. My flesh tore as this person ripped it from my shoulder like a rabid dog.

I screamed.

His grip loosened. I kneed him in the groin, knocking hot air out of him. He dropped me. I scrambled backward, tracking myself through dust, and made a frantic search for a weapon, but there was nothing within reach.

And then I saw it. On the stove top was a cast iron griddle.

Pain made my right shoulder useless, but I took up the griddle in my left hand and planted my feet in a fighting stance. The man stumbled to me, chef's apron askew and bloodied, oblivious of the weapon in my hand.

I swung the griddle and whacked him on the side of his head. Bone crunched, but he did not fall.

I readied my arm again, pivoted to put the full weight of my body into it this time, and swung again. The crunch was louder and the man fell to the floor like a tree.

My chest heaved from heavy breaths, the agony of running too hard, the pain from my bleeding shoulder. I stood over him for a long, silent moment.

I did not want another death on my hands. But it was too late.

I told him that I was sorry. I told him I hoped he would find some peace now.

Only then did I notice the low pounding sounds that said people were still trying to break down the door. Maibe stared at me across the man's dead body.

"You did the right thing," she said.

Even though I didn't think so, I was glad she did.

"Is the door secure?"

"For now," she said.

I scanned the kitchen, the gabled windows overlooking the street, the café tables and chairs, the bright green counter, the chintzy wallpaper of cowboy boots and spurs. The place seemed empty, except for the dead cook at my feet.

I waited for a memory-fever or a ghost-memory or some new damn symptom to worm its way forward and overtake me at this familiar breakfast spot, but there were only tendrils I easily waved off.

Maibe helped draw the clothing down over my shoulder and we used the bottled water she found in a cabinet and a few folded towels to clean out my wound.

"Don't hold back," I said. "Make sure you really clean it." The pain helped beat back the fever rising again in my body. I had been bitten by one of the insane people. Supposedly Christopher's inoculation would keep me from going even more insane than I had already become—but what if it didn't?

Maibe finished patching me up and threw the bloodied towels into the sink that no longer worked. "We should find a place for you to rest," she said.

I began to protest, but stopped when a wave of heat rolled from my head, ended at my feet, and then restarted. My legs wobbled and I leaned against the edge of the sink. I didn't have much time.

A sturdy wooden door led to some stairs. I remembered the owners had been this middle-aged couple with two kids who all had lived on the second story. The door stood slightly ajar, but the stairs were dark and I wanted to avoid going up there at all costs.

"Corrina!" Maibe's voice cut through my contemplation.

She had not yelled it, but the urgency in her tone was undeniable. She stood at the archway between the kitchen and serving area. Her eyes were wide, her face solemn. "They've surrounded us."

Halfway across the kitchen my legs turned to Jello. I landed feet from the crushed skull of the man I had murdered. The kitchen filled with the smells of coffee, breakfast sausage, eggs. Matilda's laugh rang out and so did the bell the cook used to signal someone's breakfast was ready.

Dylan lifted his hand in a wave from across the café. The light from the windows framed his shoulders. Our two cups of coffee sent off curls of steam. He smiled as I approached.

CHAPTER 11

A THICK COATING of dust lay heavy on my tongue again. That was my first sensation, my thick heavy tongue, dry, covered in a layer of dust, desperately needing water. That and a twilight darkness. The ceiling fan above my head sat silent, dead. One blade had broken at the gold-painted attachment to the head. Thick cobwebs and more dust covered the rest of the blades.

I pushed myself to a sitting position. I was in a sea of pillows. A glass of water stood clean and clear on the bedside table. I tossed the covers and pillows aside and drank the water without considering how it got there. How I got there. I slaked my thirst and wiped away the grime from my tongue. A hint of fermenting fruit layered what otherwise was stuffy, still air.

Worry for Maibe shot me up onto unsteady legs. I went for the door, but before I touched the knob, it opened outward. There Maibe stood, a little dirtier, a little more tired

"Oh! You're awake!" She threw her arms around my waist.

Her grip was both strong enough to knock me over and hold me in place. I wobbled and then patted her on the shoulder. "I'm fine." I said, and then took an inventory of myself.

Skin still old, head still thick with memories. "It's not any worse now than it was before."

"I was so scared," Maibe said.

"What happened?"

Maibe sighed. "You should sit."

I sat down in a chair next to the bed, my sore muscles grateful.

Maibe cocked her ear as if listening for something.

My pulse quickened. "Are we safe?"

"Enough as you can hope for right now."

I was about to press her when she saw the look on my face and said, "No, it's okay. There's just…I'm glad you're awake."

"Me too." I smiled and ran a hand through my tangled hair, trying to put it back in some sort of order, but my fingers only caught in the strands and tore at my scalp until I gave up. "Tell me what happened."

"You went into the fevers. I couldn't wake you and there were a whole bunch of zombies around the building, like they knew we were there even though they couldn't see us."

"Like the ones at the back door."

"Yeah," Maibe brushed hair from her eyes. "You said something about upstairs and I saw the door and the stairs and—"

"You dragged me up here by yourself?" I wasn't overweight, but I still must have weighed more than twice as her.

"I had help," she said in a quiet voice and looked over her shoulder.

"You came across other survivors?" I planted my feet on the floor, ready to try standing again.

"I don't think I would call them survivors."

"What?" I couldn't think of an alternative. She couldn't mean those insane, infected people helped her bring me into this bedroom.

"I don't know, it's just, there's something wrong with them."

"Show me," I said, sounding more confident than I felt. My muscles felt weak from the memory-fever and I struggled to walk across a faded area rug without stumbling.

I followed her into a living room area. A small coffee table with a cinnamon spice centerpiece stood on a threadbare patch of carpet. Two sagging love seats with unmatched patterns formed an L-shape around it.

On these couches sat four people.

Two adults, two children. Matilda the owner was one, her dark hair and plump cheeks taking me into a coffee memory, the acidic smell and creamy taste of it suddenly on my tongue. I always put in plenty of cream. She sat with a stiff upright back, hands on her knees, feet flat on the floor, wearing her chef's apron. Fly-away hair obscured her face, but, even still, it was obvious she stared at something to the left of me.

I turned, but there was nothing except for an oil painting of the family done up in their finest winter clothing, together for a posed, formal, uncomfortable-looking family portrait.

"What's she doing?" I said, but then realized they all were like that. Her husband, her two children.

"Nothing," Maibe said in a hoarse whisper as if afraid to break the spell that bound them to stillness.

But it made me want to do just the opposite. I wanted to shout or break something or pinch one of them, anything to wake them up, anything to remove the vacant gaze.

"They haven't changed for four hours," she said. "They helped me get you in here, the wife and husband did. They lifted you up and brought you to the bedroom and talked to you like, I don't know. They wouldn't talk to me. They wouldn't answer any of my questions, but they called you by your name. They KNEW you and they would talk you, but not to me." Maibe's voice rose at the end and cut off as if she felt strangled.

Maibe had bunched her sweatshirt together at her neck. Her dark hair frizzed around the edges. Her dark eyes spoke of someone almost pushed too far, someone almost ready to break.

Matilda stood up. Brushed down her chef's apron. "I'll make some tea for us. I'm so glad you decided to visit us, Corrina. You like green tea, yes?"

The room seemed to shrink. I could not speak. I wanted to step back, to step away from her, from this creature who spoke to me in a voice I recognized, who knew my name, who acted like we had done this before, this make-believe tea party.

And then the dingy carpet and cinnamon centerpiece faded. Four pink walls decorated with teacups ghosted in. Matilda had been there, getting up to make tea as the other women, all dressed in black, ate cake and whispered about Sharal, the poor woman dead by her husband's hand. Sharal had been a friend at the garden. I'd knelt side by side with her in the dirt to plant seeds. Sharal had always worn long sleeves no matter how hot the weather.

Matilda had known Sharal, and then at the memorial she had made me tea.

The pink walls faded back into gray. By then Matilda had filled the teapot and put out a cup and plate. The gas turned on and the flame licked the side of the teapot, flaring at some food scrap caught in its heat.

I moved back another step until I hit the wall. Matilda reached for the fridge door.

"No, don't!" I said, but Matilda had already opened the thing. Smells of rotted meat, spoiled milk, slimed vegetables, filled the room. But Matilda did not seem to notice the wretched smell. She rummaged around on the top shelf.

Maibe gagged next to me. The rest of the family didn't move.

Sludge dripped off the bottom shelf and pooled on the linoleum floor.

"There," she said. "You wanted cream, right?" Matilda held up a container triumphantly, then closed the refrigerator.

"We need to leave," I said. I was weak, people might still be waiting for us outside, but I couldn't stay a minute longer in this black hole with these, with whatever this was, with these monsters.

"But we can't leave them," Maibe said.

"I thought that's what you wanted to do before. They're sick, they're monsters, they're zombies, they're not people anymore." Whatever this was, it made them different, less than human, and I didn't want what happened to them to happen to me.

"But they're just kids," Maibe said.

I tugged her to the door as my mind raced. Clothes, shoes, jacket, wound freshly wrapped, no weapon. Maybe I should take a knife from the kitchen, but that would require getting close to the refrigerator. I steeled myself for the smell, but then remembered there were likely better knives downstairs. I decided to take my chances and wait.

I rested my hand on the door to the stairs. If I turned it and left these people to fend for themselves, I couldn't take that back.

Maibe shook her head in a silent "no."

I turned the knob and opened the door.

Light flared as if someone had turned on the electricity.

I stepped back into the apartment, but did not close the door. The hallway had been empty, the cleaner air refreshing, the freedom tantalizing.

Matilda poured something into a coffee cup but it overflowed the cup and oozed more onto the stove top.

I looked around but the electricity was still off.

"There," Matilda said. She capped the bottle and set it aside on the counter. An oil bottle.

She had poured oil all over her counter and onto the stove top.

The tea kettle whistled and she bustled to it. Her chef's apron dipped into the oil, brushed against the flame, and the flame caught. And engulfed. Matilda lit up like a matchstick, but she did not scream, she continued with her tea duty. She poured the oil into the cup and she turned with the cup in hand and held it in front of her and flames singed her clothes and crisped her hair and licked at her skin, blackening it. And she held out the cup and made as if to hand it to me and I screamed and Maibe screamed and I pushed her into the hallway. I slammed the door behind us and waited for Matilda to pound it down and smother me in the flames that surely would kill her.

Maibe fell to the ground and wrapped her hands around her shins and sobbed into her knees.

Something on the inside thumped, thumped again. Smoke tendrils curled from underneath the door. We should run, save ourselves from this horror, outrun Matilda's fire-wreathed face and outstretched hands and steaming tea and kind smile. Pretend it was okay to leave them because they weren't human anymore and it was worth it to save ourselves—our sick, infected selves.

And then I felt shame.

Before I knew my mind had made its decision, I threw open the door.

Black smoke billowed out but then cleared. Matilda had crumpled into her original seat on the couch. The oil tea cup spilled and a slick of fire covered the rug underneath the coffee table. The couches were on fire, their clothes were smoking. They did not move.

I coughed, raced to the bedroom, tore off the sheets. Even those precious seconds seemed like an eternity. The bed sheet caught on one corner and even a yank with all my strength did not release it. I crawled over to the corner, freed the sheet, bundled all of it in my arms and raced back into the growing bonfire the couches had become.

I threw the boy onto the floor and rolled him into the sheet, smothering the wisps of smoke that had started to curl from his collar. The girl was next.

I started on the husband, but I could not budge his body from the seat and the fire had taken over his shirt and I burned my hand and arm and ear. I used this as an excuse to not look at Matilda's slumped over form. I noticed the smell, like bacon fat frying in the pan, mixed with melting Tupperware.

"Corrina!"

I wiped the vomit from my lips and dropped to all fours because the fire had caught on a wall and we would all die of smoke inhalation soon.

"Corrina, they're coming!"

I turned and saw it, a shadow, three shadows, lurching out

of the empty hallway through the door. They went for Maibe and the two sheet-wrapped forms on the floor.

Maibe backed away from the girl, and the three shadows fell on the two children. I stepped backward into the bedroom and pulled Maibe with me. I tried to close the door but a large woman whose shirt had ripped down to her dingy white bra raised her head as if scenting prey. She lurched to her feet and went for us. I shut the door in her face, but there was no lock. She threw herself against it and I thought of the man banging his head against my patio door again and again until he drew blood.

Maibe broke the window with a lamp. The glass shattered and brought me back. Fresh air filled the room. She leaned out, so far out I thought she might fall. I used all my weight to keep the door closed but I was losing this battle inch by inch.

A hand reached through, a woman's hand, with pink acrylic nails. Though several tips had broken and several more fingers were bloody or missing.

This hand reached around, feeling the air, feeling, I knew, for me.

"There's no ladder." She peered out the window.

"There's no choice."

Maibe stepped back, looked around the room. I wanted to yell at her to hurry.

She ran to the other side of the bed and felt around on the floor.

The door moved another inch. The gap would be big enough soon for one of them to force their body through.

Maibe carried three pillows back to the window. She dropped them outside, looked to see where they fell. She went back for the rest and dumped them out the window as well.

The door moved another inch and I fought to gain back some ground, but gained nothing except for a horrible popping sound in my knee.

"Go!" I yelled.

Maibe hopped onto the window ledge, teetered, and then jumped out of sight.

I released the door and made a run for the window. I pressed my hands onto the ledge, but snatched them back when the glass shards cut into my skin. I looked back. The woman lay moaning on the floor where she had fallen when the door gave way. Another figure disappeared into the smoke. The smoke obscured everything now.

I looked out the window. Maibe stood by the group of pillows and waved me on. I held my breath, placed my hands to avoid the glass, pushed myself through.

The asphalt still jarred my legs, my bruised knee. My hands slapped the pillows and slipped between them. The wound on my shoulder stung with the impact and matched my stinging hands.

Maibe stared up at the window.

We had landed in the alley between the restaurant and another building. There were two ways out. One way led back to the tracks, one way led around the front into the neighborhood.

I edged against the wall, its textured plaster catching my clothes like fingers. I held my breath and peeked around the corner.

The front of the restaurant was covered three deep in people. People who seemed crazy and angry and infected. People climbing through the broken glass of the café windows.

I retreated, careful to step silently. I had not even brought a weapon. We had pillows.

"Corrina!"

I put my finger to my lips to warn Maibe to silence. But she wasn't looking at me. She watched the window we had just jumped out. The window that billowed black smoke and carried the aroma of cooked meat and melting plastics—where a person leaned out.

This person tipped over until there was nothing left to do but fall. She landed head first into our little island of pillows. She did not get up.

A second person appeared at the window, leaned further and further, reaching out his hands to us on the ground as if to strangle us.

I grabbed Maibe's sweatshirt. In spite of my knee and shoulder, we moved fast back to the tracks.

Something darted across the alley ahead of us.

"Did you see that?" I asked.

"See what?" Maibe responded.

We were surrounded. They would come at us from the front, from the tracks, from above. There was no other way out.

I searched the alley for a weapon. It was bare except for an orange plastic bucket someone might have used once for washing. I picked it up, even though it wouldn't do much good.

The figure dashed across again.

I lowered the bucket. It was too small to be human. It appeared again, pivoting on all fours before racing down the alley, ahead of us to the tracks.

It was in sight for only a few seconds, but it was enough.

It was Blitz.

CHAPTER 12

I DECIDED NOT TO TELL Maibe I was following my dead dog.

I think she knew I was following something from my brain, but she didn't ask. We climbed back onto the tracks because that's where Blitz went. Smoke engulfed the café behind us. The sick people inside it were burning up.

"We did the right thing, didn't we?" Maibe said.

"I don't know about that."

Maibe hiccuped.

"But I don't think there was anything else we could have done."

"They were different than the ones trying to kill us before," Maibe said.

She was right, but I had no idea what would make them so different. The Lyssa virus was supposed to be a form of rabies. It was supposed to make people go psycho. Yes, Matilda and her family were acting crazy—but they hadn't been violent. They had been sleepwalking, comatose-like at times. Matilda had clearly been reliving a memory. But none of them had the same skin issues as us, which meant they hadn't gotten the vaccine either.

I stopped walking when I realized Blitz had vanished. My heartbeat picked up speed. Maybe Blitz would come back. Even if he was a ghost, following him had felt comforting, as if he was leading me home.

I shaded my eyes with a hand and scanned the area. The run-down neighborhoods had given way to empty fields. A line of trees backed up the fields. The river cut in and out of sight between the trees.

Straight down the tracks, almost totally obscured by smoke, were the downtown skyscrapers. Though there was no fog today, the smoke smothered the color of everything except for the green fields, and something red.

I squinted, trying to make out what this red thing was in a sea of green.

It was boxy, falling apart, decaying. Like something out of the old railroad days. When I was ten and devouring the Boxcar Children book series, I pictured a boxcar like this—red and rusting, with weeds growing up past the wheel base, the sides built out of wood, and a sliding steel door.

I was sure it was some weird ghost-memory. I opened my mouth to ask Maibe if she could also see the boxcar and whether she'd ever read the books.

Then the steel door opened.

December

You make it sound like this is some kind of supernatural monster, like a great evil overtook people, when it's some virus or something that brings out the evil in people that already have it...look, can I get a cigarette? I don't actually smoke, I just—I don't know. I need to do something with my hands and it was the only thing I could think of...No, I understand. You don't want to get too close. But that's what I'm trying to explain, that it doesn't matter how close you get. There's nothing wrong with me. Actually, I can help protect you—

CHAPTER 13

THREE PEOPLE CAME OUT of the boxcar and then something was lifted down to them by two still inside the shadow of the door. The object was covered in a sheet. The shape of a body. The three were of varying ages and heights, in dark and torn clothing. One female and two males, though it was difficult to be sure from this distance and I couldn't see how many still might be inside.

"I wonder who it is," Maibe said. "I wonder who died."

"I don't know," I said. Part of me wanted to go and help them carry their burden. Part of me wanted to run far in the other direction. People were dangerous now. "We should go."

"It's too late for that," said a male voice behind us.

I whirled around. A young man with longish brown hair and a raggedy beard held what looked like a crossbow. I spoke softly, as if talking to a wild animal. "We don't mean any harm, we'll just be on our way."

"Not my decision," he said.

"What do you want?" I said.

"A hot meal and a water bed. What I get will be something different. Spencer will decide what he wants once they're done." His cheek twitched.

His eyes were wide-set. His hair was a curly, messy light brown. He was built like a football player. Markings crept up either side of his neck, pale and white like tattooed wings. From the cure. In spite of the ashy, aged look of his skin, he seemed younger than me. "Did you get infected?" I asked.

"Yeah, I was tagged with the cure," he said. "And by the looks of you two, you know exactly what I mean."

"Yeah, we know," Maibe said.

"Munchkin," he said. "I need to you to walk over this little hill and to the boxcar. Don't be stupid, just slowly walk that way."

"All right," she said as if this guy wasn't dangerous, but rather a friend pointing us in the right direction. Maibe slipped down the far side of the tracks. I followed.

"I'm Corrina and this is Maibe," I said quietly.

"You can call me Leaf."

"Leaf. Why are you doing this?"

"We're not going to hurt you if you follow directions," he said. "No promises otherwise, but we're not animals, if that's what you're really asking, but we're protecting our space from everything and everyone."

We walked through knee-high weeds and over and down a sloped hill. We reached the boxcar and he had us sit against one rusted wheel in the weeds that had grown up around and under it.

I tried to get Leaf to talk, but he wouldn't have it. Maibe

quickly fell asleep against the wheel and her head slipped onto my shoulder. She was not as scared as I thought she should be. Just because Leaf was close to our age didn't mean anything. Teenagers could be just as cruel as any adult. I knew this from personal experience.

The group returned over the hill without the body. The tallest of the five walked with his arm around one of the others. The rest trailed behind. I thought they all looked Leaf's age or close to it, but they were too far away to be sure.

I nudged Maibe awake.

She stretched, sat up, stared as the group approached.

I became nervous at their gaunt, mean looks. They fanned around us, like they were half of Stonehenge and Maibe and I were its center. All their skin had the same spidery web look. The tallest one seemed now to be the oldest and the leader the others were waiting on to speak. The rest looked younger than him. The shortest one was a girl, maybe sixteen. The other three boys seemed barely older than Maibe.

"They tagged?" The girl said.

"Yeah," Leaf said. He glanced at Maibe. "It means you've got the cure same as us."

"Some cure," the girl said.

"Quiet, Gabbi," the tall one said.

"Who are you?" I asked.

"This is Spencer," Leaf said, referring to the tall one. "This is Gabbi, Ano, Ricker and Jimmy. Ike was with us too, for awhile, but not anymore."

"Was he the one you buried?" Maibe asked.

"We had to take him out," Leaf said, shaking his head.

"He didn't let us tag him and he went V," Jimmy said, his

voice high, his dark, curly hair like a handful of corkscrews across his forehead.

"He should have let us tag him," Gabbi said.

"That's not what he wanted," Leaf said.

"Still," Gabbi said. "He should have—"

"He chose his death," Ano said, speaking for the first time. A dark, brooding look entered his eyes. I shivered. One of the other fosters had gotten that look, usually when she was thinking about hurting herself.

Something changed about their faces. Like a wave riding in, their eyes went glassy, unfocused. I scrambled back until I was hard up against the wheel. What memory was about to come alive?

Gabbi pinched her arm and came back. She slugged Ricker in the shoulder. The others shook themselves back into focus like dogs throwing off water.

"What's V mean?" Maibe asked.

"It means he went Violent instead of Feeb," Spencer said.

"Feeb?" I asked.

"Feeb, old-looking, what all of us are now. You too."

"Do you know what's going on?" I asked.

"We sort of learned the hard way," Spencer said.

Leaf cocked his head. "We made up the names ourselves."

"But where did you all come from, where—"

"You can't tell by now that we're street kids?" Gabbi said. "How dumb are you?"

I hadn't been able to put my finger on that vibe they gave off. It made sense. They didn't seem scared or all that worried about the state of the world right then, but why would they? The world had already screwed them over long before the Lyssa virus came along.

"Consider us homeless bums, if you like," Ricker said, finally speaking. He was the thinnest of them all. His cheeks were almost hollowed out. "Leeching off the system as unproductive members of society and—"

"Enough," Spencer said. "Tie them up."

"Hey, wait!" I said.

He walked away. "Gabbi, help me get things set up inside."

It didn't matter how much I tried to argue, the boys refused to answer me. As Leaf went to Maibe, he said, "I'm going to tie it loose, okay? Tell me if it hurts and I'll fix it."

"Okay," she said. "But why do I have to get tied up at all? Why are you doing this?"

"It'll only be for the night," Leaf said, but hesitated on the knots as if conflicted.

"You don't have to do this," I said. Tears creeping into my eyes. I was glad it had become dark enough now that they were probably hidden. I hoped.

"Yes, we do," Jimmy said. "We always listen to Spencer, because he always knows what's best."

"Then how come Ike died?" I said.

"He didn't listen to Spencer," Leaf said and jumped after the others into the boxcar.

Maibe and I sat tied to the wheel for what felt like hours. My shoulder ached, my knee ached, my heart ached. Tears still fell down my cheeks, making me itch. I'd followed Blitz because he was going after Dylan. I wanted to hear the truth from him and somehow everything would turn out okay. It was a foolish thought and I knew it and I couldn't help but think it. Instead I'd gotten stuck here with these six who had tied us up and planned to do who knows what with us. They should have given me the creeps, but somehow they didn't.

When the last of the twilight faded and the cold began to seep deep into my bones, a light flared from within the boxcar. I wondered at their stupidity for starting a fire inside the car until I saw smoke swirl out what must have been a hole in the roof.

Ricker jumped out of the boxcar and walked up the hill to stand guard. The other five bustled around the boxcar in the shadows, lifting down objects from makeshift shelves, putting them back, opening cans. I knew they were food cans once the smell reached us.

"I'm starving," Maibe said.

"Me too." I was about to yell out a request for food when Leaf jumped down to us with a can and a spoon in hand.

"I can either feed this to you or untie Maibe and let her feed the both of you."

I looked to Maibe. She waited for me to do something. I nodded.

"Untie me, please," she said.

I thought about how we might escape with her untied now, but all thoughts vanished as the first spoonful of beans hit my mouth. I chewed it down and took more from Maibe's hands. I could have eaten the entire can, but once I saw it was halfway gone, I turned away the next spoonful. "I'm full. You have the rest."

Leaf eyed me. He knew I was lying and I felt his approval for it. "Sometimes leaving an edge of hunger keeps the memories back," he said.

As we finished our meager dinner, Spencer and Gabbi jumped down next to Leaf.

"Why did you take us?" I asked. "And what do you plan to do with us? Why can't we leave?"

"You're the ones who barged into our territory," Spencer said. "You're lucky Leaf was on lookout," Spencer said. "He's a lot nicer than us about checking for Feebs before shooting. You'd be dead if Gabbi had been out there instead."

Gabbi smiled at me.

"That still doesn't answer my questions."

"I don't need to answer your questions."

"Then let us go."

"Eventually."

"Why not now?"

"Because." He stepped closer to my crouched body. He loomed over me and spoke in a voice that was both fierce and quiet. "We are grieving for our friend tonight and don't have time for you."

THE SIX OF THEM hiked us out to the top of their lookout hill. In the daytime it overlooked the valley, the tracks, the river. Now in the dark only the smoke from still-burning fires was visible. It cloaked the area in a sort of soupy mess.

Ano squatted on his heels and started a fire. The others sat cross-legged in the cold grass, forming a semi-circle. I drew the heavy blankets they'd given us around me and Maibe. I didn't think it said much about their intelligence as street kids that they lit a fire in the blackness, on a night so thoroughly dark it could act as a beacon for others.

Maibe shifted next to me. I helped her fix the blanket underneath since our hands and ankles were still tied. She huddled against my side and I used her counterweight for support. There was no sound except for the crackling of the fire and the random mini-explosions that seemed to haunt the city now that some of it was burning. But those sounds were muffled booms that felt far away.

Spencer took out a knife. Gabbi lifted the shirtsleeve of her left arm. He carved a line of blood into her bicep, and then another. Gabbi grimaced but held still.

After he was done, Ano came to Gabbi, wiped the blood away and rubbed a dark paste onto the wound.

Spencer held the knife into the fire for a couple of minutes, waited for it to cool, and then repeated the act on Jimmy, Ricker, Leaf, and then himself.

In the flickering light, I saw that Leaf's and Spencer's cuts were far lower on their biceps than some of the others. Shaky, scrawling, gray-black letters filled the upper part of their arms. Everyone had at least two names carved, but Leaf and Spencer had at least half a dozen.

When Spencer had carved everyone, they cleaned the tools and returned to the half-circle. Now all sat cross-legged. I knew I was in deep darkness, and with the firelight there was no way for them to see us, but I thought Spencer looked right at me.

Ano passed the bowl around. Each added more paste to their wounds.

When they emptied the bowl, they sat in silence for a moment, and then someone doused the fire.

I was blinded by the lack of light, and then a low howl echoed across the darkness. I flinched from the shock of the noise. Another low howl, and then a "yip, yip, yip." I almost scrambled to my feet, almost woke Maibe from her coma-like sleep, and then realized the sounds originated not from the darkness, but from them.

Their voices rose into the orange starlight like a pack of coyotes. It didn't matter that coyotes didn't run in packs, their chorus of voices sounded real and chilling and fitting. Coyotes were the outcasts, the throwaway predators of the world, the scavengers, the ones no one cared to protect, and yet, they still survived. The coyote had outlasted the wolves and the bears and the mountain lions and thrived in the very places the other animals couldn't.

Their howls stopped and there was silence for a long time. I began to nod off in spite of the shoulder wound that still ached. A soft thump landed next to me. I started awake. "Shh," Leaf said. "I'm going to untie you. We're going back to the boxcar and closing the doors."

"Aren't you afraid the Vs heard you?"

"Sure we are," Spencer said out of the darkness. Warm hands fumbled at my wrists. "That's why we did it out here."

"But then—"

"Some things are worth the risk."

"I don't understand."

"I don't expect you to."

There was a long silence.

"I'm sorry for your friend," I said.

"He was more Mary's friend than mine," Spencer said.

"Who's Mary?"

"No one you need to know about."

"I'm still sorry."

Spencer grunted and gathered up Maibe. I ignored the shock of cold at her departure. I scrambled for the fallen blankets and an instant's thought crossed my mind about running off.

I let the thought pass without action. There was Maibe, and there was something about this group.

I climbed into the boxcar. The others were already laid out across the floor in a haphazard pile of limbs, blankets, snoring, dreaming. Leaf dropped our blankets in a pile on the floor.

Spencer lifted the still-sleeping Maibe to me. I went to my knees and guided her onto an open spot.

Spencer jumped into the boxcar. He handed me the blankets.

"Thank you," I said.

"Tomorrow we're going to visit Officer Hanley at Cal Expo. "

"I'm looking for my boyfriend," I said, cringing even as the words came out. I didn't know what else to call him, but it didn't seem as if that word could possibly fit anymore. Not after Jane. Not after getting infected with this cure. I explained how he'd been captured and about the radio broadcast.

"If he's been captured, he'll be held there," Leaf said.

His words made hope rise in me. He sounded so sure.

"But he might already be dead," Spencer said. "Whoever is running the show over there needs cattle."

"Needs what?" My voice rose sharply. One of the boys groaned and tossed around in his sleep.

"Mindless followers, test subjects, laborers, nay-sayers, foot soldiers, do-gooders, loyal subjects—"

"—What do you mean about who is running the show?"

"Some sort of military thing running not exactly by the book," Spencer said. "Or maybe it is by the book. Or maybe by police or politicians. It doesn't matter. What matters is that Officer Hanley is going to pay. If you want to help us, we'll help you get inside Cal Expo."

I'd had experience with deals like these before. The group

home hadn't exactly been Disneyland.

"That is where you want to go, right?" He said.

"What do I have to do in exchange?"

"We'll talk about that tomorrow."

"I won't help you kill anyone," I said. "I have never—" and then I stopped that sentence because I thought about the woman on Mr. Sidner's front yard and about the chef and Matilda and her family.

"We're not killers, no matter what you think of us," Spencer said, disgust in his voice.

"No, I didn't mean—"

"Yes, you did."

The door creaked as Spencer pulled it closed. Darkness filled the boxcar. I suddenly felt suffocated by the smells of unwashed bodies, musty blankets, the spent ash of the fire, my own stink. I tried to think of some way to respond and came up with nothing.

"We'll help you get inside, if that's what you want," he said. "But we're not going to help you back out."

For all Spencer might know about surviving on the street, that didn't mean he was right about Cal Expo. If that was where people were organizing, where the police or military or government were, that was the safest place to be. I hadn't liked the foster care system, but it had been better than running away and becoming homeless.

Cal Expo, with its walls and guns and military protection would be a hundred times safer for Maibe than out here, even with this fierce group of six.

CHAPTER 14

I WOKE UP GROGGY and with the aftertaste of bean paste in my mouth. I desperately wanted water and noticed a glass jug and a few plastic cups. I untangled myself from the blankets and quietly stepped over still-sleeping bodies. Light entered through the smoke hole, and also through cracked walls.

Leaf lay in a fetal position on his side, his blankets wrapped into a lump against his chest as if he were holding a beloved stuffed animal. Gabbi jerked and mumbled in her sleep as if from bad dreams, or bad memories. There wasn't much difference anymore. Ano, Ricker, and Jimmy looked like puppies who had fallen asleep at the comforting, interwoven touch of a brother. The pup-brothers, pup-boys, I named them in my head.

The wispy bodies of my old foster mates ghosted into appearance. They overlaid the sleeping forms of these runaways in a mismatched silver border. I realized why I felt both uncomfortable and unafraid of Leaf and the others. This was a sort of end-of-the-world group home. In the old version, my parents had both died and the state took over. I had hated how the foster parents always got into our business, how everyone pretended to care about each other, how we went through the motions of being a family. How they had asked me to find a new place to live when I turned seventeen. They'd wanted to make room for a pair of ten-year-old siblings. I'd been hurt, even as I understood they had meant well.

In this new version, I lost my life all over again with the infection and the cure. I was outside this makeshift family. I was always on the outside. It hurt worse this time because it didn't feel fake here like it had in the group home.

Spencer stood leaning against the wall of the boxcar. It took me a startled moment to realize he was staring. I could not read his expression, but guessed all the same what he might be thinking. If I put his family of runaways in danger, he would make me pay.

A dull ache I easily recognized as loneliness settled into my chest. Before I could protest his silent accusation, he spoke. "Good morning, rejects," he said in a loud voice, and then paused. Bodies stirred under blankets. "Life is good..."

"...until it's not," Gabbi and Leaf said in unison. Ano, Ricker, and Jimmy repeated the answering phrase a second later.

Spencer nodded in approval. "Now get up and get some damn breakfast into you. We've got to take care of Officer Hanley today."

Ricker and Ano grinned at each other and jumped from the blankets to rustle food out of a stack of cans. Gabbi pulled out a little propane stove and set about boiling water. Leaf gathered up the blankets and Maibe and I helped him.

Gabbi finished the oatmeal. Jimmy heated up the rest of breakfast—beans in a can they passed around. We each dipped in our dirty fingers for a sweet, dripping section of peach.

As the light grew brighter in the boxcar, I saw how the infection sat on each of us. Ashy skin, fine wrinkles like a spiderweb, sun-spots and veins showing clearly across paper-like, fragile skin—it didn't matter what color skin: brown, black, white.

"Gabbi, examine the perimeter before we open the doors," Spencer said.

She wolfed down her last peach section and wiped her hands on her jeans. She came back with a telescope. Leaf grabbed a stool. The pup-boys cleared breakfast.

She positioned the telescope and moved in a careful circle. Her ankles were eye level with me. Dirt blended with the ragged edges of her jeans so as to look like dark socks. She wore torn-up tennis shoes and angry bug bites laced her exposed skin. The same bites covered the exposed parts of her arms.

"All clear," she said.

"All right," Spencer said. "Weapons check, bathroom, trash duty."

Leaf opened the boxcar door and blinding white light streamed in. Once my eyes adjusted, I saw an open field and open horizon, and the smoke haze keeping the sky a sickly orange, blocking the skyline.

We jumped out of the boxcar and trudged a quarter mile to the makeshift port-a-potty latrine. Ano, Ricker and Jimmy took turns standing guard, but it didn't feel like danger could be possible this early in the morning.

I took my turn and found the dispenser still contained anti-bacterial gel. This little gift made me smile. I thought it was probably Leaf's doing. He seemed thoughtful like that. When I was done, Leaf motioned me back to the boxcar.

It was still early yet, and the morning frost made the weeds crunch under my shoes. At a particularly loud crunch I looked down and saw I had stepped on wild chamomile. It wasn't supposed to flower in the winter, but here it was. A seed had gotten just enough water, nutrients, and sunlight in this forgotten field to bloom in spite of winter. I thought about Gabbi's angry red bites. I shaped my fingers like a fork and harvested the last few flowers. I cupped my hand into my chest as if protecting a baby kitten from the cold.

Spencer stared at me, but did not say a word as I scrambled into the boxcar with my flowers. "Do you have a pot?"

Spencer wordlessly handed me the oatmeal pot and I left the bits of oatmeal inside. They would help. I grabbed a spoon, the propane stove, the oatmeal pot, some water, and my weeds. I smashed everything together and then heated it. By the time it had boiled and steeped, everyone had returned to the inside of the boxcar to watch me work.

As the concoction cooled, I motioned Gabbi over. "I have something that will help the itching."

Gabbi's hand froze in the act of scratching her ankle as if she'd been caught stealing. She looked to Spencer and then me. "I'm fine."

"If you keep doing that, they'll turn into sores and get infected," I said.

"I'll volunteer," Leaf said. "I've got bit a million times on my back and can't reach any of them. It's driving me crazy." He lifted his shirt and turned his back to me. Angry welts from who knows what—fleas, spiders, mosquitoes—crisscrossed his spine.

I dabbed the watery paste onto his skin.

Leaf's profile showed he had closed his eyes.

"Is this okay?"

"It doesn't…it doesn't itch anymore." He grinned and stretched his back. "This is fantastic, Gabbi. You gotta get some."

She didn't move. Ano, Ricker and Jimmy lined up to expose limbs and backs and stomachs and necks, and Maibe had me paste a welt on the inner part of her arm. I also used the paste to clean up my shoulder, which still hurt, but hadn't gotten infected and at least seemed like it was healing.

Gabbi came over when I was finished with my wound. By the look on her face I knew she didn't want me to touch her so I handed her the rest of the pot. She jumped out of the boxcar with it and went out of sight.

"Oh," I said, realizing Spencer had not received any of the paste. I looked at him and said, "I'm sorry, I—"

"Explain to Leaf how to recognize the plant you used. I'll get some later," Spencer said.

I went outside with Leaf and showed him the wild chamomile. I explained the few other things I knew it could be used for.

"This weed, all of this? The entire patch?"

"Yeah."

"All the nights I spent itching myself crazy." He shook his head. "Thank you. Spencer would thank you too, or I mean, he kind of did, asking you to show me how to do it. That's the best you're going to get, but—"

"—No, it's fine. I get it."

We returned to the group. The boxcar was closed and locked and the chain of the key glinted around Gabbi's neck.

"We should leave Mary a note," Gabbi said.

"She's dead," Ano said.

"She's not! Take that back."

Ano stood there with his arms crossed. The others looked uncomfortable.

"You don't know that," Gabbi said. "Not for sure."

"You're right, Gabbi," Leaf said. "Not for sure." He grabbed a rock from the ground, examined it's edge and handed it to her. "You should leave a message."

We watched in a sort of sacred silence as she scratched letters into the wood next to the door.

Mary, we'll be back.

When Gabbi finished she dropped the rock. I noticed that everyone, including Maibe, had a weapon of some kind. A bat, a stick, a crossbow, a rock. Spencer held out a knife.

"So you trust me now?"

"Let's say, we trust you're not going to kill us yet," Spencer said. "If we're going to help each other, you have to defend yourself."

"What did Officer Hanley do?" Maibe asked.

"He's responsible for Ike needing to be put down," Ricker said.

"It's his fault Ike didn't get the cure in time," Leaf said.

"I'm not going to help you kill a man," I said. "I told you last night."

Leaf sucked in a breath.

Gabbi laughed. "You're a dumb towelhead."

"We're not killers," Leaf said to Maibe.

"This is an information collecting trip," Spencer said. "Nothing's happening today." He looked at each member of the group. "Got it? No stupid moves today. We're going to plan this careful." He turned to me. "I thought you wanted information. If so, Cal Expo is the place to get it. Come along with us. Or not."

CHAPTER 15

WE TOOK THE RAILROAD TRACKS into the neighborhoods and into a clothing store where we all abandoned our grubby clothes for dark, thick, clean clothes.

It was cold enough to see the mist from our breaths well into late morning. We took a zigzagging path, sometimes following the train tracks, sometimes dipping into the neighborhoods and back alleys, sometimes skirting along the roads, across parking lots, and through strip malls.

We saw people from a distance, but Spencer seemed to have a sixth sense for avoiding close contact. Not as many as I would have thought after that first horrifying day, but they were there, and we heard screams echo across the eerie silence of a city gone dark and motorless. Gabbi walked on the other side of Leaf. Maibe was to my right, Spencer in front, and the pup-boys in back.

A few birds chirped, a cat howled, some stray dogs ran away

as soon as they saw us. The fires must have taken out the electricity. Sometimes mini-explosions sounded, like a gas tank had exploded or someone had set off fireworks.

"Where is everyone?" I asked Leaf. "Where are all the people?"

"Well, we're not totally sure, but a lot of people got out. We think that's how it got here, you know, other people from other places brought it. A lot of people got out, a lot of people are dead and a lot of people might as well be dead."

"What do you mean they might as well be dead? I'm happy to be alive, I—"

"I don't mean Feebs, people like us," Leaf said. "A lot of people are locked inside their memories. They haven't been able to beat them back. You go into any of these houses, you'll find them. Standing, sitting, lying down. Like in a coma. Sometimes the memories make them act like a V or a Feeb in the fevers, but after the memory is finished they go back into a coma. We call them Faints. It happens if they're only infected with the bacteria."

I thought about Matilda and her family. "You know about that? The virus and the bacteria?"

Leaf squinted at me. "How do you know?"

"I..."

"Never mind," Leaf said. "Don't let it trigger a memory."

"A memory-rush," I said, using Christopher's name for it.

"Yeah, that is kinda what it's like. A rush. The worst kind of high." He shook his head. "Anyways, yeah we know about the memory-rush. We know a lot more than people give us credit for. That's pretty much how it's always been. Runaways aren't exactly seen as trustworthy."

"I trust you," I said.

"You probably shouldn't," Leaf said. "You don't know us. If it comes down to you or one of us, I won't think twice."

"I don't believe that," I said.

Leaf shrugged. "We think the crazy violent ones are trying to fight back the memories and can't. Us Feebs, maybe it overtakes us sometimes, but the double infection helps push it all back. The zombies don't have that kind of luck, they're stuck. The virus makes you crazy angry, the bacteria puts you into a sort of memory-coma. Together they balance each other out in a totally awesomely horrific way."

"They're not zombies," I said. "Don't make them into crazy supernatural monsters. They're sick and crazed, not risen from the dead."

Gabbi gave me a withering look over her shoulder. "We'll call them whatever we want. Anyways, it's not like we think they died or whatever, they're just locked in, under the control of their memories. In Haiti, that's what makes you a zombie, when you aren't in control of your own actions or thoughts. When you're somebody's slave, you're their zombie. These people, they're slaves to their memories, so we call them zombies, because that's what they are."

I ignored the anger in Gabbi's voice and thought about her version of zombies. It made more sense than the movie version. People under the power of memories, of their past selves. They were trapped—like a form of paralysis or locked-in syndrome, except it was their memories they couldn't escape—good or bad. Lost either way.

"You're smart and not just street smart," I said. "That Haiti stuff involves book smarts. How did you learn all that and end up homeless?"

Her face contorted and she turned away. "People were violent long before these zombies showed up. Or did you get to have one of those happy childhoods from out of a fairytale?"

She walked away before I could tell her she was all wrong about me.

We stopped a few times and Spencer would tell us to wait and he would duck into an alleyway or behind the gate of a long-abandoned building. After a while, I realized he was checking up on people. He'd come back and say someone had gone V or was in a coma. I had thought the city was empty but began to realize how wrong I was.

"Could that happen to you, to any of us?" I asked Leaf, continuing our conversation after Spencer returned from another side trip. "Going V for a time even though we've been tagged?"

"If you can't control the memory-rush, and it's a violent one, who's to say what we're capable of?" Leaf said.

I thought about Christopher and what he had done to us. Maibe said she couldn't remember much of what happened in there, except that Christopher always seemed next to me. The idea that I could lose enough control so that a memory might make me hurt someone else—this repulsed me. I would not let that happen.

"That's what we think, anyways," Leaf said. "The city has filled up with zombies. Some violent, some not."

This time I didn't contradict him. What better word was there for people like us? People who zombied-out at a memory trigger? "We're sick, but we're not hopeless."

"That's not what Cal Expo believes," Leaf said.

"They're screwed up," Gabbi said, slowing to walk beside us. She kept her eyes away from mine, but must have decided she forgave me for my offense. "They think we're zombies, and they have the weapons and the desire to back it up." She shifted her stick to the other shoulder. "They're taking the Normals, or anyone they want to run tests on, and killing anyone they think is a zombie."

I looked at them in disbelief.

Leaf said, "It's true."

Gabbi shrugged her shoulders. "You'll see."

We came across a burned-out neighborhood. The six-lane street had acted as a fire gap. One neighborhood was reduced to ash and soot, and the other neighborhood was untouched. Well, untouched by fire. Likely all its residents had been touched in other ways.

There were people. Of course there were people around. I couldn't believe I hadn't felt it before now. You could feel them walking around, staring at walls, gazing out windows, but there was no way to know if they were Normal or Violent or lost in a memory-rush or had just gone nuts.

A sudden thought occurred to me that I still didn't understand. "But how does the bacteria spread by itself?" The Lyssa virus spread itself just fine, but who had infected Matilda and her family?

"We don't know," Leaf whispered and motioned me to silence.

"We're jumping on the tracks until Exposition Boulevard," Spencer whispered to the group.

The tracks were raised and paralleled the freeway which was about a half mile away. I'd imagined the freeway jammed with cars of people trying to escape. And there were cars, but no people, and all the cars had for the most part been pushed to the shoulders. We cut over and across Exposition Boulevard, skulking in the shadows. The wind had shifted, blowing the smoky haze at us. It hung heavily, altogether obliterating the downtown landscape. When we stopped for even a moment, our new, warm clothing lost some of its effectiveness.

The crack, crack of shots sounded, then silence, then shots again. Spencer led us through and behind several warehouse buildings, around a closed-down department store, and then sent us up into several large oaks.

"We'll watch for awhile," he said as he boosted Maibe up. I pushed back a memory of climbing trees as a kid and positioned myself on a branch high enough to give a direct sight line to the main gate.

Cal Expo's fairground fencing had grown taller since I last worked there and now sported barbed wire and military-like vehicles and lookout towers.

We watched for about an hour. That's how long it took me to determine things were as Spencer said. That's how long it took me to feel sick over what I saw.

There were men in fatigues at the gate. People stumbled up the wide street, almost freeway-wide, and made their way to the gate. Some passed through. Many were turned away. Some were shot. The old and infirm, the ones who limped, whether from age or injury or the cure, those were the ones the guards didn't bother checking.

When the bodies were shot down, a front-end loader dumped them into a burn pile along the interior of the fence. Part of the haze came from that fire. I had thought to challenge Spencer's notion of how things stood. Cal Expo was a place for refugees, a place of safety. So the radio had said.

Leaf shared a branch in my same tree. He spoke softly.

"They took a lot more inside at first. Like they said on the radio. Rounding up people for their own good, they said. Shooting anyone close to looking sick, shooting people like us. Asking questions later. Or not at all."

My parents had told me stories. I had watched the news of what happened in other countries. People with guns and too much power had always shot first and asked questions later.

Someone whispered. Spencer was at the base of our tree. He motioned for us to come down. No one spoke until we had regrouped blocks away from the gate.

"Officer Hanley isn't on duty yet," he said. "But he'll be on tonight. Do you still want inside?"

I thought about backing out. How could I disguise myself, how could I possibly find Dylan in this mess? The situation was hopeless, yet I needed to try or I might as well limp myself to the gate and let them shoot me. "Yes."

"If your guy is alive, he's probably somewhere near the old Waterworld section. Officer Hanley will be on duty where the fence backs up to the bike trail and river. We could pick up Old Bully, maybe bash our way through. The fence isn't so high or as controlled as here."

"Actually, there's a gap in the fence," I said, remembering my state fair smoking days. "If they haven't sealed it."

"Do you remember where the gap is?" Spencer asked.

"Yeah, I remember," I said. "Who's Old Bully?"

Leaf shook his head and grinned.

"You'll see," Spencer said. He turned to Leaf. "Tell the others we're opening the shop again."

THE FOG ALWAYS CAME in at night along the back end of the grounds, waist-high along the sandy field behind the racetrack. Even with all the lights on, I remember thinking the fog was thick enough to cover anyone with the courage to crawl through, military-style, for a free ticket to whatever event was being held.

"There'll be coyotes and stuff now though," Ano said. "Now that people aren't around."

"And others like us. Or Vs," Maibe said.

"There might be some," Leaf said. "We'll need to be on lookout."

I shook my head. "But if you can't see them, they won't be able to see you, and the fog covers all the smells."

"As long as we get to the fog in one piece," Spencer said, "you won't have a problem, unless you do something like stand up."

Coyotes, jackrabbits, owls, dogs: the bike trail was a forest avenue through the city. Its own kind of no-man's land. A strip too intimidating for most, even when the city had thrived. The bike trail was a few dozen miles of semi-wilderness long, but less than a football field wide, on either side of the river. I thought through how the plan might work. The trees would protect us until we reached the fog. We could enter Cal Expo the back way, under full lights, protected by fog. I felt excitement. This could work.

If the gap in the fence still existed, it was behind a livestock building. People washed their prize-winning llamas and goats and pigs with a spigot attached to the outside wall of that building. It was flat there, empty of trees.

If the fog wasn't as thick as I remembered, if there were too many Vs, if the gap in the fence was fixed, we'd be lost. But there was no other way to get inside. There was no alternative but to break in.

"Maibe should stay behind," I said.

"No!" Maibe said.

"There's no reason for you to do this," I said. "It's too dangerous. If they see you, see that you're tagged, they'll kill you."

"I'm not getting left behind," Maibe said. She whipped her hair around and pulled her hood tight around her face.

"But Maibe, the Vs."

"There's no point in telling her she can't do something," Leaf said.

"Unless you want to tie her up and make her a prisoner," Gabbi said.

"No, I—"

"Vs will be out there," Leaf said, "but most are locked in weird zombie states. If you don't make any loud noises or fast movements, they'll miss you."

"Or they won't," Spencer said. "Keep a weapon on you. Just not a gun. The noise attracts them, and they come fast, but they don't have very good balance. Tip them over, slit their throat, but you gotta do it before they latch onto you cause their grip is like a vise. They'll never let go."

"I still think—"

He jerked his thumb at Maibe. "You can't leave her behind or lock her up. She plans on sticking with you, get it? I'd hate to see another one of you mess up a kid because they decide they know what's best. Hell, it wouldn't be the first time. But you don't know what's best. No one does. No one ever did. It's people like you—"

"—Spencer," Leaf interrupted.

"I'm more like you than you think."

"Yeah," Spencer said. "Whatever," Spencer said, but he lessened the edge in his voice. "Just don't let them kill you and you'll be fine."

"The zombies or the guards?" Maibe asked.

He turned a critical eye on Maibe. She shrunk under his gaze. "Both, dumbass. Both."

CHAPTER 16

SPENCER, MAIBE, AND THE PUP-BOYS came out of Ike's Bikes. We were a gang of bikers now. Pink bikes, blue bikes, green bikes, yellow bikes. Banged-up steel, scratched paint, disintegrating rubber grips, creaking chains, flat bars, drop bars. Gabbi's bike displayed silver streamers, a skull and crossbones sticker on the head. A bat was strapped to her back with bungee cords. Someone had taken black paint to Leaf's army green bike and striped it with an unsteady hand. Foot bars attached to his back wheel, like he was planning to do tricks, except the bars had been filed to sharp points.

I fixed the seat of Mary's bike to my correct height and ignored the ghosts crowding around me. Gabbi avoided looking at me or the bike, I wasn't sure, but I didn't blame her. It was hard not to look at Dylan or jump at his touch when he checked to make sure my brakes worked. But it wasn't his hand, it was Spencer's.

I rode the bike around in circles, hoping to beat back the ghost-memories. It helped. I flipped through the gears, rechecked the brakes. The blue aluminum was flecked with dark red spots that looked more like dried blood than rust.

Spencer came out with a contraption that looked like an oversized tricycle with a snowplow attached to the front end.

"What's that?" I asked.

He adjusted the seat and checked the attachments. "Old Bully. We'll be traveling fast, right? What do you think will happen if you're traveling at twenty miles per hour on a flimsy road bike—into a zombie hanging out on the trail?"

I tried to picture the outcome of such a crash and then decided I didn't want to. "Why didn't we use the bikes before? Why did we walk?"

Spencer fiddled with his brakes.

Leaf finally answered, "We put them away after Mary. Mostly it's safer to walk and hide. To stay invisible. These bikes are the opposite of invisible."

"We'll be going about fifteen miles per hour in the dark. They'll be invisible tonight. I'll go first with this." Spencer patted the handlebars. "We'll push any bystanders out of the way. They might get scraped, but a crash would hurt them, and us, a lot more."

I didn't know how to answer his matter-of-fact response, as if it were the most natural thing in the world to talk about bulldozing zombies off the trail.

"Old Bully's helped us escape some tight spots in the last few weeks," Leaf said with affection.

There was no wind, only a thick blanket of cold and silence. The oak trees were like statues, the street lights were dark, traffic noises were nonexistent, the grass did not rustle, no human voices spoke.

I was anxious to move. "Are we ready yet?"

Spencer adjusted his seat. "No," he said.

Anger sparked in me. His arrogant dismissal of everything I did was getting old. Wasn't I the one who'd remembered the gap in the fence and told them the fog would be thick cover for our break-in?

Then I realized that if anything went wrong, if it all wasn't how I'd said, I would be at fault. This group had based their plan on me. I couldn't remember the last time such trust had been given to me.

Spencer stood up and brushed his hands on his jeans. "Load up," he called out.

Leaf jumped, as if coming back from the dead and I realized maybe he had. I thought he'd been standing guard, but now I realized he had been lost in a memory-rush.

I walked my bike to where Maibe stood, also entranced, and gently shook her. "Maibe, time to move."

She shivered, shuddered, and scratched, and then focused her eyes on mine. "My uncle taught me how to ride a bike. It was the first thing we did together when he took me in."

Spencer positioned his behemoth of a tricycle at the head of our group and pedaled off. Gabbi took the rear position. I stayed behind Maibe. We shot down the trail and the wet fog banished the memories that had edged forward.

Goosebumps raised on my arms. Instead of zipping up my jacket, I let the cold air wash over me. Every pedal increased my heart rate and sent the memory-ghosts back a step. Yet Dylan continued to pop in, riding his bike next to Maibe, as if we were on a date. I knew it wasn't real. Yet. I unzipped my jacket further. I saw others did the same. We rode with our jackets open and hats off. Anything to keep the ghosts at bay.

Spencer's snowplow tricycle was difficult to make out in front. No working street lights meant we saw by the glow of the firelight reflecting against the fog. I wondered how long the fires and the fog might last, how difficult it might become to breathe. There was a reason so many of the city's high pollution days took place in winter. The fog trapped everything, as if it were a plastic bag wrapped around a person's head.

I took out a scarf and folded it across my mouth. Better. I pedaled to catch up to Maibe, motioned for her attention, and then to my scarf. She took one hand off the handlebars to fix her scarf around her mouth.

I dropped back behind her. I squinted to make out Spencer's position. An impact sounded and an object flew off the trail. Maibe didn't look to the side as she passed the object, but I did. Someone lay face down in the starthistle. It twitched as I rode by but did not get up. Then I was past it and put it out of my mind.

Another hit sounded down the trail. My anxiety ratcheted higher. We'd covered several miles without seeing a soul and now Spencer had hit two bodies within a hundred yards of each other. How many more were there in the next five miles? How many more were hiding in the fog just off the trail, and how many would respond to the sounds of our pedaling, our wheels, our snowplow hits, and how many more would be drawn to us like a moth to flame, like iron to a magnet, like a tongue to a toothache?

Maibe slammed on her brakes. I almost ran my bike into her back tire before I could stop. I also swore out loud and then caught myself. We were making so much noise.

Spencer stopped a few yards up the trail, just before a blind curve. He left his tricycle and jogged back to our grouped bikes.

"We have a pretty big tail forming," Gabbi said. She took her beanie off and rubbed the side of her face as if trying to remove a stubborn piece of dirt. "They're not that far back."

"How far?" Spencer asked.

Gabbi rubbed her face harder and looked up at the surrounding fog bubble. I wasn't alone in feeling suffocated.

"Gabbi!" He said.

"Less than five minutes if we just stand here."

Spencer glanced at each of us. "All right. There's a group of about six Vs ahead. We're going to sprint this next section, but," he paused, "the plow won't get all of them. So, you know, watch where you're going."

Gabbi paled. Leaf swore quietly under his breath. The pup-boys traded looks. I caught Maibe's eye. "Ride behind me," I said. I gave her a confident smile I knew she couldn't believe. "We'll get through."

Spencer jogged away and then pedaled the tricycle around the corner, disappearing. I coughed once before suppressing the next.

I bore down on my pedals and stood up to both increase my speed and give myself a chance to guide how I might fly off the bike if I hit something, but, god, it was dark and thick and the fog seemed determined to choke me. I twisted my handles away from what I thought was a hand reaching out but was only a thread of water vapor.

What would I do if the plow didn't push them out of the way? I sat back down on the seat and pictured kicking out my leg against an impending shadow, and then pictured the shadow bowling me over, falling on top of me, biting me. I stood back up, ready to launch myself off a V, even if that meant losing the chance to speed away on my bike. I sat back down as I imagined myself stuck on the trail as more and more of them caught up with us.

I heard a hit and then another hit, but I couldn't see worth a damn what Spencer was hitting or if he had gotten them all. All I could see was Leaf's tire in front of me, and then I saw Leaf stand up on his pedals and kick out at something to his right side. Leaf quivered, wobbled and jerked, and managed to keep pedaling. The something fell backward, half of it across the trail. I tightened my thighs around the seat, stood on the pedals and lifted my front tire over the body. "Go to the left!" I yelled over my shoulder, hoping Maibe would hear it in time to steer around the fallen body.

Then a shadow came lurching across the trail. I had a split second to think I couldn't let the bike take that hit, not if I wanted to ride it out of here. I twisted the bike away and launched myself into the collision and hoped that the bike would coast and fall gently to the ground, and then I tucked my head and hit the V sideways, as if my back were a clothesline. I flew through the air and closed my eyes and protected my head and told myself not to lose consciousness. My legs whipped around painfully. I felt the impact of stopping, felt the cloth and smell of a person I didn't know, felt my organs slam against my skeleton, felt myself almost go dark. I couldn't afford it. I needed to spring up from the ground, bounce back, run off. My legs were like jelly, and I wasn't quite sure where they were.

"Get up! Get up!"

Maibe's voice, or my own. I couldn't tell. I told my arms and legs to move. I told them again. After the third time a part of me moved. Someone gripped my shoulder, lifted me up. I fought the touch, I punched out.

"Open your eyes!"

I opened them and saw Maibe's pink hoodie and held back another punch. I splayed my hands on the ground and tried to still the dizziness, peer down the trail, and look for my bike all at once. I collapsed on the ground as Gabbi and the pup-boys whizzed by on their bikes. They did not stop, though Gabbi frantically waved for me to get up.

Shadows stumbled out of the fog. The others had caught up with us.

"Maibe," I croaked. "Get on your bike."

"Get up!" She whispered frantically.

"I'm right behind you." I stumbled to my feet. "Go!"

She rode to where mine had fallen about twenty feet ahead. She stopped. She reached down, picked up my bike and looked back at me. "Come on—"

The V loomed up from the trail, halfway between me and Maibe. He, she, it, made small wrenching noises, like it was sobbing, like it was hurting, and then lurched to Maibe with its arms outstretched.

I learned to walk and then run again in the space of twenty feet. As I came alongside, I kicked out at the Vs lifted foot, pushing it into the other leg, tripping her. Her, I decided. It was a her. I tripped her and sent her tumbling to the asphalt. I grabbed the bike from Maibe. She pedaled off and I followed. My leg felt as if someone had taken a cheese grater to my skin. My head throbbed. My hands felt skinned. The bike creaked in places it shouldn't. I looked over my shoulder and saw a mob less than a hundred feet back. I passed three more shadows on the trail, swerved, narrowly missed the first one, rode over the second one who had fallen, and then kicked the third one over while keeping balanced on the bike.

This was a bad plan. This was a very, very bad plan. They would know we were coming. There would be no way to sneak in, no way to hide out, no way to get inside. The trail funneled the mob directly to our destination. Our noises were drawing them from their homes, their hovels, their hideouts. We would not lose them all before reaching Cal Expo. And how many were still ahead?

This was a bad plan.

I caught up with Maibe and the others. Spencer's tricycle took an uphill side trail and the others followed. The trail flattened out to a staging area and Spencer and the others stopped.

I braked and set my foot down, and then pain lanced through my knee. I set my other foot down. We were screwed.

"All right," Spencer said. "Couldn't have planned it better."

CHAPTER 17

"WHAT ARE YOU TALKING ABOUT," I blurted. "We can't see. A mob of Vs are following us. They're going to know we're coming. There's no way to sneak—"

"Who said we were sneaking in?" Spencer arched an eyebrow.

"I thought—"

"Yeah. You thought. You thought and thought and still came up with crap for a plan."

"Hey," I raised my hands. "I'm trying to understand—"

"There was never a way to sneak in. We're going to storm the castle and give Officer Hanley a nice little surprise."

Gabbi snickered into her glove.

"What are you going to do?" I asked.

"Bite him," Gabbi said.

"What?"

Silence reined. I hadn't meant to lace my response with judgment, but there it was.

In that silence, the cold seeped through my layers. My shoulder still ached from the bite, my exposed skin felt damp and clammy. Some sort of water dripped nearby, pinging on metal. I flexed my fingers on the handlebars and focused on the ridged pattern of the rubber grips. The fog covered what would otherwise be an overwhelming smell of body odor from our adrenaline-laced ride, our boxcar living, our shower-free days. Yet still, the fog contained a hint of rotting organic matter, a swampy smell I hoped was the river and not us, or others. At least my knee felt better.

Finally Spencer sighed. "We're going to bite him to save his life. We're going to inoculate good old Officer Hanley."

"Yeah, but if he has a heart attack while we save his life, we're okay with that, too," Gabbi said.

"I still—" I spoke with care, keeping my tone and words neutral, "—don't understand."

Leaf shifted the bike back and forth between his hands. "We're Officer Hanley's stray dogs. When he felt sorry for us, he'd help out with food, a blanket. When he didn't, we got a nice beating for trespassing. He saved Gabbi and Mary once, but then he got Ike killed, so—"

"Enough," Spencer said. "She won't get it." He turned to me. "We're bringing the mob to them. The fog will cover us so that we're all just blobs in the whiteness. You use the chance to get inside. We'll use the chance for some payback."

I shivered and pictured the scene. I saw lots of ways for things to go wrong and few ways for things to go right. Spencer's plan involved bringing together a mob of Vs on one side, people with guns on the other, and us in the middle with the fog for protection and a fence in the way.

Yet. Dylan waited on the other side.

And he was right. I didn't have a better plan.

"Where's Maibe going to be in all this?" I asked.

"I'm going through too," she said.

Gabbi opened her mouth, her brow furrowed. Spencer held up his hand.

"Maibe," Spencer said.

"I should go through. I can do it. I can help."

"Maibe, we talked about this," Spencer said. "I need you to help with the most dangerous job of all. We're depending on you to help us get back alive."

"I need someone to watch my back as I watch out for the others," Gabbi said. "I need you outside with me. I need you to help me once they've all gone through, to get them back out."

"I—" Maibe looked at me.

"You don't have to do it," Spencer said. "If you're too scared, you can go through with us. But we were counting on you."

"I—"

I held my breath and hoped Maibe would agree. No way would I risk putting her in the middle of a bunch of Vs and guns and chaos.

"Okay," Maibe said.

Gabbi nodded. "Thanks."

Spencer looked behind us, down the main trail. "There."

Dark shapes curled out from the fog, as if they were walking through water. I focused on breathing through my mouth to avoid taking in the swamp smell.

"The field is around the corner," Spencer said. "The perimeter lights will trip and then the Vs will be drawn that way. We'll use the Vs as cover. That means you don't want to be first to the fence line. The fog will do the rest. The guards won't be able to see. That's how we'll get across."

I used the back of my hand to wipe away the moisture beading on the tips of my nose and eyelashes. It felt as if I scratched myself with sandpaper. I licked my upper lip and tasted salt, water, dirt. Even though we could see the mob, we couldn't hear them, which made the whole scene more disturbing.

"Gabbi and Maibe, this is your spot until the Vs clear out. After that, do what makes sense."

Maibe nodded with solemn attention. Gabbi put an arm around her shoulder.

I lifted my leg to swing it over the bike.

"Leave the bikes," he said. "We've got to look like them."

Of course. I cringed at the tongue lashing I deserved to get from Spencer, but he said nothing, except, "Good luck finding your person."

I looked at him for a long moment, seeing someone only a few years older than me with aged skin who was even more wise and experienced in the crueler layers of the world than me. "Good luck biting your officer," I said.

He nodded.

I hugged Maibe. If she hadn't been there for me to take care of I knew I wouldn't have made it this far. But she couldn't go where I needed to go next. If any of us survived this, it had to be her. At least her.

"Stay safe," I said. "I'll be back."

"You too," she said and let go.

I nodded a goodbye to Gabbi, who returned it. I didn't know how, but I had earned a little respect from her. The rest of us walked as a group down the trail, behind the Vs, careful to stay far enough back to prevent triggering them with either our sounds or smells.

Finally, we rounded the trail's corner and Spencer pulled out a flare gun, I thought maybe a token stolen from Officer Hanley before the world had fallen apart. He lifted the gun, aimed, and shot it into a tree outside the Cal Expo perimeter. The flare brightened, then disappeared for a moment in the fog. Then the fog lit up, red. Then everything went blinding white. Cal Expo had turned the lights on and made it impossible to see, but it drew the Vs to this new sensory input like Spencer had said it would. Did they follow the white light at the end of the tunnel? Did they look for relief?

The fog muffled the first shots.

Leaf shoved something into my hand. I looked down and reflexively tightened my grip. My chef's knife. I blinked. It wasn't my chef's knife, that one had been lost long ago, but rather a pocket knife.

"It's time," Spencer said. The three of them drifted into the fog, disappearing, leaving me alone.

I felt a memory-rush brush the edges of my brain, tendrils of state fair exhibits brought in on the fog. I began to run.

I focused on breathing steady and deep and went to where the light shined brightest. A lone V crossed my path and I dodged him. My feet sunk into the wet weeds, my pant legs became soaked to the knee. I lifted my feet high above the vegetation, waited for my knee to pop, but it felt fine. There was no pain. I leapt over a fallen tree trunk. I swerved away from another V sprinting in my direction.

I couldn't see the line yet.

I hoped I had been right. I hoped Spencer and the others

had found the gap in the fence. I hoped there still was a gap in the fence. But if not, I coached myself to jump and climb and sacrifice my hands to any barbed wire.

A snuffling sounded on my right.

A big, middle-aged man with vacant eyes and a torn, red plaid shirt ran faster than I thought possible. To me.

I froze.

A loud crack sounded, and then his head exploded. He was there, and then he wasn't, and blood drops were suspended in the fog for a horrible moment before everything dropped to the ground. I lost my footing, stumbled to the ground, my knees and hands and forehead falling into the wetness that was part water and part middle-aged man. Metallic, swampy muck hit my nose and mouth. I snapped my mouth close, held my breath, and crawled to the fence. Panic increased my speed.

Before I covered ten feet, something grabbed my shirt and hauled me up. I fumbled for the knife at my waist. I hoped it was Spencer or Leaf or Jimmy.

Hot breath, stinking like fermented cheese. A dirt-smudged face, crazy long brown hair, a gaping mouth with two broken front teeth. She was taller than me, impossibly tall, and she gripped my clothes like a vice.

"Let go!" I screamed.

She shook her head, as if throwing off my words like I was a bee that had buzzed too closely. She pulled me against her. I saw the bits of grass and blood and dirt stuck in her gums.

Her face bobbed to the side, out of sight. Her teeth punched through my clothes and the skin of my shoulder. The same shoulder that had already been wounded once. As if she had smelled the wound, the weakness, and went straight for it. The pain burned like fire through my body. I screamed and plunged the knife into her chest. The Vs flesh resisted and then gave way like I was carving a roasted chicken.

She remained latched to me. I feared backing away might tear my skin to shreds. I pressed into her instead. A sucking sound filled my ears as I drew out my knife. This time I aimed higher.

She growled into my neck. I pulled and twisted and plunged the knife into her cheek. She released and sent me spinning backwards. She fell to her knees, clutched her cheek. I swear she looked at me with clear and horrified and knowing eyes. I ran away, into the oblivion of the fog, not sure of my direction now, only knowing that it was away from her and that human look in her eyes, that look that said she realized what had happened to her, she realized what she had become.

My shoulder throbbed and shot waves of pain up and down my body. The bloody knife slipped out from my hand and was lost in the weeds. I was lost in a white tunnel to hell.

I couldn't stop running. If I stopped running the memory-rush would come—it was here. Time and place disconnected. Running after Dylan, running from those school girls, running from the Vs, running from the Vs, running from the Vs.

I tripped and fell to the ground. Water soaked my upper body. Whiteness encapsulated me in a cold glove.

I was nowhere. There was nothing. I was going to die without ever seeing Dylan again.

There.

A faint gleam of light reflected off metal.

I crawled forward.

The fence.

No Vs, no guards in sight. Just me and an uncut fence, and

a hint of luck—no barbed wire. My shoulder felt paralyzed. I used my one good arm and two good legs and climbed over the damn fence.

The fog revealed a rusted truck—a place to hide, to tie up my wounds, to fight back the fever that was going to come. I scooted underneath the bed, ignoring the wetness on my back, grateful for the smell of rust and oil to replace the other smells of muck and rot and blood.

I tore a piece of my undershirt for a tourniquet, wrapped my shoulder. Everything went blazing white with infection. I never hated a color as much as I did in that moment.

The memories tornadoed in.

THE PARTS OF MY BODY I could still feel seemed frozen from the cold. My face and hands and feet I could not feel at all. There was no way to know how long the memory-fevers had kept me numb. I knew at least that something had disturbed me enough to interrupt the fevers.

My eyes focused on the truck's pipes, barely illuminated. They were crusted in dirt and rust and mineral build-up. The truck had sat abandoned for some time.

I tried to see outside the border of the truck, but the fog, the dull, gray fog, no longer lit up by artificial lights, obscured the view. I breathed through my mouth and then regretted it as ice seemed to touch the back of my throat. My tongue felt heavy and coated in a layer of grime. I shifted and pulled away from the foliage. The weed's succulent leaves and stem spread web-like across the ground all around me. No yellow flowers bloomed, but I knew its form all the same. My old friend, purslane.

I caught up a broken stem with several leaves. A drop of its clear fluid remained on my fingers as I pushed the leaves into my mouth. It tasted a bit like tough lettuce with a hint of lemon. I felt comfort at its familiar taste, even as it triggered gnawing stomach pains and a burst of saliva. I thought from my level of hunger that the fevers had lasted for only a few hours, but I couldn't be sure.

The silence disturbed me. The only sounds were the crackle of weeds near the edge of my body line, my own breathing, my own heart beating. I had broken into Cal Expo yet there was no sound to indicate it was anything more than a grave.

My joints popped in quick succession as I pulled my belly along the metal underside of the truck. Rust and dirt rained on me. I had my mouth open like a fool. I spit and thanked the purslane for producing saliva.

Had something crackled in the weeds just along the far edge of the truck?

My heart beat increased and filled my ears with a roar.

I forced myself to go slow and silent, using only one arm as my other shoulder was locked up. I could see only inches ahead, everything beyond the border of the truck was blurred, and I did not know if it was because of fog or fever.

A woman's head reared into view. Stinking breath, dirt-smudged face, crazy hair. I jumped away, banged my head against the bumper, jabbed my injured shoulder against a sharp corner. I fell back to the ground in agony.

The woman hadn't died. She was alive and had searched for me and—

She disappeared into the fog like evaporating water.

A ghost-memory, I told myself. That's all.

The fog parted, forming a small circular stage, and Mr. Sidner was there, and the other woman I had almost killed, alive and well, on top of him, hurting him. I scrambled up, ignored the pain in my shoulder, and tried to outrun these nightmares. Instead, I barreled into a wall.

Pain bloomed on my face, along with embarrassment. Running from a ghost-memory in the fog was one of the more stupid things I could do.

After the pain lessened I opened my eyes. The damn fog still surrounded me. My nose was on fire. I forced my numb fingers to touch the edge of the pain. No way to tell how bad, but my fingers came away blood-tipped. At least the cold might keep the swelling down.

I forced myself to walk on, using the wall as a guide.

The truck that took Dylan away drove into view. Dylan locked inside but not more than a hundred yards away.

A strangled moan left my throat and slapped back to me. I beat away the instinct to run. I locked my legs, locked my mind. I would not run after a ghost-memory. I would not become a V. I would not.

An eternity passed.

Then a new fear sprung my legs from their lock.

Neither did I want to become one of the Faint.

I shuddered, licked my cracked lips, and hobbled away from the van mirage. One creaking foot after another. One step away, two steps away. Three steps. Four. My hand against the wood wall kept me steady. Five steps.

The van disappeared.

My fingers caught on something other than wood.

Six steps and my hands fumbled at the latch. Seven steps and a creaking door, and I was inside. Smells of hay, dust, rotting wood. Metal animal stalls crisscrossed the room.

I stumbled into a stall full of clean hay, not looking or caring about what else might be inside.

The metal latch to open the stall might as well have been padlocked. My hands could not budge it. I draped my upper half over the stomach-high top bar, leaned and pushed and struggled and flipped onto my back on the other side. I lay there stunned for a moment.

I shimmied deeper into the hay, heaping it over me while I sneezed and itched. I ignored the ghost-memory that appeared outside my stall. Another woman, locked in a fog of memory, old, like a grandmother, like the one I had hurt, yet different. I couldn't place her, couldn't remember what ghost-memory this was—when had one of the sick ones shuffled her way to me, staring vacant, arms pinned to her sides, stopping feet from me, not seeing me? The fever rose in me again, obliterating the question from my mind. I welcomed the heat the fever would generate under my layer of hay.

I awoke all at once as if someone had sprayed water in my face. Yellow hay stalks filled my vision, hay dust tickled my throat, my rhythmic breaths counterpointed with someone else's.

The woman whose arms were pinned to her sides, whose vacant stare did not see me, whose body pressed against the stall bar. She was no ghost-memory.

I thought about staying hidden in the hay, maybe she would leave, and then I thought about all the time I had already lost.

And then I thought, what if she wasn't the only one? I couldn't see her, only hear her breathing. What if more had shuffled in from the corners of the building and surrounded this stall three lines deep, breathing, frozen, locked-in?

I shot up from the hay, stalks flying in all directions and clinging to my hands and clothes.

Only her. She was alone.

I calmed myself down. I was almost warm and the memory-fevers had left me with a clear head for the moment. My shoulder throbbed, my face throbbed, my hands and feet throbbed. The pain was a good sign.

The light signaled early morning. The fog was still thick but dissipating. A full night had passed—I hoped not more than that.

The woman did not look dangerous. Only very sick.

I backed to the far end of the stall, caught my foot on some sort of cloth. A stall blanket, like those clipped onto livestock to keep their fur clean before the show. I wrapped it around my shoulders and warmth flooded into my core. I clambered over the bars again, determined to find some water and begin my scouting, to find Dylan and never, ever come back to this place. The bare dirt floor was damp and there were two sets of footprints. My own and the woman's.

When I reached the open door, the woman mewled behind me. She still pressed against the stall bars. Tears streamed down her face. She had wrapped her bare arms around her. Blue tinged her lips. She shivered uncontrollably.

I told myself to keep moving. I told myself to get on with it, there was nothing I could do for her. I turned back, took off the cloth, and clipped it around her shoulders.

She dropped her arms, and I thought she meant to attack

me. Instead, she fingered the corner of the cloth, rubbed her cheek against it, and smiled.

I opened a stall and led her inside. It took coaxing, but she sat and allowed me to arrange hay around her to create an insulating nest.

"Stay here where it's warm," I said, when I had finished. This was what the bacterial infection did. She was like Matilda and her family. She was a Faint now. The virus I understood. The instinct for people to go V—to bite and injure and infect—was obvious. But how did someone catch the bacterial infection? How did it get passed from one person to another?

"Stay here until I come back," I said again.

Her mouth curled into a slight smile.

I feared she would wander away but was afraid to lock her inside. I didn't know when I would be back and didn't want her trapped, banging against the inside of the stall until she died of dehydration.

I limped my way to the sink next to the stall. The tap ran for minutes—cold, almost frozen water—then gushed glorious hot water. I quickly stripped, ignoring my various injuries, and stepped into the deep sink. My toes and fingers stung as they came back to life. The shoulder wound was an ugly, swelling injury I cleaned as best I could. My face was next. Except for some tenderness, I did not think I had done much damage to my nose after all. Hay became my towel. I climbed back into my filthy clothes. Steam rose from my body in thick waves.

A dirty mug rested on a wood beam next to the sink. I washed it out as best I could, filled it with warm water, and carried it back to the old woman. I held the water out to her, guided her hands around the cup. Being this close to her, I saw the dirt that filled the lines around her eyes. A chalky line of something else crusted her face from her eyes to her jaw. Maybe dried salt from old tears. She smelled no different than the building. A mix of dry hay, soil, wet earth, and decay, but not so bad really. We were in a barn after all.

When she did nothing with the cup, I splashed the liquid onto her lips. With that vacant stare still in place, she opened her mouth and licked. She jerked from the taste of water, raised the cup and drained it.

"Thank you, Lorraine," she said, surprising me. Her voice cracked from disuse, but otherwise sounded steady, modulated for politeness and control. "I knew you would come back and take care of me."

My mind raced, would she hear me, listen to me? I had to try. "Of course, but you're sick and need rest. I've made the bed. You need to lie down and rest. Wait for me. Don't go anywhere."

Her laugh tinkled like glass. "Of course, dear. Where would I go? This is my home. Thank you for the soup. I will be fine now. Go look after your children and I'll be here." She finished the water, moved the cup as if placing it on a side table, but since there was none, the cup disappeared into the hay. She lay down on the ground as if relaxing on a couch, folded her hands underneath her cheek like a child would, sighed, and closed her eyes.

I tucked the hay around and fought back a sob. This horrible disease trapped people, and it scared other people so badly they became willing to kill because of it. I had killed because of it.

My stomach rumbled and I wondered how long ago my meager purslane meal had happened, and then I wondered how long she had gone without food.

I strode out of the barn, surveyed the area, and dropped to my knees to pick as much purslane as I could carry. When I returned with my bounty, I rinsed the weeds and set a pile next to the woman. I guided her hand to it and said, "Here's a nice finger-food salad before dinner."

"Thank you, dear." She proceeded to munch on the purslane and I did the same. It would not satisfy our hunger, only take the edge off for a short time.

I stretched to warm up my joints and muscles and practiced walking around like a normal person. They'd shoot me on sight if they thought I was infected. I put my hair down and arranged it to cover the ashy, webbed cast of my skin that would give away my true state.

The woman was as comfortable as I could make her. I promised myself I would come back for her.

CHAPTER 18

"MEETING…" THE HISS AND CRACKLE of a stereo interrupted the message. I crouched behind a metal trash can big enough to hide my body from view. No smells of rotting food. I looked inside. Empty. Not even a plastic bag lined it. There were no people in this section.

A speaker popped again and I found the source. A dozen feet away from where I hid stood a tall metal pole with a speaker attached. The fairground's music and announcement system.

"Meeting at Stage 1…Fifteen minutes. All must attend. Meeting at Stage 1…"

If they used the same names as the state fair, I knew where to find Stage 1.

The quality of light made me guess it was late morning, though even a vague outline of the sun wasn't visible through the fog. I skirted along the edge of buildings, sidewalks, grassy areas, the skeletons of vendor stations. The building the old woman and I had taken refuge in was one of several animal housing structures near the horse racing stadium. There were no sounds of people or activity, but I thought maybe this was for safety reasons.

Stage 1 was near the exhibit buildings, on the opposite end of the fairgrounds from where I was. Those multi-storied cement fortresses encircled a cement-stepped amphitheater and were partially surrounded themselves by canals used for paddle-boating during better times. They would form a type of castle, moat and all.

There was no one in sight. This made me uneasy. I reminded myself Cal Expo took up hundreds of acres and I was still along the edges of it. But how long had I actually been in the fevers? Hours? Days?

Stage 1 opened to air, except for the backside, which opened to a cement walkway that connected several warehouses. The layout made it easy to see people coming while also drawing the eye to it like a magnet. Dozens of people milled around the opposite side of the stage across the algae-filled water. People lined up underneath tents with tables that displayed huge, open pots sending curls of steam into the air. My stomach cramped.

People lined up with bowls in hand, waiting for their turn at this outdoor soup kitchen. Winter clothes obscured faces, genders, ages. I thought I might pass through unrecognized. I thought it might be worth the risk of getting caught for a chance at a bowl of food.

"Ladies and Gentlemen. Sergeant Bennings would like your attention." The electronically amplified voice sounded tired. People shuffled and faced the stage. The food servers paused.

I walked on a curving asphalt ramp, lost sight of the stage

and the crowd for a moment, and then suddenly became a part of the crowd. No one questioned me. No one seemed to notice me. People focused on eating or on the stage. Those few people who talked seem to do so in furtive whispers as if trying to hide criminal activity. The smell of unwashed bodies reminded me of fermented pickles, which only made my stomach rumble louder. Now I could see the dirt caked onto clothes and exposed skin. Now I could make out genders and guess at ages.

I drew my clothes tightly around myself, arranged my greasy hair to obscure my face, used the bulky bodies of two men facing the stage to hide me from the sight of others.

A man in army uniform took up the microphone. He stood in front of scarlet stage curtains that must have been commandeered from a game stand. He stood spread-eagled and looked out across the water over the crowd for a long moment. Once the few whisperings fell into a strained silence, he spoke. "We're all hungry. I'll make this quick and to the point. We are all survivors, some of the last human beings in this great city. We've lost communication with the outside which means one of two things: the CDC is following standard quarantine procedures, or this is countrywide. Maybe worldwide."

A person behind me gasped. Others stood in grim silence.

"We will hold the line here. We must. All of us are responsible for the safety of our new home. We have survived for over a month already because we follow the rules. You must follow the rules. There are no exceptions. There can be no mistakes when our very humanity is at risk. Therefore, anyone caught breaking the rules," his voice deepened and he pressed his mouth closer to the mike so that his voice distorted, "will face a hearing and execution."

Sergeant Bennings turned, as if to cue someone offstage. The curtains trembled and moved apart. They revealed a gallows stage with a noose already around the neck of a woman, plump and pear-shaped, in a sweatshirt and jeans, wobbling on top of a wooden box.

"This must be a joke." The words left me before I realized I'd spoken.

The two men I hid behind shifted at my voice, and I quickly lowered my head to stare at their shoes, hoping they would not look at me, see me, see my infection.

They did not turn around, but one said, "This is no joke. It's what's kept us all alive and uninfected for this long."

"Doesn't make it right," the other guy whispered.

"Shut your mouth. Better not let any of them hear you."

"In accordance with standard quarantine containment procedures," Sergeant Bennings said, speaking into the microphone like he was reading from a script, "and the prevention of bodily fluid transfer and the limited supplies of drugs available at this time, Fillipa Stenfor, you are hereby sentenced to death by hanging for helping a known infected escape detection—"

"Her own grandmother, for God's sake," the first man whispered.

The second man said, "If you're determined to get yourself killed, I'll not be a part of it." At that he walked off, exposing me to the wind and a better line of sight to the stage.

"Please confirm to all of us gathered here that you received the hearing as promised in the bylaws of this quarantine site."

The woman hung her head, tucking her chin around the rope. She did not move, not until someone in soldier's fatigues prodded her with the butt of a rifle.

She nodded slightly.

"Now you may share any last words before you are hung until you are dead." Sergeant Bennings held the microphone to her mouth.

After a long moment of silence, she said, "Sometimes doing what is right and doing what is good—sometimes they are not the same thing. I do not regret my choices." She stopped talking, and then nodded to show she was finished.

Sergeant Bennings stepped off the gallows box and held the microphone away, but it still captured his words to her, floating them to us like whispers on a pillow. "You should not have protected her. This could have been avoided." Even from this distance, there seemed to be real sorrow etched on his face.

She did not answer him.

He waited another moment and then backed up several paces. With a sigh into the microphone, he said, "Proceed."

Another soldier on stage kicked the wooden box out from beneath her feet. The sharp crack of boot against wood shot across the water like a slap.

I did not watch. Instead I examined my shoes as if my very survival depended upon tracing the mud-crusted laces, the little seed stickers attached to those laces, the colored scuff marks that were a mix of more mud and grease from being under the truck, a rust-colored streak that was likely dried blood.

By then they had hung her until she was dead and closed the stage curtains.

Sergeant Bennings came out again to speak against that scarlet background. "Shift change in two hours. Food served until 6 PM." He left the stage.

I tried to process what all of us had witnessed in silence,

without protest, without chaos, as if normal life now included hanging a woman on a stage.

But maybe it was normal now.

People milled around, talked in close whispers, lined back up for food. No one seemed to notice that the curtains had opened again.

The woman and her gallows were now missing, but five figures remained. Three stood in a semi-circle talking and gesturing at each other on the side of the stage, almost hidden, but not quite. They wore army fatigues. The fourth and fifth figures wore regular layers of winter clothes and pulled electronic equipment off the stage. There was something familiar about the fifth man. Something about his outline, the way he walked, the way he coiled wire, lifted a speaker off the stage floor. I squinted and my eyes swam and my heart lurched.

It could be Dylan. It could be.

I stuffed my infected hands in my pockets and approached the moat. I ignored the pain that made me want to limp like an old person. Even with everything I knew, my heart felt glad to see him alive.

Adrenaline made saliva flood into my mouth. I backed away from the moat's edge at the last moment. People would see me. They would stare. They would know I wasn't like them. They would know I was infected. They would show me no mercy.

I veered to join the end of the soup line. Maybe I could lose myself in the commotion of people moving and eating while I figured out if that was really Dylan I had seen, or if it had only been a ghost playing tricks on me.

I pulled my hair and hood over my face and shuffled along with the others to the pots of food. I made and then discarded a dozen frantic plans to bolt to the stage.

"They lost control of the fence last night," a man in front of me whispered to his female companion. "Sergeant Bennings is stretched too thin. He says he's going to put civilians on the perimeter."

"It won't do any good," she said. "This place is too big, not enough of us came together."

"When you kill half the refugees because you suspect they're infected…" he let his voice trail off.

His companion grimaced. "It was the only thing to do. It's a quarantine."

"You wouldn't say that if you'd had people—"

"My father was…but he was infected. Went crazy, tried to kill me. I would do anything not to get infected," the woman said. "Sergeant Bennings is doing what has to be done. We'll worry about whether it was right if we're still alive when all this is over."

Her companion grunted, but otherwise kept his thoughts to himself.

The fifth man, the one who could be Dylan, still had his back turned to me as he coiled another cable.

Someone behind me cleared their throat. I shuffled to cover the space in line. The stage guy turned to drop the coil in a pile with other cables. My heart lurched into my throat.

Dylan.

I'd imagined him dead, imprisoned, infected, wounded. Yet he looked like none of those things. He walked with a strong gait, with a purpose. Only a few yards of water and asphalt separated us. He was breathing and alive and healthy and young. I had to get to him.

It was my turn to pick up soup from the table. Without

thinking, I grabbed a bowl and spoon and looked up, straight into the eyes of my soup server.

Straight into Jane's hazel eyes.

CHAPTER 19

THE PLASTIC SERVING SPOON froze in Jane's hand. The liquid half-splashed back into the pot.

My arms stopped halfway outstretched over the table. My wrinkled, infected hands held the bowl in front of me like a fool. I smelled the soup—a chicken, rice, and vegetable medley. The taste of ash sat on my tongue.

"What are you doing here," she hissed.

My brain locked up except for one thought: she must not know I was infected otherwise she would scream instead of whisper. And then another thought: put your damn hands down before she notices. And then a third: but no, Jane wouldn't betray me. And then a fourth: but she already had, in more ways than I could ever have imagined.

"You left," I said, because I could not, would not, talk about Dylan with her.

"Shut up," she said. She looked to my right, to the next person in line, but he was lost in a whispered conversation with the person behind him. She stared at the spoon in her hand, deliberating. Finally, she glanced at the stage, dumped a full spoon of soup into my bowl, and without looking at me again said, "I'll be done in five minutes. Meet me at the bears."

I cupped the bowl of soup to my chest and scurried from the table. I retreated to the edge of the crowd and devoured the soup so fast it burned the roof of my mouth. I tongued those burned ridges of skin and a spark of anger surfaced. How dare she run, how dare she act indignant.

Her glance at the stage told me she knew Dylan was here.

She'd found Dylan and neither one had come looking for me. Neither one.

I TEMPTED MYSELF with the thought of not meeting her, of fading away into the fog and leaving Dylan and Jane together. Maybe I would first exact my own bit of revenge by biting her, aging her, wiping that smooth skin off her face. This last thought spurred me into meeting her instead of leaving. Part of me hoped I was a better person than my current thoughts, part of me knew I wasn't.

We met at the pair of bronzed grizzly bears that stood sentinel a hundred yards or so from the soup line. The statues represented California's state animal and had served many times as a way to find members of your group otherwise lost in the sea of people that wandered the grounds during state fair season.

I stood on the side of the bear that kept me out of sight of the guards. I leaned against its hip so that all of me fit within the boundaries of the bear's hind leg.

A string of uniformed guards lounged while watching the exterior parking lot. Soldiers maybe, but they looked unkempt, unwashed, unsure of themselves. They guarded the front gates from above, using a tram's second-story access to keep lookout.

They were the gates I had been outside of with Spencer and Maibe and the others just a day past. I hoped Spencer and Leaf and the rest were still safe somewhere with Maibe.

Jane walked up, her hair wrapped in a scarf, wearing jeans, boots, and a thick jacket with fake fur that rimmed her pristine skin. "When did you get here?" She avoided my face as if ashamed to look at me.

I felt thankful for that because I had been thinking that as soon as she noticed I was infected with the cure I would slash her arm open with my teeth and watch the horror dawn on her face once she realized what I had done to her. I was a horrible person.

"Last night," I said, finally.

She looked away from the bear and the gates and the guards—to Stage 1.

"I...Christopher escaped and I thought he was going to infect me and I needed to get to Cal Expo. To someplace safe."

To Dylan. Before me. "Stop lying."

She didn't respond, other than stiffening her back.

"Is this place safe?" I shot at her. "They're killing old people, or anybody who looks old, not giving them a chance—"

"There's no way to test for the infection," Jane said. "They're not taking any chances. There are two infections running through the city—through the world for all we know. There's no cure."

Hopes tumbled into ash. I'd known deep down there must not have been a cure, otherwise why would they be killing infected on sight? It was still tough to hear my fate was sealed out loud. The truth hurt, especially coming from Jane.

"But they're still searching for a cure? They must be."

She nodded. "But they say they aren't even close."

"So that's how they can justify killing innocent people," I said, thinking about the ones I'd seen shot, the ones responding to the radio announcement, the ones seeking help.

"It's the quarantine. It's for our protection. If you'd seen what I've seen, what the infected can do—"

"I have—"

"Some people are calling them zombies—"

"They're sick. They need help, not bullets—"

"It's like nothing we've ever seen—"

"No, we've seen it. Rabies, Alzheimer's—"

"Corrina, it makes you disappear. It turns you into something other than human—"

"Which makes it okay to murder ?"

She whirled and faced me. "Yes. Yes!" She yanked her scarf off and waved it around. "Yes! Anything not to catch it, not to turn into—" She froze. "What's wrong with your face?"

Panic fluttered in my stomach. "I was busy surviving out there. No thanks to you." I turned so my hair better obscured my profile. "Have you talked to Dylan? Is he okay?" I asked, desperate to change her focus, and desperate to know what had happened. "Why didn't he come after me?" That last question sounded petulant even to my own ears, but it was too late to take it back.

"Answer my question," she said.

"No, Jane. You answer mine," I said. Suddenly Jane's seventh-grade self materialized next to adult Jane. Yes, we'd had this childish argument before.

"I told him you were dead."

Her words punched me in the gut. "What?" I asked in a strangled voice.

Seventh-grade Jane stood next to adult Jane, stiff-legged, pouty, arms crossed on her chest, hair flipped over her shoulder. I leaned my forehead against the bear, felt its slippery surface, its coldness, smelled a hint of the metal underneath the bronze-colored paint.

A couple of guards yelled at the gate. Several shots were fired. Silence returned. I used the sounds to distance myself from this conversation and bring me back to reality, back to survival. None of it mattered, these details that came before, these petty decisions about loyalty and desire and betrayal. None of it mattered in the foggy, cold light of this new world.

I couldn't stand still a moment longer. My heels dug into the ground and I pivoted away from the bear, away from the front gates, back to the soup line, back to Stage 1.

"Hey!" Jane yelled, but there were no following steps.

I quickened my pace until a building hid me from sight. The handicap rail bit into my stomach as I leaned over it and gulped quick, panicked breaths. I didn't know who's version to believe. Jane's, or the one I'd lived through, the one where Dylan and I made up and forgave each other and it had nothing to do with guilt, but instead because we belonged to each other. I wanted a memory-rush or ghost-memory or some damn something to wash away Jane's words.

But none came.

Instead, another thought teased me.

I was one of the infected, aged, sick. I had never belonged
with Dylan, and I didn't belong here. If I hadn't been worth
anything to Dylan before, now it was doubly true. And if I loved
him—and in spite of everything, I knew I did by the wrenching
emptiness I felt at thinking I might never see his smile again
or touch his shoulder or feel his kiss on my neck—how could
I make him take care of someone like me now?

Something pink caught the periphery of my vision. I
blinked and focused. Not Maibe, but it reminded me of her
and reminded me that I wasn't completely alone. Others needed
taking care of. Like the woman I'd left in the hay. Like Gabbi
and the pup-boys.

The pink caught my eye again, along with a flash of movement. And even though I knew it couldn't be Maibe, I felt
compelled to follow. The pink disappeared around a corner. I
hurried after it, thinking I would discover who it belonged to,
and then I would track Maibe down and I would leave Jane
and Dylan and everyone else here to their moat of false safety.

Better that Dylan think me dead than see the new, old me
with cracked skin, deep wrinkles, demented thoughts.

Clanging, like from a bell, tripped my feet. People shouted
and the pink disappeared in a crowd that had re-formed near
the soup table. I slowed down and repositioned my clothing.
It wouldn't do to get caught now.

People edged the moat, staring across the green water to the
stage. A shaved ice cart with pastel-colored lettering appeared.
The woman manning it sprayed dark blue syrup on a cone and
handed it to a toddler in a blue and white striped shirt, but this
ghost-memory was easy to ignore. I pushed my way through

people with thick coats that smelled of musty cloth, unwashed bodies covered in filth, incoherent rumblings of distress and anger and fear. I burst out the front of the crowd and almost fell in the moat.

I squinted to better see. My stomach sunk.

The old woman had escaped the hay nest.

She stumbled, trance-like, across Stage 1, arms out as if she was going to hug someone. Dylan stood in front of her. There was no doubt in my mind now that it was Dylan between her and the guns pointed now at his chest.

"Move away," one of the soldiers said, his voice echoing across the water.

Dylan held his hands up, palm-faced and open, and shook his head. Another soldier came running. He held a different kind of gun in his hands. He charged Dylan and tackled him to the ground.

The first soldier raised his gun. A sharp crack snapped across the moat.

I looked away and then forced myself to look back, to be a witness. The old woman had fallen to the floor in a heap, but there was no blood.

A few cheers sounded behind me. Another person screamed "That's right! That's right! That's right!"

A man next to me hunched his shoulders and shook his head as if in disapproval.

The stage filled with people in uniform. They dragged both Dylan and the old woman away. They used a dog-catcher stick on the woman so they wouldn't have to touch her. They handled Dylan roughly, slapping him around the head, kicking his shins when he didn't move fast enough. I felt the acidic remnants of the chicken soup return to burn the back of my throat.

"What are they doing?" I dared to ask the man with the grim lips. I tried to swallow away the acid and my fear for Dylan's safety.

"You don't help the sick. He'll get a hearing and she'll go to the experiments. Those are Sergeant Bennings' rules. Don't you know that?"

I felt his eyes rake my face. I pretended to shiver and closed my hood closer. "I got here last night," I said. "I forgot."

"After they're done with him, you won't want to remember. But you will."

I melted into the crowd, skirted the soup table, failed to see Jane, and then there she stood, off to one side of the moat, arguing with a guard. She tossed her blonde hair back over her shoulder, fiddled with the scarf she'd repositioned on her head and let tears stream down her face.

The soldier shrugged. He seemed young, grim, annoyed. "Probably to…" I couldn't make out his last words and then he walked away.

Jane looked across the moat, at where the guards had disappeared with Dylan. I crept up behind her, and when I was within a few feet, I whispered, "Jane." Her back stiffened. She dropped her hands from the scarf down to her sides.

"Jane, where are they taking him? Tell me, and I'll help any way I can."

"He thinks you're dead," she said, without turning around. A slight shift in the breeze brought the smell of algae to me. Two men dressed as lumberjacks did the log roll on a large rough redwood trunk in the moat. I ignored the illusion of their plaid-covered contest and waited for Jane to realize keeping

Dylan alive was more important than keeping her lie alive.

"There are holding cells in Building B for problems. For their experiments."

"I thought they killed anyone sick."

"We're not animals, you know. She was only tranquilized."

"No, I don't know that. They were killing people at the gates for looking old."

She shook her head. "No, that's not how we do things. He said he always checks first, just in case."

"You believe that?"

"They tranquilized that woman, didn't you see? They didn't kill her."

What I had seen was Dylan stepping in to hold back bullets until the tranquilizer gun arrived, but I bit back my words. There was no point in trying to reason with Jane. Plus, one of the men had fallen off the log and splashed into the moat, causing the winner to do a quick tap dance to stay afloat.

"We've got a better chance of helping him if we work together," I said, even though I thought maybe my help might get me killed. But I couldn't leave. I accepted that now. I cared too much, even if the same wasn't true for him.

"All right," Jane said.

The men and their log disappeared, leaving only the empty stage someone had forgotten to draw the curtains on. I suddenly wanted water, anything to wash away the taste of the chicken soup that burned my throat.

However large a part of me hated her now, at least I knew she cared about Dylan. And maybe they belonged together. Neither sick, neither—I shook my head and told myself to stop. My plan hadn't changed, only taken a detour. I could feel despair later, but I would never live with myself if I didn't help Dylan now, no matter what he thought of me or of Jane. I wasn't that kind of person.

"People who break the rules always get a hearing, but—"

"But what?" I examined the skin on the back of my hands. I was disease-ridden, Jane-betrayed, falling apart physically and mentally. It didn't matter whether Dylan had meant it when he said he loved me and wanted to work things out. That was before this new world. That was in the past now. Before I became old and decrepit and ugly and infected.

"Then they're executed," Jane said. "Sergeant Bennings says it's the only way to make sure people follow the rules. He says it's the only way we can last long enough to find a cure."

CHAPTER 20

JANE AND I FOLLOWED the group dragging Dylan and the old woman along. The few guards and refugees nodded at Jane as we passed. Working the soup table must have made her well known.

By now the diffused light of winter had faded, signaling late afternoon. The fog rolled in more thickly, further blocking out the faint December sunlight. This was in my favor. I focused on working through the pain in my shoulder.

An empty chip bag floated across our path, its shiny orange color in contrast to the dull gray sky and faded blue buildings. Sometimes my mind wandered with ghost-memories and I caught myself limping. At least the exercise helped push them back.

Dylan and the soldiers crossed to the backside of Building B, a place once used for vendor exhibits. Even from this distance I could see they had modified the concrete space into a series of human cages.

There were more guards here and we stopped before getting close enough for them to question us. I didn't have any sort of military background, but even I could see the 'prison' wasn't well protected. In fact, everything about my entrance and movement around the Cal Expo fairgrounds spoke of deep security problems.

The men took Dylan and the old woman. The windowed walls showed them disappearing into an aisle of cages.

We hid behind the wall of another building, out of sight of the guards and anyone who might decide to walk the route we'd just taken.

"Why are there so few guards?"

"This is where they keep the infected," Jane said. "The crazy, violent ones are held somewhere sturdier, but the quiet ones, like the old woman, they don't climb or fight, so this is easier."

"What do you do with them?"

"We…I don't do anything," Jane said. "They're trying to find a cure or vaccine or anything that might help us figure out how to stay human."

"What do you mean, stay human?"

"The infection changes DNA. That's what they said at least. It swaps out a bunch of our DNA with something else, making us less human."

"That woman looks human enough to my eyes."

"The ones that attacked our street, they're more like rabid dogs that need to be put down. They say the same thing happens with the quiet ones, but they go quiet instead of violent."

"They're lying," I said quietly.

"You have no idea what you're talking about." She looked at

me over her shoulder. Red rimmed her eyes, but not a speck of dirt marred her face. "How could you possibly know?"

"I just do."

Jane turned back around. "Excuse me for taking their word over yours."

I told myself to shut up. The infection had changed me. It had changed the old woman too, but to my eyes she still looked human, just sick. And I definitely believed I was still human. I thought Spencer had a better sense of what the disease did to people than these scientists.

Two men in uniform ran up to the guard at the doors, yelling about an assault at the gate and Vs getting inside. All three dashed inside. A third uniformed person limped up. He held his rifle low and loose at his side. His shoulders slumped and he was missing his left boot. A half dozen people in fatigues streamed out from the building. One of them spoke into a radio. It squawked back. The group ran back the way the first three had come. The remaining bloodied soldier slumped to the ground, using his rifle as a supporting cane. He stared at his bare foot.

"It's Stan," Jane hissed.

The guilt I felt over leaving him punched me in the gut. A part of me felt glad to see my old neighbor alive. A part of me knew he probably wouldn't feel the same way about seeing me now. I wasn't much better than Jane, abandoning someone when they needed you most. "Does he know you're here?" I asked.

"Yeah. He's part of the guard at the front gate now."

I flinched at that information. He was one of the ones shooting and killing people infected with the cure like me.

"He makes sure he's always in my food line, brings me news."

Shoots you like you would a dog too old to walk, I was

tempted to add. "Talk to him then. Distract him, anything. I'll go inside and find Dylan."

She paused, bit her lip. She looked ready to disagree, but then nodded. "Dylan's going to be shocked to see you."

"I can't do anything about you lying to him," I said.

She winced. "I deserved that," she said, and without waiting for a response, she walked confidently forward. As soon as Stan heard her steps he jerked his head and swung his rifle point at her, but she didn't pause, only raised her hands to show they were empty. "Stan, it's Jane."

He slumped his shoulders and pointed his rifle down.

Jane stopped within a few steps of him. They talked too quietly for me to hear their conversation. After another minute, she helped Stan up and supported his weight. I didn't know what she said or how she managed it, but Stan didn't resist, just let her lead him away.

I got to the doors and no one yelled out or shot at me. In their rush the guards had not yet turned on the interior lights of the building. Only dim natural light filtered in. Even though I couldn't see what all filled the space, I could smell it. Unwashed bodies, the peculiar scent of sweat, fog, mud. Precise rectangular rows of cages created aisles to walk down. Each cage near me included a dark shadow, a person. They had filled this building with human prisoners.

I walked the first aisle, the shuffle of my shoes against the linoleum floor a calming swish. I heard shallow, stuttered breathing, turned to find its source. A Faint pressed himself against the bars on my right. I knew he must be a Faint. In the dim light, his skin was clear of markings, his eyes were lost in a coma, he didn't seem dangerous. Even though there were bars, they were probably unnecessary. The disease wrapped his mind in a prison thicker than the metal.

He wore a brown suede coat that had seen better days and a red plaid cap with ear flaps. He stared unseeing at something behind me. I looked over my shoulder. Nothing there. Nothing except for the old woman in another cage, the same woman I had tried to keep warm with the hot water and hay so many hours ago in the barn building.

A memory-rush took hold. The building, the man, the woman, the bars. They all disappeared. I relived the hot water bath, the pleasure at being warm and clean.

When it was over and my mind cleared, the building still felt unguarded, but if anyone had come upon us three just then— the man, the woman, and me—they wouldn't have found any difference. They could have taken me into a cage without a fight and left me to my coma of memories.

I had one advantage over these two. I could walk away from the memories. They did not hold me in a permanent state.

Though I could not feel grateful for what Christopher did to me and Maibe, I did admit at that moment that he had provided me with an advantage to live in this new world. Without the double infection, I could turn into a V or a Faint. Getting the hybrid virus was a poor vaccine I wouldn't wish on anyone, yet—

A voice startled my thoughts. I cocked my head, trying to better listen.

It wasn't a whisper or a conversation. It was—

Singing.

I drifted in the sound's direction. Took a few false turns before the singing became unmistakable.

"Corrina, Corrina…"

The words floated along the linoleum floors, past the sick people making no noise, past the animal corral bars turned into human cages.

The words hit me like a knife in the stomach.

I went after those words like I was starving and had found a trail of breadcrumbs.

CHAPTER 21

THE BREADCRUMBS STOPPED at a cage with bars taller than the others. This cage had a roof. This cage was meant to hold people with minds intact enough to climb out.

And there was a man. It seemed as if a spotlight shined on him. It highlighted his layers. The scarf and jacket and shirt, all some mottled brown. His dust-covered jeans. His brown hair was messed up, tousled, and I almost couldn't resist reaching out to smooth it all down, to touch him again.

He sat, back against the bars, profile to me, his hand resting casually on the metal. Singing.

"Dylan."

His singing cut off. He tensed his arm and closed his fist around the metal. He tilted his head.

I held my breath. Of course I wanted to scream and shout and run to him.

Yet.

I was sick. The spotlight showed beyond a doubt that his skin was unlined, untouched, his face only rough with beard not sickness.

I was—

"Who's there?"

I thought about running. The light made it easy for me to see him and impossible for him. Maybe it would be best to keep things that way.

"Is someone there?"

I stepped forward, to the edge of the light. "Dylan."

"Corrina?" In a flash he stood up and pressed himself into the bars. "Corrina? Is it really you?"

"It's really me." Before I could think about what I was doing, I rushed into his outstretched arms and buried myself into the metal bars, into his clothes, his heat, his familiar smell, like how he'd smell after a long day of work in the yard.

His hands explored my back, my shoulders, my head. His fingers ran through my hair, like he was afraid I was an illusion.

"Jane said—"

I froze. All the pleasure I felt at being together again died. I shouldn't have let myself touch him. I shouldn't have given in. My face pressed into his shirt between two bars, my breath hot and humid, my nose full of cotton and Dylan's earthy smell. Water filled my eyes. He was the most beautiful being I had ever known, and he was no longer mine.

"I thought I'd lost you," he said. "I thought—" He tightened his embrace and my shoulder burned where the fresh scab must have split open under my shirt.

I remembered who I was now. I tried to back up but his arms felt as if they were made of steel. Finally, I said, "Dylan, we need to get out of here."

He released one arm, but kept his other hand against my neck. "The key, it's hanging on the rack."

I stepped back from his heat, away from the light. I saw the rack about fifty feet away. Next to it hung someone's scarf, left behind in the rush of whatever had sent them running after Stan's message.

I returned with the key. The metal clanked but the bars did not release. Dylan rattled the bars in impatience.

Finally, the lock clicked.

I retreated into darkness and choked back my longing and despair as he swung the gate out. I knew I had only a few more moments before he discovered the truth. If I could just pretend for another minute that we were really together again and everything was going to be okay now—

He rushed to me and framed my face with hands the texture of fine sandpaper, his blue eyes large and glowing, his three week old beard long and dark. He tilted my chin for a kiss, into the light—

"No!" I said.

But it was too late. The joy on Dylan's face froze, half-formed.

He dropped his hands.

He backed up one step.

I flinched.

"How is it possible? You're walking and talking. It's not possible."

I closed my eyes so I wouldn't have to witness the moment when the joy on his face vanished altogether. "It is, if you're infected with the Lyssa virus and the bacterial infection that keeps it in check."

"Oh God."

Anger seeped into my next words—better anger than hurt. "You can feel repulsed by me later, after we get out of here."

"Corrina, that's not—"

There was a rush of slapping shoes, a rush of loud male voices, a rush of fear.

Jane ran into view at a dead sprint. She saw us, tried to stop, slipped on the concrete floor, and crashed into me. We tumbled to the ground in the center of the spotlight. My head cracked against the floor hard enough for stars to burst across my vision.

Jane gasped above me. "Oh my God. Oh my God. You're infected. You're, you're…"

The slapping shoes grew louder.

Her blonde hair brushed across my eyes, stinging them, then she looked at Dylan. "Over here! There's an infected loose over here."

Memories of our love and friendship might haunt me for the rest of my life, but these people I still cared about whether I wanted to or not—they no longer saw me as human.

Something yanked her off me.

My vision cleared.

Dylan held her back from me, protecting her from my infection.

I didn't give in to the pain at his actions. I could feel sorry for myself later. Now my only goal was to survive.

I jumped to my feet and ran, but my head left me dizzy and unstable and I knew I weaved from side to side. Dylan appeared, arms outstretched, standing in my way, blocking my path, ensuring my capture. It felt too much like the embrace we had shared, and the ghost-memory of a moment ago overlaid this moment and I wanted to cry out at this last betrayal. I had expected revulsion, disgust, distance, but not this. Not this.

And then I teetered too far in one direction and welcomed the familiar feeling of an oncoming memory-rush. It took over as the guards rushed into view. It took over before I hit the ground, before Dylan caught and held me down for the guards.

CHAPTER 22

I AWOKE WITH A DESPERATE THIRST for water, my tongue thick and dry, and with memories of all the deaths in my life crowded on top of each other, my parents, acquaintances, those I had murdered. When I became aware enough to notice my surroundings, I saw they had locked me in a cage much like the one I had helped Dylan escape from. Exactly like that one. It was the same one.

A guard held a rifle crooked in his arm and stood at attention a few feet away from the bars, in the shadows. The spotlight filled my cage, making it difficult to discern what lay beyond its edge.

Ghost-memories materialized in front of me. Dylan and Jane outside the cage, the looks they exchanged, as if they knew each other better than I knew either of them.

I jumped up from where I'd lain in the grip of memories and startled the guard into an alert stance. I wanted to run and beat away their faces. Those looks. I paced up and down that small cage with barely enough room for four steps together. Not enough room to hold back the memories. When I moved I smelled my own mix of sweat and fear, as if my cleansing hot water bath had never happened.

I shook the bars in frustration.

The clanging metal echoed through the building.

The guard lifted his rifle and pointed it at my feet, but I knew it would take less than a second for him to change his aim. He stared at me, unblinking.

I sunk into myself almost instinctively and smelled the metallic residue of handling the bars. The light likely threw my papery, infected skin into high relief for the guard.

I raised the back of my hand to my cheek, wondering what he thought as he stared, wondering how old I looked now and whether the disease stalled its aging or if it continued to progress. His stare reminded me of my creaking joints, my fragile bones, my list of injuries.

I shook the bars again.

"Stop the noise," he said.

As if by their own mind, my spindly-knuckled fingers grasped the bars again a third time. The metal clang took several long seconds to fade into the darkness. I never looked away from the guard's stare.

He stood straighter, shifted his rifle position, took a step toward me, crossed the edge of the light. I still couldn't tell if he was a grizzled veteran or a young and cocky recruit.

I shook the bars a fourth time. His outline became rigid and the rifle moved. I bet the butt now lay against his shoulder.

I silently dared him to kill me and readied myself to shake the bars again, out of spite, out of despair, out of plain stubbornness.

"Stand down," said a voice from outside the perimeter of light.

I shielded my eyes.

The guard stepped out of the way, rifle now at his side, a salute at his forehead. "Yessir," he said into the darkness.

"You're Corrina." It wasn't a question, but a statement of fact. His voice sounded full of gravel and somehow familiar. I shivered.

"I'm sorry we had to cage you like this, but you put up quite a fight. He never mentioned you were such a spitfire."

"Where's Dylan?"

"Safe, for now. He's made some poor decisions, but he's still valuable to us. We've lost too many good people in the last few weeks. Too many to those animals. Dylan is one of the few here who knows how to work the electronics. It's an interesting predicament."

"Who are you?"

"Apologies. We rarely have time for niceties these days, but it's still rude of me. I'm in charge here. You may call me Sergeant Bennings."

I expected him to show himself, to step into the light and reinforce the authority he carried. He did not. It angered me. "Show yourself, Sergeant Bennings."

The blobs engaged in whispered conversation, then, "No, that will not be necessary yet," Sergeant Bennings said. "The doctor still doesn't know how contagious your kind is—"

"My kind?"

"Please do not interrupt me."

Silence reined.

I thought I heard the creak of soft, aging bodies pressing

against other cages.

Finally, Sergeant Bennings continued, "The infected are dangerous and our science staff was drastically reduced last week. Because of your kind—"

"I did nothing!"

A long pole and a disembodied hand appeared in the light and snaked through the bars. Light glinted off the pole's metal surface as the blunt end jabbed into my ribs. The breath was knocked out of me. I fell to my knees gasping for air.

"Please do not interrupt. I know sometimes it is difficult for your kind to understand language now, but there are other ways of helping you remember."

Tears leaked out of my eyes and I cursed myself for showing such weakness. Under the lights, I could not hide the glisten of saltwater. I was a zoo animal and Sergeant Bennings the bully someone had let loose inside.

"I am not an animal," I said between gasps. My papery hands wiped the tears away and I stood on shaky legs. Damn his shadow.

"You are somewhere between an animal and a human," Sergeant Bennings said. "The doctors are trying to find out exactly what, but that venture has not yet succeeded. Your kind—the aged, yet walking and talking kind—are in some ways the least and most dangerous. Easy to overcome with force, yet the dual infection allows you to think—"

"That's not true. I'm hu—"

Another thud in my ribs and I heard a crack. A burning sensation bloomed on my side. Taking a deep breath intensified the pain enough so I saw spots.

"The old, locked-in bodies are to be pitied, yet must be

eradicated so as to not infect others. The ones most dangerous, the ones who seek out violence, are the most predictable
and, except for a few mistakes early on, the easiest ones to
protect ourselves from. But things like you, yes, you are the
most dangerous, the most likely to make people doubt the rules
that protect us here. The most likely to spread the infection,
like a rabid dog not yet frothing at the mouth. Like the mad
cow packaged into a thousand different freezers, a time-bomb
waiting to decimate what's left of humans. It's quarantine procedure. Not that it matters so much on a city level. The disease
has likely gone around the world. Still, we must all do what we
can with what we have."

"Why bother telling me all this?"

"I am curious about how much human is left in your type.
And you've been outside the fairgrounds recently. I wanted to
appeal to your sense of duty to humanity. We need information
that you could provide. The outside conditions, the numbers
of various infected, whether certain resources remain intact.
I thought to see whether there was enough human left in you
to help us."

"All I see are men with guns imprisoning and murdering
those less fortunate."

"We're holding out, surviving. Protecting the human blood-
line or DNA or whatever the doctors call it. To keep humans,
human. As many of us as we can."

"I am still human," I said. If I could explain to him what it
all felt like. Tell him about Maibe and Spencer and Gabbi. We
might be sick, but that did not mean we could not feel or love
or hate—or remember.

"No, I'm sorry. That's not going to work."

"I can explain—"

A sharp prod made pain explode in my ribs and drove me back to my knees.

"Please answer one question. A yes or no will be sufficient. Please think carefully about your answer. It is more important to your...safety...than you can imagine. Did you come here with others like you?"

I thought about Maibe and the pink something I'd glimpsed what felt like days ago, but had only been hours. Spencer, Gabbi, the pup-boys, they were not supposed to be here, they were supposed to have taken care of their police officer and left. I hoped it was so.

"No," I said.

I received another jab of the pole. It was the Sergeant's monstrous metal finger, the stick poking a decrepit lion.

"Yes. As I expected." He spoke too softly for me to hear for a moment, then, "I promised Dylan I would at least try to help you see the human parts that still exist inside of you. I promised this knowing I would fail, but I always keep my word. He will be disappointed."

"Dylan? Are you there?" Had he watched through all this and not said a word, not tried to stop it?

"Of course not. I am not a monster. You may have aged thirty years, you may have to be executed, but he can still see parts of his wife in you. I would not put any healthy human through such a thing." He paused and lowered his voice. "Still, he will be required to watch your execution like everyone else."

"My execution?"

"Usually we shoot those like you on sight, or send you to the camps, but people need a reminder of the rules. The New Year is almost here and there have been too many close calls over the last few days. You showed up at the right time."

I wanted to ask about the camps, but the shuffling of shoes against concrete told me he was leaving.

"Wait! That's it? No...no...trial?" I said.

The shuffling paused. "No, of course not. But you will get several chances to wrestle with whatever humanity you have left. Our doctors will check you over and add your medical information to our growing database. We are trying to find a cure for this. Whatever you think of me and my methods, there is a noble purpose behind all of it. My remaining advisors and I will ask you to share any information you have gleaned from your trek through the city. But I can't say I'm hopeful. It's easy for your kind to degenerate into a rather self-serving brute of an animal."

"And if I share information?"

"Then you can die knowing you helped to save humanity. Guard, she may receive water but none of the food we have left."

He did not wait for a response but walked away with what looked like three other outlines. My original guard stepped back into the edge of light. He seemed to smirk.

"Do you enjoy killing grandmothers and sisters and aunts and brothers?"

The smirk left his face and something more dangerous glinted in his eye. "Sometimes."

The pain in my ribs felt unbearable. I'd bet money that at least one had cracked. I still smelled the metallic odor of the bars on my hands. I still smelled me and all the mud and panic of the last hours. I wondered what Sergeant Bennings had meant about whether I'd broken in with others. I hoped Maibe and

Spencer and the others had found safety. In an insane world, people like them made sense. People still willing to do right, regardless of the danger it put them in.

Or maybe Sergeant Bennings was right. Maybe I deserved whatever came next. Maybe I'd deserved all the names at school, deserved losing my mother and father, deserved Jane's idea of friendship. Deserved losing Dylan.

But part of me rebelled at my cowardliness. It didn't want to give up. It didn't care whether Jane or Dylan cared.

What mattered was I cared. What mattered was I believed the people who had shared my life—the people less fortunate than me, the people who couldn't take care of themselves anymore—deserved protecting. They did not deserve abandonment or death and it didn't matter if they could not, or would not, return the favor.

I slept fitfully. The spotlight never flickered in its intensity. They would not allow me any privacy and I used the latrine bucket in full sight of the guard, though he gave me the decency of looking away. They provided me enough water only to drink, but I used some of it to wash my hands. Each action caused my shoulder wound to flare in sympathy with the pain in my ribs.

In the morning, the dark gray interior of the warehouse lightened to medium gray from the bit of sunlight that entered through the bay of windows. There was no hiding my skin as I used the latrine bucket, but to hell with hiding anymore.

In the dark, with the spotlight shining on me, I had felt isolated and alone and in a small place. Now I could see the cages I had first walked by in search of Dylan. Dozens of cages spanned several rows. Most of them contained at least one Faint. I didn't want to believe that Sergeant Bennings really did kill every Feeb he encountered, but the surrounding cages implied this was the truth. I tried to find the old woman both Dylan and I had ended up helping but could not. I wondered why he'd tried to help her, or if I even remembered the situation rightly.

When the guards came, two of them wore white latex suits with masks. I swore Stan was one of the guards even with the mask making it impossible to be sure. If Stan was one of these pillowed-up freaks, he didn't say a word to me, didn't look me in the eye. Just as well, any actions from him might otherwise tempt me to spit and share my vaccine. He did not deserve it.

They brought the stick back. But I saw it wasn't only a stick. They'd found a dog catcher noose. Maybe the same one they'd used on the old woman. They hooked that noose around my neck, forced me out of the cage. Each step woke up nerves that had gone numb overnight, igniting my chest and shoulder with burning pain. My stomach grumbled because they had not wasted any of their resources by supplying me with breakfast. But my guards had eaten. I could smell the coffee at least one of them had drunk before coming for me.

CHAPTER 23

"WE WILL BE MOVING YOU now. It's best if you cooperate."

My muscles tensed, but I knew I was too weak to put up a fight. A part of me didn't care beyond thinking about Dylan's last betrayal. He had thrown me away and yet I wasn't angry. I was sad.

The nylon braiding of the noose tightened into my skin. This was their way of telling me to stop while one of them opened the doors. No warning, just the same pressure you might use to rein in an unruly horse.

Sergeant Bennings waited on the other side of the door. He ushered me and my guards outside. "Follow me," he said.

We left the warehouse, crossed under a cement pathway, and Sergeant Bennings opened the door to another building. I stumbled and anticipated a choking, but the man holding my noose accounted for my stumble and moved with me to keep me comfortable. I did not understand this kindness, but that's what it was.

Sergeant Bennings held the door open. "This way, please."

"And do you feel so sure of yourself, you don't wear a suit? How can you be so sure I can't infect you from here?"

"I trust my men," he said.

"Dad? Dad!" A young voice yelled out.

A boy, maybe fourteen, wearing a black jacket and a dark beanie pulled low over his head with little sprigs of brown hair escaping it, ran to us.

"Alden! Don't come over here," Sergeant Bennings said. He dropped his hand from the next door and allowed it to close. He nodded at the two men holding me. "Stay here."

"Yessir."

Sergeant Bennings loped a few yards away until Alden caught up to him.

Even though Sergeant Bennings lowered his voice, I could clearly hear his conversation. I wondered if he knew that and spoke so loudly on purpose.

The boy had lanky brown hair. A gray stripe circled his dark beanie and set off his dark eyes. He looked young, his features set in that typical angsty, almost sullen, teenager frame, ready to demand something unreasonable and deprecate you for your response. But maybe I was being unfair, maybe I only wanted to think so badly of him because he was the son after all, the son of a man capable of hanging people and doing who knew what else to people like me.

"I told you not to come over this way," Sergeant Bennings said.

"There's trouble at the gate," Alden said.

"Why didn't someone else come? Why did they send you and not one of my soldiers? And what were you doing at the gate?

I told you not to go over there either!"

"I can't just sit and do nothing. Not with mom…the guards needed me. They sent me because there was no one to spare. And I stayed safe. I stayed out of sight like you taught me. I didn't—"

"Stop, Alden."

I wondered what Sergeant Bennings' first name could be. I tried to picture the mother, the woman who could love someone like him.

Alden bowed his head when Sergeant Bennings' hand touched his shoulder. "Just—tell me what's happening."

"There's a rush of people, of the sick ones. The guards aren't sure what drew them in, but they're having a hard time, and it looks like something is organizing them."

"What did you say?" Sergeant Bennings asked.

"I don't know—that's what they said to tell you. It doesn't look random."

I shifted my weight from one leg to the other. The cold was starting to sink into my legs, stiffening my knees. My animal handler did not move, other than to flick his eyes at me. Definitely Stan. Even with a mask covering most of his face, the lines around his washed out blue eyes were instantly recognizable.

"It must make you feel so good, knowing you've got the best of me now. I left you, and now this is payback," I said to him in a low voice.

His eyes squinted in a pained expression. "I'm sorry, Corrina. This is not by my choice."

"I'm sure."

"We can't let the sickness spread. Otherwise no one human will be left."

"How does a sickness turn someone sub-human? Doesn't it just make them sick?"

He didn't answer.

I returned my focus to Sergeant Bennings and son. The two of them parted ways and Sergeant Bennings hurried back to us while Alden disappeared around the building.

"Take her to the chair. Strap her down, lock the door. Then get to the gate."

Without pausing for the "yessirs," that both men responded with, Sergeant Bennings pivoted and went the opposite direction, following Alden and disappearing around another building.

I thought for half a second about escaping, but the men, even Stan, were good at their job.

The warehouse was a dank, dark building with ceilings three stories tall, skylights yellowed and fogged. They pushed me into a side section, down a makeshift hallway with a lowered ceiling that made it feel claustrophobic compared to before. Multiple doors on either side lined this hallway. Something moaned behind one of them.

The men pushed open the fifth door down. Before they could force me inside, I walked into this plaster-walled, cement-floored, windowless room the size of a walk-in closet. There was a cot, two buckets—one empty, one full of water—and a door on the other side.

The men followed after me. Stan still held my noose. The other man opened the opposite door into a room that gleamed with sterile white light.

This room had a chair. An all metal, dentist-like chair, in the center. Various cords and wires attached to it and snaked across the floor to the opposite wall, to a bank of windows and a type of control room. This one looked triple the size of the last room and while it was still a makeshift setup, a lot more care and equipment had been used.

Lights on floor stands created a halo effect around the chair. A set of metal roller trays with tools laid out on sterile blue hospital paper were positioned near the chair. Leather straps were attached at the arm and leg rests.

My legs jiggled with fear and I almost lost my balance. Stan grabbed my arm and lifted me up. The other man helped him position me in the chair.

I rested the crown of my head on the cold, metal surface behind me and looked forward to nothing, a blank wall. The chair was turned away from the windows and control room.

The two men strapped me down. I held my breath, anticipating the too tight straps, the way it would cut off my circulation, a way to cause me pain just because. But that didn't happen. Yes, the straps were secure, but they were not too tight. Instead, both men took care to make sure the straps did not dig into my skin, or pinch it, or otherwise hurt it. Once they were done strapping me down, they pivoted the chair so it faced the windows where more lap equipment and computers were setup.

I started rattling off questions, hoping this would stall the two men, keep them from leaving me here alone to dwell on what would happen to me next.

They worked in silence except once. Stan said, "We used to put your type in the cages along with the comatose ones, but you all talked too much to each other."

And then the second guy elbowed Stan and he shut up and it didn't matter what I asked or that I had begun to shout my questions. They finished their work in silence and left through the door to the windowless closet.

I WAITED FOR what seemed hours, but may have lasted only minutes. In these moments of stillness I inventoried my body, its dry, cracked, aged skin, its looseness, its papery texture. My mind, its fragile state, as if it balanced on the middle of a tee-ter-totter and while I stood in the middle, everything was clear, but weather or people or my own miserable balance threatened to push me onto one side, into memory-fevers or ghost-memories or a memory-rush.

But my mind was still sharp, and my heart still pounded, strong and regular. I did not think it had also aged, I would not think so. I could still run, I could still fight, I could still think. Those were what mattered.

The door clicked behind me. I did not bother to look.

"Hello, Corrina." Sergeant Bennings had returned and brought along with him a middle-aged female doctor who wore a stereotypical white lab coat, sneakers, blue jeans. A stethoscope lay on her collarbone and she held a clipboard.

She was as tall as the sergeant's shoulder. Her brown hair was pulled back into a tight bun. Her eyes glinted with intelligence when she looked up. Her gaze slid over me, past my eyes, down, around, as if I wasn't really there. As if there wasn't a person strapped to the chair, only a specimen to observe.

"Let me introduce you to Dr. Ferrad. She will be conducting a number of tests on you today." Sergeant Bennings paused, as if his next words pained him to say them. "She is infected, like you."

My heart pounded. The bright lights had washed out the

telltale lines, but I saw it now. The ashy paleness, the almost papery quality. Dr. Ferrad did not look me in the eyes at first, but then as if by some internal decision, she stiffened her back and met my gaze. "It is my job to find a cure, or a way to contain this, or a way to destroy it. If you have any sense of responsibility left, you will cooperate."

Confusion surrounded me. They treated the infected like animals, like less than human, like vermin to exterminate, yet here was an infected doctor, standing alongside Sergeant Bennings, as if they were almost equals. She was ready to experiment on me and he stood there unprotected—

But I realized he wasn't unprotected. His hand rested on his holster and another guard I had not noticed before was standing silent against the wall with a gun leveled at the doctor.

"Yes, I can see you have questions," Sergeant Bennings said. "It would be easy to dismiss us as monsters from your viewpoint. It would be easy to label me a tyrant or a murderer. But you may come to see that I do all of this out of a deep sense of responsibility, a deep love for humanity, a..." He trailed off and looked away, into the shadows. "The more we learn about your kind, the more dangerous we know you are to keeping humans human, yet some of you can be reasoned with still, and so we must try, must we not try?"

Dr. Ferrad reached out to touch Sergeant Bennings' shoulder.

"Sir!" The guard in the shadows yelled and stepped into the halo of light.

Dr. Ferrad withdrew her hand as if struck by lightning. Sergeant Bennings stepped between Dr. Ferrad and the guard. "Hold it right there, soldier. It's fine."

"I will find a cure for this. I will," Dr. Ferrad said.

They stood there for a long moment. Sergeant Bennings and Dr. Ferrad locked in a staring contest.

"She is your wife," I said.

As if my words broke a spell, Sergeant Bennings flicked his eyes at me.

Dr. Ferrad turned her head down as if ashamed. She returned her focus to the clipboard and began taking notes. She looked up at me every few seconds with that impartial, emotionless stare that made me feel like an apple in a still life painting.

"She is not my wife," Sergeant Bennings said finally. "My wife is in a coma from the bacterial strain. Dr. Ferrad and I have worked together for many years. She happens to be the best doctor we've got and whatever part of her is still human, it is enough to allow her to continue her work, to help us save what is left of the rest of us."

"So she's sick like me, less than human, but gets special treatment because you slept with her once."

Sergeant Bennings flinched at my words. "You cannot be trusted, yet there is no one else to do this work, and the work must be done, and so—" Sergeant cut himself off and shook his head slightly. "It is so easy to try to reason with your kind. The spark is missing, yet you act so—"

"Let me get on with my job," Dr. Ferrad interrupted. "We are wasting time."

Without another word, Sergeant Bennings left.

The guard remained at his post against the wall and faded into the shadows. The doctor lowered her clipboard. I smiled tentatively. She would tell me the truth now. She was like me. She would help me escape, she would understand—

The clipboard snaked out and hit me alongside the head. The

blow was more of a shock than anything. My ears rang, blood rushed to my head, my ear became hot.

"Let's begin." She set the clipboard down and grabbed a needle from the blue-papered tray. She held the needle high over her head like a maniac before plunging it into my shoulder and drawing out what felt like a pint of blood.

When she finished she deposited the needle in a case and the case in a bag. She unwrapped the stethoscope from around her neck, listened to my lungs and heartbeat, cuffed my arm, took my blood pressure, poked and prodded me in a dozen other ways, all in silence. If I could convince her, reason with her, there might still be a way out.

Though the sting of her clipboard would say otherwise.

"When did you get infected?" I asked quietly so the guard could not hear.

She froze for a moment, then continued her work.

"Oh," I said, trying to connect the dots. "You were part of the vaccine program."

A muscle in her cheek twitched.

"You were infected from the very beginning, even before they all started killing the old people. How come Sergeant Bennings wasn't vaccinated. How come—"

"Do you remember the numbers from your last checkup? Blood pressure, cholesterol?"

"Maybe."

She sighed. "I could ask the soldier over there to make you more cooperative. Just like we would a dog."

I glanced at the man staring woodenly at us from yards away. He gave no sign he heard either of us, but maybe he was trained to do that. "You don't have to threaten me, " I said.

"Answer some of my questions. Give me information, I'll tell you what I know."

She set the medical equipment down on the blue paper, grabbed both sides of the tray with her hands as if to steady herself. Anyone who knew anything about the co-infection could see she was fighting back a ghost-memory right then.

"Do they know you see the ghosts?"

Her arm snaked out and she slapped me on the other side of my cheek. Anger lashed up in me. Only one other person had slapped me in my entire life and I had punched her in the ear for it. Any thought about reasoning with her flew out of my mind. How dare she help them, how dare she act like she was better than me, how dare she—

"No questions about me. Otherwise you have a deal."

I stopped straining against the straps. My anger cooled, but my distrust remained. She was crazy and she was working for them. For the people who would as soon kill me as experiment on me. For the people Dylan was with now.

I closed my eyes and forced that thought away. This was not a good time to think about him.

"Why do you want to know my numbers," I asked, my eyes still closed.

"To compare them now that you are infected."

"What do you think you will find?"

"If it matches the pattern, your numbers should be the same, even improved, from before you were infected." She said this matter-of-factly, as if this bit of information were rather inconsequential.

"But I'm old now," I exploded. "How could it, how…"

She looked up. Her eyes were brown, a hard brown, there

was still no softness present. If anything, I swore I could see a crazy glint in them.

"The co-infection changes many things about the body and mind. Most are detrimental, some are neutral, or may even be considered an improvement."

I tried to digest this information. My skin might be old, my mind might fail me too many times to count, but, "The rest of me, my insides, my heart, my muscles, that all will still be normal, like before?"

"If you fit the pattern we've seen so far, yes," she said. "I must always confirm, although I have yet to see an exception."

"But…" I tried to think this through. "What about all the times my knee gave out? All the times I felt sore and stiff and old, just plain old—"

"You were likely out for a couple of weeks after being infected. Laid out somewhere, immobile, muscles atrophying, and then when you awoke, did you give yourself any rest? Did you build up your muscle strength and stamina slowly, or did you overdo it?"

I opened my mouth.

She held up her hand. "Don't bother, that was a rhetorical question. Of course you didn't. Any normal person would have strained muscles and joints, along with pain from the sudden amount of exercise you likely engaged in, and you did all that after laying out somewhere practically comatose weeks."

I couldn't argue with her logic. I had jumped out of buildings and fought people to the death. I had feared the last few weeks of injuries weren't the normal consequences of an overworked body but instead a horrible part of the disease I lived with. And here she was, smirking at my ignorance.

She asked again for my numbers and I rattled off what I could remember. I hadn't had health insurance for months. It wasn't much, but it seemed to satisfy her. She wrote it all down on her stupid clipboard, left the room with my vials of blood and returned a few minutes later.

"So," I said. "Is it true, are my numbers the same?"

"Too fast to know, it will take 24 hours to get the results back, but everything else I've looked at says yes."

"I don't understand," I said. "If I'm so normal, if so much of me is like before, if I'm so goddamn normal, why are you all treating me like I'm not even human anymore?"

The light cast weird shadows across her facial features. It deepened the bags underneath her eyes, but smoothed out the wrinkles and webs of her skin. The corner of her mouth lifted in a small smile, as if she was telling herself a silent joke.

"Because you are not human anymore. Or, you are not JUST human anymore. The virus has made sure of that." She looked about to explain further, then stopped. A coldness seemed to wash over her face. I wondered who or what she saw instead of me. It felt strange to see this happening so clearly in someone else. It felt as if I were invading her privacy.

"Who did this?" I said in a quiet voice.

"We don't know," she said, her answer automatic, as if she'd had to answer this question a million times and had gotten bored with it.

"We just happened to discover a mutated rabies virus and also happened to discover a bacteria that can fight it off?"

"Oh no, we genetically engineered the bacteria. That was us."

"You're kidding."

She shook her head. "Unfortunately, no. The only compatible

bacteria was in the family that causes Lyme disease. It fights off the Lyssa virus, but buries itself in the nervous system. Specifically the memory center of the brain."

I knew all this. Well, I hadn't known it was a genetically engineered version of Lyme disease, but this wasn't exactly new information. "When it's just the bacteria that infects somebody, it turns them into Faints—"

"Into what?"

"Puts them in a coma. That's our name for them. Faints."

"Okay," she said.

"How is that possible?" I thought about Matilda and her family, and how they had saved me and Maibe, and how they had burned themselves down soon after. "How does something that puts people into a coma end up infecting anyone if it's not being purposefully injected?"

"Normal Lyme disease spreads by way of the tick. Maybe something like that," she said.

"So you don't know. Not for sure."

She shook her head. "Not for sure. But we're working on it."

"So this entire camp of people could be turning into Faints and you wouldn't know it."

"It's a risk. But it's one that Sergeant Bennings and the other camps have decided is worth it."

"What other camps?"

"It doesn't matter," she said in a clipped voice. She collected her equipment, put away her notes, took off her gloves.

"Wait," I said. I felt deflated. This woman was playing games with me somehow. She was getting a twisted satisfaction out of providing partial answers, half-truths, leading statements. But that didn't mean she wasn't telling the truth, that didn't mean she wasn't right. She acted so sure, and she was like me. Infected. And she acted like it was this easy thing to just go ahead and judge herself now as something less than human.

The straps being undone from my wrists wrenched me from my thoughts. She was going to help me after all, she—

But it was the guard. Dr. Ferrad had left and the guard was taking me back to my room. To my cage with a cot, two buckets, and four dingy white walls.

I lay in the cot that night in total darkness. They'd turned off the single bulb that hung precariously rigged from the center of the room. Moans filtered, muffled, through the walls. My muscles ached, my joints ached, they always ached, but for once I did not assume it was a result of the infection. Maybe it was normal.

What did it mean to be human? I could still think and talk and love. Yes, I lost myself sometimes, but I came back. I came back.

Tears leaked, leaving cold trails down my cheeks. I did not make a sound, I would not give into such weakness, but I could not keep back the tears. I balled up the rough blanket and tucked it under my chin. No one, not Dylan, not Maibe, not the pup-boys, no one could get me out now. A part of me thought I deserved this.

I turned my head to the side. Snot leaked out of my nose. Memories of past moments of despair threatened to rise up and take over—grieving for my parents, for Dylan, for not trying harder—

A scratching noise broke through and allowed me the strength to push back the memories. I stopped breathing. I listened. Groans from some other prisoner in pain, the clomp-clomp of steps in the hallway outside my room.

There.

A scratch, and then another. Somewhere in the darkness, but very close. In the room with me. The scratching increased, became more insistent.

I got out of the cot and followed it to the opposite corner of my cage. The wall felt smooth and cold to my hands as I searched down it until I almost hit the floor.

There.

An edge of something rough and uneven. It moved and I gasped and shrank back.

"Hello?"

"Shhhh." Someone said through the walls.

I sat back on my heels and waited. I could not see a thing other than the faint outline of the walls, but I could feel.

When the scratching was done. I returned my hand to the wall. The slight lip I felt earlier was now more like an inch. Big enough to grab and pull. I did so, and a small section of wall, just a couple of square inches, came away in my hands.

My calf muscles tensed and I waited for what would happen next. I thought it must be the prisoner next door, someone like me. Someone I wasn't supposed to talk to. Someone who may have found a way to escape.

The scratching noise started again, different in timbre. An almost hesitant sound. Something white uncurled from the gap in the wall and fluttered to the floor.

"Close it," said a female voice. "It's from Spencer. Say nothing."

I quickly returned the piece of drywall to its hole and grabbed up the paper.

I explored every inch of the room, looking for a hint of light strong enough to allow me to read the words I knew must be scrawled on the paper. But I found none.

My heart pounded with excitement and frustration. What good was a message if I couldn't read it? I scrambled back to where I thought the hole had been made and tried to find the lip, but I had returned it too neatly. My fingers grazed the wall a dozen times and found no purchase and I couldn't be sure I was even in the right spot anymore.

I thought about banging on the wall to get next door's attention and had raised my fist in the air when I scolded myself for such stupidity. I would bring the prisoner to the wall, along with who knew how many guards.

I forced myself back to my cot and lay with the paper pressed between my hands and chest. I thought of a million things the message could say: maybe it was warning me to get ready for an escape attempt, maybe it was directions for escaping on my own, maybe it revealed the secret for taking down this whole farce of a refugee center.

I decided to force myself to stay awake until there was enough light to read the message. And I did manage to keep sleep at bay for several hours. At least, I think it was several hours.

SOMETHING POKED INTO my chest. I was walking alongside a faceless friend. It felt like this friend had just elbowed me in the ribs. "Look," the faceless friend said. "Look at that."

I looked across the street, to where she pointed, but there was nothing except fog, even though on our side it was a bright, sunny day.

My friend elbowed me again in the ribs, harder now.

"Ow," I said.

My eyes flew open.

The one bulb still hung from the middle of the small room, swinging gleefully, as if on holiday. Dr. Ferrad loomed over me, not afraid to touch me, yet still treating me like a dog about to bite. She carried a stick, a short one, some broken off handle from a broom or rake or something, but a stick all the same. This is what poked me.

"Get up," she said. I thought about jumping her. There was no guard with her. But then I heard the faint crackle and sizzle and saw where the noise came from. A taser in her other hand.

I pushed myself up on my elbows. The threadbare blanket fell away. Something white fluttered onto the cement floor.

The note.

"What's this," Dr. Ferrad said.

I jumped off the bed to grab it. My heart rocked in my chest. I had been so careless. She used the stick to poke me back, but I resisted.

She held out the taser, its crackle of electricity clicking like an insect. I backed up a step. Dr. Ferrad took the paper and began to uncurl it.

I bowled into her and the taser. The paper fluttered to the floor. The taser clicked like an insect. My body went rigid with pain. Everything turned red and then the pain vanished.

The taser hit the ground next to my face. I didn't know when I had fallen to the floor, only that I was there, gasping for air alongside Dr. Ferrad's unconscious body. The paper tickled my nose. I snatched it up and read the words:

We have a plan.

That was the message? That's what I had gotten tasered for?

Another guard burst into my room. I stuffed the note into my mouth and mashed it into something swallowable. The paper edges scratched my throat on the way down. Without thinking it through, I tripped over Dr. Ferrad and charged the lone guard. He held a stick and taser and wore a white suit. One of the uninfected. I blocked his stick and smashed my fist into his temple.

He fell like a rock, his head bouncing on the edge of my cot railing. Blood began to pool underneath his head, onto the cement. Light from the hallway cast ugly shadows across his still form.

He looked dead.

No, no, no, no.

He was someone's brother, someone's father, someone's son.

The guard groaned and twitched. His eyes fluttered.

I thought about grabbing the taser and running, but he needed help. My hand itched for the weapon. My body demanded I run. My mind screamed at me to escape.

I yelled for help.

I backed into the opposite corner of the room as three men rushed in.

One guard took Dr. Ferrad's and the unconscious guard's pulses. The other two advanced on me. I held up my hands to show I was defenseless. They tasered me into unconsciousness.

CHAPTER 24

THEY SAT ME DOWN on a hard-backed chair in the middle of the room. Someone had placed other chairs far away from me. I'd been drugged for days into a forced coma. They'd woken me now for some reason I could only guess at.

Six chairs, including one for Sergeant Bennings. All but two people in those chairs wore fatigues. One seat remained empty.

I had a sudden flash of insight. "That was Fillipa's, wasn't it?"

The side conversations stopped. Most looked at Sergeant Bennings to see if he would say something.

He nodded. "Yes, that's right. It's a reminder to all of us. Now. The New Year's celebration will begin in a few hours." He looked to the other five members. "Shall we hurry this along?" They nodded. Male and female faces, various ages, all exhausted, all looking at me like a creature under the microscope.

"Excellent," Sergeant Bennings said. He looked at me. "Let's begin."

"What's there to say? I'm infected."

"There is no question about what we are required to do with you. I hope you've given some thought to what we asked?"

"Yes, your Dr. Ferrad gave me a lot to think about."

"Whatever stunt your friends are trying to pull," one of the other six said, "it won't work."

"She's the one who entered my cell late at night without a guard," I said.

"What are you trying to say?" One of the men in fatigues spoke. He looked younger than Sergeant Bennings but not by much. His hair was short and stiff, his chin doughy.

I kept my face emotionless. I didn't know exactly what good this lie would do me, but any trouble I could bring Dr. Ferrad's way seemed justified since she didn't seem to care how she experimented on us Feebs. Anything to help throw them off the scent of whatever plan Spencer had cooked up couldn't hurt either.

"Maybe she was trying to help me escape and we got unlucky when one of the guards caught us."

"This is becoming a circus," Sergeant Bennings said.

The two men glared at each other across their little semi-circle. All other conversation and movement stopped to watch the power struggle between the two of them.

"If there are accusations against Dr. Ferrad's loyalties, we should hear them."

"She is casting dispersions on Dr. Ferrad to waste our time!" Sergeant Bennings said.

"You have a biased opinion on this matter," the other soldier said.

"I have killed plenty of infected," Sergeant Bennings said. "I have proved my loyalty."

"It's Dr. Ferrad's loyalty in question here."

"It is not," Sergeant Bennings said. "This is a hearing to follow standard procedure. Nothing more."

"Why was she in the room with this infected?"

Sergeant Bennings sighed. "I ordered her to do so. It was under my orders. Is that sufficient?"

"It breaks protocol."

"So it probably would, if there were any protocols for this."

He stroked his chin. "Camp Mendocino—"

"Camp Mendocino gave me full authority in this situation."

"Camp Eagle is who I'm worried about," an older woman interrupted. "Especially when they find out the two of you have been bickering in front of the infected like you're five year olds. They're making fresh bread tonight to celebrate the New Year. I don't know about you, but I might kill someone if I miss that. Can we get on with this now?"

The doughy-chinned soldier coughed and folded his hands in his lap. "We can continue this conversation later."

Sergeant Bennings tilted his head as if trying to stretch the tension out of his neck. "Very well. Is there anything you would like to share with us today? Anything about the companions who helped you break into this protected space?"

"Except it's not the last holdout, is it? There are other camps after all."

The older woman sighed and threw up her hands.

"One of our guards died in that attack," Sergeant Bennings said. "Dr. Ferrad's assistant is now in a coma. They were both innocent. Guilty only of trying to find a cure to all this."

"I…I don't understand." Only Dr. Ferrad and a guard had

entered my room. I thought I'd killed him, but he had moved. I had seen him move.

The woman gave me a quizzical look.

"Why are you looking at me like that?"

"She doesn't know," the woman said.

"She knows," Sergeant Bennings said. "She's acting."

"I've been drugged for I don't know how long," I said, a headache creeping in between my temples. "I have no idea what I'm supposed to know."

"Two days," the other man in fatigues said. "You've been out for two days."

"And during that time you're friends came to bust you out," Sergeant Bennings said. "They showed us certain weaknesses in our security here. Thank you for that. We're on watch for them now. It won't happen again."

I folded my hands in my lap. I hoped Spencer and Maibe and the others were far away from this place, but either way I wouldn't give him any information on them. Even if I did know anything.

"Your silence speaks for itself. This is disappointing but not unexpected. We often find a certain weakness in those who are infected. They are no longer truly human and do not have human concerns at the forefront of their mind."

I only cared to know one thing. In spite of feeling betrayed and abandoned, I did not want Dylan hurt. "What's going to happen to Dylan? Why did you imprison him?"

"Yes, your husband. If I were a crueler man, I would use threat against him to get you to talk, but I am not capable of such things today."

Another panel member, a man dressed in civilian clothes

sniffed and wiped his cheek.

A woman in fatigues spoke. "Fillipa was a vital member of this panel. No one is above the rules of this facility."

"But that does not mean we are immune to the heartbreak inherent in our decisions," Sergeant Bennings said.

"What about Dylan," I prompted.

"We have decided that he did not mean to protect the infected woman," the doughy-chinned man said, "but instead wanted to prevent potential bodily fluid contamination."

"We do not shoot anyone except from at a distance," a woman said. "The risk for infection is too great. Your husband did us a service by preventing the poor decisions of exhausted soldiers. He has been given another chance to return to normal duties."

"You should know," Sergeant spoke. "Your husband was very difficult to handle when we first brought him to safety. He wanted to immediately set out in search of you. He tried to run off alone with weapons and a vehicle. Not until that woman in your party, Jane? Not until she arrived and said you were dead did he give up."

Dylan had tried to come after me.

Sergeant Bennings' words heartened me, though I did not understand why he had decided to share them.

"Is there anything else you would like to share with this council?" The woman said. "We will not threaten your husband. Yet, your refusal to act now could well undo all that we have built here to keep people like your husband safe."

I huffed a laugh. That's why they had chosen to share those details about Dylan. They hoped it would somehow change my mind enough to spill my guts. For all I knew, they had made up every word.

I sat straighter in the chair and held my silence.

"Unless there is anything else," Sergeant Bennings said, he looked to either side of his panel members. They shook their heads. "Excellent. All in favor of execution by hanging of this individual say 'Aye.'"

All members of the panel said, "Aye."

"Opposed?"

Silence.

"Make the announcement. Take this prisoner to the stage."

The guards fitted the animal control loop around my neck as Stan whispered, "Sorry about this, Corrina."

The loop found the groove of my skin that had not yet bounced back from the last time the dog-catcher's noose had been used on me. The rope settled back in as if it had found its home, raw and burning.

CHAPTER 25

WITHIN FIFTEEN MINUTES Sergeant Bennings had me taken to the stage, behind the closed curtains, up on the gallows, next to three unused ropes.

That first breath of air outside had been a relief, its cold freshness wiping away the hot, humid smells of so many humans breathing, urinating, defecating, sweating in those cages. Rope bound my hands behind my back, cutting into my skin, stretching my chest so that my ribs ached with each step and breath. I did not begin to shake until they replaced the animal noose with the human one. Plastic nylon for thicker plastic nylon. Slip knot for noose knot.

Executions made excellent examples of what happened to people who did not follow the rules, especially on New Year's Eve. Sergeant Bennings must have had a flare for the dramatic. What better way to set the tone for the New Year than to usher it in with a hanging?

I wondered if Jane would watch in her soup line. I wondered if Stan would be one of the guards on the stage. I wondered whether Dylan had set up the electronics.

A ghost-memory of a bright, clear day spent on the beach in Santa Cruz rose up. Sand and surf and stunning moments of peace. The smell of saltwater, the crust of sand between my toes. The sound of those ocean waves matched the blood pounding in my ears.

The scarlet curtains opened. The ocean waves overlapped the moat and the people standing on its other side. They looked so small from here.

I thought of Fillipa's last words. Mostly I wanted sleep, mostly I wanted to curl up in Dylan's arms. Something wet tickled my cheek. I tasted saltwater and knew it must be tears. I turned my head and wiped the water off with my shoulder. They would not see me cry. At least that.

Jane and Dylan belonged together now. This was their world. The world of the uninfected. The remaining humans—

But even as I played the pity game, my mind rebelled. Being infected changed nothing about who I really was. It changed nothing about Maibe and Leaf and the others. We were still people—people with problems like memory-fevers and ghost-memories and memory-rushes to deal with now.

Sergeant Bennings stepped onto the stage next to me.

He began speaking but I did not hear the words. Instead, my eye caught on movement, a figure in dark clothing, a dark mask over his face, creeping onto the stage, unnoticed by the two guards standing on either side of Sergeant Bennings.

He rushed at me but I could not make out the face. It was Spencer or one of the pup-boys making an impulsive decision.

He must know he would get caught. Why would one of them take the chance?

Someone from across the moat shouted and pointed.

Sergeant Bennings and the guards turned.

The figure crashed into me and the noose tightened and the pressure made me gag. He steadied me and I took in a ragged, shallow breath, the sharp pain in my ribs at the crash keeping me on the edge of suffocation.

As if in slow motion, the guards raised their guns, but Sergeant Bennings waved them off. He held out hands to me as if in supplication.

I saw the glint of a knife and understood my rescuer meant to cut away the bonds. The rope loosened and fell away.

Sergeant Bennings yelled something, but the ocean roared louder than ever in my ears and I could not make out any words. I raised my hands to loosen the noose around my neck, not sure what the next move would be. I decided to trust that Spencer would have a plan for this, even if I couldn't think of any way out.

Before I reached for the rope around my neck, before I barely moved, he yanked my arm back down. I felt a sharp slash on my left hand.

My hand was pressed palm to palm with my rescuer's.

He tore off the mask. Dylan's blue eyes looked at me, wide and sorrowful. His hair was wild, the look on his face even wilder. He held his bloody knife in one hand and his other hand pressed against my cut.

"What did you do?" I tried to take my hand away, but he wouldn't let me go.

"What was necessary," Dylan said.

CHAPTER 26

"I TRIED TO LOOK FOR YOU," Dylan said. "When Jane told me you had been killed. It felt as if it was my sister all over again. They wouldn't let me leave."

The fog rose like steam from the moat. A soldier dressed in one of those white pillow suits adjusted the noose around my neck. The blood on Dylan and me had required the suit.

I couldn't look at him. It made me sick to think of him infected and executed alongside me. "You shouldn't have done it," I said.

Dylan stood a few feet away from me. A noose now around his neck. Both our hands were tied behind our backs.

"I can't stop them from doing this, but I can make sure I go with you."

"I'm not your sister."

"I don't want to live without you," Dylan said.

People gathered around the food tables on the opposite side

of the water as Sergeant Bennings lectured everyone on the importance of the rules. The bread the woman at the hearing had wanted was laid out in trays. I could almost taste the fresh bread, the way it would tear apart in my hands, the way it would smell warm and yeasty and like home.

"You held me down for the guards," I whispered, remembering the look of horror on his face when he'd seen I was infected.

"Corrina," Shock washed away the feverish glow on his face. "I pushed Jane away. She was yelling. She had called the guards. They were coming and you were falling. You were falling and I caught you."

I shook my head, feeling the rope scratch my skin. I remembered being held down. I remembered thinking Dylan was holding me down and I deserved it. My mother had left me. My father had died rather than live for me. My foster parents had asked me to leave to make room for someone else. Dylan and Jane—

"I was going to make you run, but you blacked out. I carried you. We made it all the way outside. You don't remember? They caught us outside."

I remembered waking up in the cage. I remembered feeling abandoned. I had believed for so long that no one could love me like I loved them. Had I wanted to believe in the lie so completely that I could see his act of courage as a betrayal?

My brain roared with these thoughts. I lost the feeling in my hands. The noose around his neck and the blood on his hands told me the answer was yes. He had infected himself and he was going to die—because of me. Because in spite of the mistakes we'd both made, he loved me too much to let me go.

Candlelight lit the tables across the moat and made the

people around them look ghoulish. Sergeant held the microphone to Dylan. "Any last words before the New Year?"

"I love you," Dylan stared at me not bothering to address Sergeant Bennings or the crowd. His words echoed across the darkness. Redness flushed his cheeks. Sweat gleamed on his forehead and trickled down his temples. The fever rising in him made him glow. He was beautiful. "You may have feared I stopped," he said. "I was afraid of that too, but I realized…I don't want to be in this world without you. " He turned to the crowd. "Fillipa was right."

Sergeant Bennings gently pulled back the microphone with his gloved hand. He spoke through the medical mask. "As we usher in this New Year, remember that this fight isn't over. We will not give in to the darkness. We will not give up without a cure!"

Dylan stood tall on the box.

Sergeant Bennings turned the microphone in my direction. "Let no one say we cannot show mercy. Do you have any last words before we give you release from this terrible disease?"

I shook my head, no. There was nothing left to say, I was sorry for my own part in all of this. I hadn't trusted my own worth. Now the person I loved most in the world would die because of me and—

A flash of pink at the edge of the crowd caught my eye. A small person in a pink sweatshirt had climbed onto a stairwell and was making a "keep rolling" motion like out of the movies.

Sergeant Bennings signaled to a guard.

"Wait," I said. "I have something to say."

January

***

"...I came here out of love, not violence. I came here to save someone I love. That's what I tried to do. I tried my best, even though I knew my best might not be good enough, not even close. But you've got to know that deep down—"

CHAPTER 27

"—I AM YOU. I am a real person. We are real people. We are not—"

Screams from across the moat interrupted my speech. The food table lay turned on its side on the ground. The soup, the fresh bread, the coffee, all of it was splattered onto the ground, a mix of colors mashing into a dull brown glop. Candles guttered and snuffed out. Trickles of soup streamed into the moat.

More people screamed and began running. The generator lights revved on, drowning everything in an eerie silver relief. It looked as if something red, almost black, had been added to the soup stream. Sergeant Bennings and the guards began shouting into their radios. Had the Vs gotten in?

"Corrina?"

I tore my focus away from the commotion and saw Dylan flushed, sweating, his eyes glazed.

His legs wobbled and his weight gave out.

"Dylan!" I lurched to him. The noose tightened around my

neck. His body dangled from the rope, his feet limp, his knees bent and inches from the ground.

My hands were bound. The rope bit deeply into my skin and cut off my breath but it was not enough to close the distance.

Dylan's face turned red and then a deep shade of purple.

I screamed, pulled close, inches away now, so close. The rope dug a sharp ditch of pain into my neck. Lights burst in front of my eyes.

I fell to the ground.

My chest bloomed with pain from hitting my cracked ribs, but the ache around my neck lessened. Somehow, the noose no longer held me back.

I scrambled over to Dylan, turned my back to him, fumbled with my bound hands until I caught his belt. I strained upward. My knee popped. I added the pain to the list of injuries to ignore, continued to lift, to try to ease the pressure of the rope, to get air back down his throat.

I draped his weight over my back, and then I was stuck. I had locked my injured knee and knew if I moved it, both of us would go down and the noose would tighten again.

"Dylan!"

He gasped for breath across my back. His weight brought me to the point of collapse.

I tilted my head, tried to breath, tried to think, tried to keep my legs locked even as I felt my knee begin to fail.

Then there was someone, Leaf, using a knife to saw through Dylan's rope.

My knee gave out. I fell hard onto my stomach. My face slammed into wood. I breathed in dust and tensed, waiting for Dylan's weight to hit me. Nothing.

He still hung from the noose.

I scrambled back up as Leaf cut through the last threads. I could not stop Dylan from falling, only help control it.

Leaf waved to me, a goofy grin on his face as if this was all one big game. His hair was tousled, his shirt bloody. He ran for the other side of the stage.

There was a crack of a rifle.

Leaf's chest bloomed red. Shock overcame his grin. He fell on his face.

I screamed but before I could move, the soldier turned his gun from Leaf to me. I shielded Dylan's unconscious form with my body and waited for the inevitable.

The gun dropped from the soldier's hand. An arrow sprouted from his chest. Blood spread from the hole. He fell to the ground like a domino.

Gabbi stood behind him, in the moat, the muck up to her thighs, crossbow in hand. "Get off the stage," she yelled. "The goddamn guards let the Vs in." Then she leapt out of the moat and disappeared into the chaos that included Vs tearing into those people not fast enough to escape or strong enough to fight back.

I knelt next to Leaf and checked for breathing, for a pulse, for anything.

There was nothing.

I smothered a cry and left him. There was nothing I could do.

I limped back to Dylan and rolled him onto his back. He lay still. His eyes were closed, his mouth hung slightly open, his hair was tangled, his clothes were askew, his face was still and an unhealthy red. I stroked his forehead and held my breath and leaned my cheek over his mouth.

Hot breath caressed my skin.

Dylan was breathing.

I smelled the coffee he must have had that morning. I smelled him, alive. I pressed my hand against his beating heart and bent my forehead so that it touched his chest for a moment.

He was alive.

I sat back up and made a more thorough examination of his body. The changes from the infection already showed. He was unconscious from the fever. A muscle in his cheek and neck began to twitch.

I dragged him off the gallows and the stage, not very gently.

Sergeant Bennings leapt into the moat and climbed a light pole. He hung on it with one arm, directing soldiers and people, firing shots. His pants were wet to the waist, he'd lost one boot, but he did not stop his work until he caught my stare. He lifted his gun and aimed in our direction. One of the Vs jumped into the moat, catching his remaining boot and hanging from it, began to climb. Sergeant Bennings shot the V in the head dropping the body into the water.

I dragged Dylan out of sight before Sergeant Bennings could return his attention to us. Snot ran down my nose and I coughed around tears. It wasn't fair to leave Leaf there, alone, but I didn't see any other way. I searched for something, anything, to help me carry Dylan. I found a wheelbarrow of garden supplies, overturned it to make room, and maneuvered Dylan into it. For a moment, I swore an almost-dead blueberry plant rested in the wheelbarrow between Dylan's knees.

The fog hung thick in the air. It sent tendrils across our path like fingers ready to pull us away into its depths. The sounds of fighting and screaming and dying mixed with ghost-memories of Sergeant Bennings' soldiers, Vs attacking, people appearing out of nowhere. The only way to tell they weren't real was a faint translucence that took a moment for my brain to register. If any one of them had been real, I would not have acted in time.

I steered us away from the fighting groups, into the silence of the empty state fair buildings. The tire pressure was low, which made the wheelbarrow unstable. Dylan almost tumbled out twice. Not that he would have known it, unconscious, sweating, his skin developing this weird, aged, gray. The infection worked so fast.

The silence became thick like a blanket. My panicked escape settled into a steadier pace. We were far away from the moat, the gallows, the cages, the fighting. A part of me wanted to go back and help. Leaf was dead. What about Maibe and the others? But I couldn't leave Dylan. Not like this, not when he was so helpless. If anyone found him, V or uninfected, he'd be dead within seconds.

I focused on slowing down my breathing, on pushing us onward, on not looking at Dylan's sick form. I could do nothing for him until we reached the safety of the only place I could think to take him: the barn.

Dylan's weight shifted and caught me off guard. I lost my grip on the handles. The wheelbarrow screeched to a halt. I waited for someone to hear it and come running. No one came, no one other than the ghosts.

When I picked up his weight again, I pushed myself into a slow jog, ignoring the pain in my knee and ribs and chest. I used the momentum to steer us around another building's corner. The barn came into sight, it's rectangular form appearing out of the fog like a dark brush of paint.

It took precious seconds to register that someone real stood between us and the building.

The wheelbarrow slowed to a stop. There was no way to know from this distance if it was a Feeb, V, Faint, or an uninfected. So many labels for people. I didn't like any of them.

I decided I had to leave Dylan and check out the situation. I hated to leave him. But Dylan's unconscious body would only hinder my ability to deal with whoever was ahead. I kissed Dylan's fevered forehead. He thrashed for a moment. Said something in a whisper. It was in the grip of the memory-fevers, I knew it was, but I thought I heard—

"Jane," he said again in a long whisper, as if caressing the name.

I stumbled back. I feared—I could not stand the thought he was remembering being with Jane at that moment as if it were happening right then and there, as if he had traveled back in time and—

I closed my eyes. Stop. Stop it, stop it. I began to run. Anything to push back the bile that had risen in my throat and the hot tears that threatened to pour down my cheeks. It didn't matter what was up ahead. If it was a V or someone ready to kill me, so be it.

The figure did not acknowledge me as I approached and I knew it must be one of the Faint. Her back was to me, but I recognized the clothes from somewhere. Blue jeans and a sweater set.

My old woman. The one who had met me in the barn, the one Dylan had saved, the one captured and in the cages. She might as well have had nine lives though she looked the worse for wear now. Dirt covered her previously pristine clothes. Holes dotted her jeans. Something dark and crusty smeared her face. Blood most likely. She stared out into the nothingness of space, at the river and bike trail, but really at nothing at all.

Some noise I couldn't place whipped me around. It was off in the distance, as if a puff of breeze had moved the sound in just the right direction. Groans and screams and the pop-pop of gunfire.

I hurried back to Dylan. His eyes were closed, his body feverish, his neck bent at an awkward angle, resting on the edge of the wheelbarrow. The building was right there. I would settle him in a stall and then lead her in as well. I'd done it once before, I could do it again.

The stillness inside the barn was different than outside. More complete, more solid, as if entering a church. I dared not whisper for fear of offending something. The stalls were open, inviting, the sweet smelling hay still in piles. The open door let in enough light to see the hay, but not enough to see into the dark corners.

I left Dylan at the door. My steps dragged, my eyes drooped, Entering the building somehow signaled to my brain that we were safe now. But we weren't. There was no way to know until I had checked. Exhaustion came quickly and heavily anyway. I did my best to scare myself awake by imagining Vs and soldiers hiding in corners, ready to tear me limb from limb.

After I checked, I dumped Dylan rather unceremoniously onto the hay, stretched him out, and then I went back for the woman. I would bring her in, then I would care for Dylan until he was well enough to walk. We would all go back to the bike shop. If the pup-boys and Maibe weren't there, we'd go to the boxcar. I decided not to think about what would happen if they weren't at one of those two places. I allowed myself a moment of grief for Leaf's death. He had been the nicest one of them all. Without him, we would be hanging from the gallows.

I stepped out of the barn. Someone yelled.

I dropped to all fours, sleepiness gone. Was it Maibe? No, it had been a male's voice. One of the pup-boys?

There was nothing in my field of view except for the truck I had spent so many hours under when I first broke into Cal Expo. I pressed my back against the exterior wall of the barn and crept to the corner. Slowly, like a snail, I edged around it.

Two men stood a few feet back from the woman in the sweater set. Sergeant Bennings' soldiers.

They seemed about to shoot her down. I held my breath and waited. Instead, one of the men, bloodied and stoop-shouldered from exhaustion, pulled out a dog noose. I turned away from the sight of her being led away, back to whatever experiments they did. I should not have left her.

My mind whirled with all the things I could have done to stop her from being taken. I returned to the dark barn. When I didn't see Dylan my breath quickened and my heart pounded.

There.

The hay covered him almost completely.

I settled in to watch. It was in our best interests for me to stay awake and stand guard. The fatigue I had pushed back until now washed over me like an ocean wave. It pulled my eyelids down, forced me into a crouch, a sit, and I leaned back and tried to force open my eyes again. Failed.

I remembered the hydrophobia. Dylan needed water. I forced myself back up from the weight of sleep that wanted to keep me in place. I searched for the cup I'd used once before. I filled it with water and propped Dylan up to drink. His eyes were closed, but when the water touched his lips he grimaced in pain.

I kept the water at his lips and he finally took a little of it. He flashed open his eyes for a second. I wasn't sure if he saw me or an illusion.

"I always wanted—" his voice cracked, "—to grow old with you." He smiled to make his joke clear.

"I guess you'll get your wish sooner than you thought." A half-smile forming on my lips.

His hand wrapped around my head and pulled me deep into a kiss. He smelled like home and my skin electrified at his touch.

"Corrina," he breathed out when he released me.

"I'm here. I'm here, Dylan."

I pressed myself against his side and felt his fever burn like a fire against my body.

CHAPTER 28

THE WHEELBARROW WAS made of metal. The paint the color of a banana peel, chipped and flaked.

I noticed this when I woke in the morning. The wheelbarrow was inches from the stall, right where I had abandoned it after dumping Dylan out of it.

I sat up, felt for Dylan. There. Still under the hay, still breathing.

He needed to drink and maybe eat if I could get food into his mouth. I had no idea how long I'd slept or how the situation outside the barn might have changed. I decided not to beat myself up for falling asleep. What was the point? I would have to sleep while Dylan went through the memory-fevers. If it was anything like mine, it would last for weeks. I didn't think the wheelbarrow or my muscles were in a state to carry Dylan miles away to safety. At least not today.

I scouted the buildings near the barn. I kept low to the

ground and came back as soon as I found a jackpot of canned food in the cabinet of a little kitchen off one of the buildings. Sergeant Bennings' men might come around at any moment, so I made my shirt into a bag and stuffed it full of canned beans and apricots. I grabbed a kitchen knife at the last second, remembering I needed a way to open the cans.

I returned to the barn, gave Dylan some more water, but he was in no state to eat. My stomach rumbled. I would not dare start a fire, so I ate the beans cold, the rough texture welcome in my mouth even though I had always thought cold beans were gross. The sweet apricot slices went down more easily.

In the dim light of the barn, I could not be sure, but I thought I saw the beginnings of web-like lines appear on Dylan's skin. He shouldn't have done it. He shouldn't have risked himself for me.

"Corrina, I'm sorry. I'm so sorry," He said this softly, great pain in the words. His eyes remained closed. He moaned and thrashed about. He mumbled something and I feared what he would say. Feared it would be about Jane again.

"It's okay. I'm here. It's okay."

His blue eyes blazed open and stared at me but did not see me at all.

I tried an apricot slice, the juice dripping into the hay around us. This he opened his mouth for. He always did favor sweet food. He chewed it mechanically, opened his eyes again and locked them with mine. This time I think he did see me.

"It matters to me that you know—I thought you were dead. That's the only thing that made me stop looking. I thought—"

"Shh." I caressed his face. "I know." But it mattered that he said it. It helped erase Jane's name a little.

Dylan slumped back, gone in the memory-fevers again and I wished him a good one, whatever that meant to him.

I ate more of the beans and apricots, then saved the rest for when Dylan woke again.

I used the next few hours to scout further out from the barn.

My loops lengthened, always bringing me back to check on Dylan, until I had almost returned to the stage, to the gallows. I found no one alive. Bodies lay out in a sort of grotesque display of blood and mayhem. A soldier here, with his uniform bloody and flesh missing. Better not to look too closely. A civilian there, propped against a trash can, dead from an obvious bullet hole to the head, but I didn't look closely enough to figure out whether it was a Feeb or an uninfected. My gag reflex worked on overdrive so I didn't dare venture closer.

The metallic smell of blood was faint on top of a layer of garbage, but it wasn't bad—yet. I tried to put my thoughts together. Stan and at least one other soldier were alive and organized enough to round up more Faints, but whoever had survived wasn't organized enough to clean up the dead bodies, yet.

Suddenly I pictured Dylan missing, someone having come and taken him from his stall. The feeling felt so real, I raced back to the barn. But there he was, sleeping on his side, face still flushed, mumbling softly.

I steadied myself against the wall and decided to be done for the night. I closed the door, it's every squeak jarring my heart. I stumbled back to Dylan's stall, felt for his sleeping form and curled myself around him and slept.

When I awoke next, Dylan's arm draped across me. The hay and his fever made me warm. Light filtered in. Another day had passed. More prominent webbing showed up on Dylan's skin now. My fingers traced some of the lines along his cheek.

He opened his blue eyes. Our faces were inches apart. His eyes looked clear, coherent, calm.

"Hi," he said.

"Hi," I said.

His hand traced my cheek, echoing my touch.

He started talking. He started sharing his memory-fevers with me.

CHAPTER 29

"YOU NEED TO EAT while you're awake."

He took the opened can I handed him and dug into the beans. When he had finished, I passed him a can of apricots. I opened up more cans of food and he ate those too. I didn't bother rationing the cans. Who knew when he'd feel well enough to eat again or how long the next memory-fever would last.

"They feel so real," he said, once he polished off the second can of beans. "Did yours feel so real?"

"Yes," I said.

"What did you relive?"

I told him, briefly, quickly, without emotion, about his parents.

His face became sad. "They should never have acted like that. They—"

"Are your parents," I said.

"No. It's not right."

"It is what it is. But they weren't all like that. Some of them were nice to relive." And I told him about the first time we met.

"That was one of mine too," he said quietly. "And then one of just watching you sleep. Just that calmness, that perfect peace. It was a bright morning and you slept in, and I'd woken and watched you breathe and it was perfect."

I looked down, blushing, embarrassed.

"Except for the morning breath, that is."

I sucked in air and looked up. Dylan smiled. "Joking."

I smiled back, my face cracking. I couldn't remember the last time I really smiled. "Funny."

"You're perfect. You never have morning breath."

"Oh, now I know you're lying."

Dylan sobered. "No, really, it was perfect."

We sat in silence for another moment. I knew I should go back out and stand guard, but I didn't want to leave him, not while he was lucid, not when I had almost lost him for good.

A flush began to creep up his neck. Sweat broke out on his forehead.

"I think it's coming back," I said.

He set the empty can down. It tipped and became lost in the hay.

Suddenly I needed to know. I couldn't bare not knowing for another minute. "You said Jane's name. You said it like a caress. Were you, were you—" I couldn't finish. Tears sprang to my eyes, my stomach twisted. I shouldn't have asked. This wasn't fair, not like this.

Dylan's eyes glazed, he struggled to stay upright. He shook his head as if to clear it but I knew it wouldn't work.

"It doesn't matter, Corrina. I chose you. That's what it made clear. I will choose you, again and—"

He slumped over. I jumped up to lay him back out more comfortably. I kicked the hidden can, bouncing it out of the stall so that it skipped onto the cement floor. Its sound was shocking and intrusive.

Once I knew he was safe and comfortable, I left. To scout, I told myself. But now I was the liar. I couldn't stand to be in there with him another moment, not when the first thing he had relived, not when—

I burst into silent sobs. Of course I wasn't good enough, of course I had never been good enough.

But he'd gotten himself sick for me, he'd exiled himself from everyone normal now. For me. I let that fact plant itself in me, take root, blossom. I would not dismiss his sacrifice because I wanted to have a pity party. I could not forget what Jane had done, what Dylan and Jane had done, but he had infected himself to prove he loved me, that he couldn't live without me. Either I moved on or I let the past control me.

Two figures stumbled out from behind the truck, limping, dirty. A dozen thoughts tumbled through my brain. I should have been watching. I should have taken my chances with the wheelbarrow.

"Corrina?" A young voice called out across the distance between us.

"Maibe?" My heart pounded.

The two came closer. Maibe and Gabbi. Gabbi raised her crossbow at me and let lose an arrow. I screamed and raised my hands. When I lowered them, a V was dead in the dirt with an arrow buried in his back. Gabbi shot off another arrow, but this one only nicked his shoulder and almost embedded into my foot. I jumped, surprised.

"You idiots need to get inside," Gabbi said.

I locked the door as best I could behind us.

Dylan moaned and thrashed around. Gabbi swung up her crossbow again and crouched, scanning the barn.

"It's Dylan," I said. I went over and pushed her crossbow to point at the ground. "He's in the fevers."

I HAD SO MANY QUESTIONS, they tied my tongue in knots. Where had they been? What had they done? Who was still alive? Why was Gabbi so angry at me?

"Thank you for coming back for us," I said simply.

Maibe was eating from the last apricot can, but Gabbi stopped and jerked her finger at Maibe. "Don't thank me. It's this one who made it happen. She was ready to get herself killed for you. I couldn't have cared less."

I reached over and hugged Maibe. "Thank you."

"You're welcome," she said, smiling.

"But what kind of idiot intentionally gets himself infected and hung from the gallows and—"

Maibe stared at her.

"Sorry," Gabbi said, not looking at me.

"That's okay. I kind of thought the same thing when it happened. All that trouble I went to trying to find him and keep him alive, and—" I laughed and it wasn't a fake laugh. Gabbi and Maibe were here now. Dylan was here.

"We can't stay here," Maibe said. "I think things are going to get much worse very soon."

"But I can't move him, not when he's in the fevers," I said.

"But they're waking up," Maibe said. "The Vs wake up first, and then the rest."

"Those who survive the fevers anyway," Gabbi said.

DYLAN STOOD ON UNSTEADY FEET, shirtless, the fevers too hot for him to keep it on. I went to get him some water.

"We should get out of the city. Go into the foothills," he said, and crumpled. I was too far away to help, but Gabbi jumped in time. I ran over and helped bring him back to the stall.

He kept mumbling something about Dutch Flat—where his grandparents had owned a little house before they died. I told him it was going to be okay. Just rest. He pulled me into him for a kiss. When he let go, Maibe was by my side, holding out a cup of water.

I thanked her and helped him drink and he settled back into a troubled sleep.

Gabbi slammed the door behind her.

"What's wrong with her?" I asked Maibe.

"I don't know," Maibe said.

"WE HAVE TO LEAVE. Right now," Gabbi said, bursting back into the barn.

"What happened?" I said.

"Sergeant Bennings is alive. He's here. He's still here," she said.

I didn't make her explain further. The panicked look on her face said enough.

Maibe helped me position Dylan in the wheelbarrow. He woke and helped us pack as many supplies as we could fit around him.

As we left the barn, a low train whistle sounded across the sky. After all this time, the noise seemed strange, almost creepy. It filled the empty sky with its howl. When the sound drifted back into silence, an aching loneliness filled my heart. The world had been ripped apart and emptied out and the people still living in this world weren't safe.

"What do you think that was?" Maibe said.

"You heard it too?" Gabbi said. "I thought it was a ghost-memory."

"I heard it," I said quietly.

"I don't think it means anything good," Maibe said. "Stuff like that never means anything good in the movies."

I wanted to contradict her but stopped myself. She'd been right too many times.

Gabbi paced around us, scanning the area for trouble. "We can't worry about that right now. Spencer and the rest will be at the boxcar. We have to meet back up with them."

I realized there were still some people in the world I could consider safe. Maybe not many but enough. Spencer and Gabbi and Leaf and the others had taken care of me and Maibe. I decided to do the same for them, if they gave me the chance.

"How do you know?" Dylan asked.

"That's the place. It's always been our meeting place," Gabbi said.

"And after the boxcar?" Dylan asked.

Gabbi huffed and turned away.

"What's her problem," Dylan whispered to me.

"She doesn't trust most people," I said. "With good reason."

Dylan nodded. "Until I get through this, this, whatever this is—"

"Memory-fever," Maibe and I said at the same time.

"Until the fever passes, I'm in your hands. Tell me what you want to do."

Gabbi turned back and examined him for a long moment. "How long have you had the fevers now?"

Dylan turned to me.

"Four days," I said.

Gabbi looked out into the distance as if remembering. "Sometimes the fevers pass in as little as a week, sometimes as long as three weeks."

"He's already been awake for longer stretches than I remember when I went through it." I shuddered, remembering the Army surplus store and how Christopher had died.

"So maybe you get lucky and have the fevers for only a week," Maibe said.

"But that's still three days of hauling around someone who could go comatose any minute," Gabbi said.

"There are still Vs on the trail. More of them than before," Maibe said.

"We'll get through it," I said, resting a hand on Dylan's shoulder and looking Maibe and Gabbi in the eye. Dylan clasped his hand over mine. "We'll figure it out together."

WE DID FIGURE IT OUT, and it ended up being the beginning of something much bigger and darker than we could have imagined.

But all of that is a story for Gabbi and Maibe to tell.

Mine ends here: we made it to the boxcar, to Spencer and

the pup-boys, and we headed for the foothills.

We are all of us together.

Dylan and I are caring for each other, and it is more than enough, and whether you believe we are human or not—we are surviving, and we are not going away.

WHY DID THE TRAIN WHISTLE? FIND OUT IN...

Infestation (Book 2)

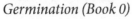

Germination (Book 0)   *Eradication (Book 3)*

Get the complete Zombies Are Human series
Available in ebook, paperback, and audio.

ABOUT THE AUTHOR

Jamie Thornton is the *New York Times* and *USA Today* bestselling author of the Zombies Are Human series and the Doormaker series. She lives in Northern California with her husband, two dogs, a garden, lots of chickens, a viola, and a bicycle. She writes stories that take place halfway around the world, in an apocalyptic future, in a parallel universe—her books don't always stick to one genre, but they always take the reader on a dark adventure.

Join the Adventure through her email list to receive freebies, discounts, and information on more of her dark adventures.

Sign up at:

ZombiesAreHuman.com

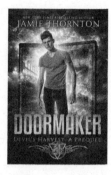  

Made in the USA
Coppell, TX
10 March 2022